SOMERVILLE'S WAR
PROOF COPY

SOMERVILLE'S WAR

ANDREW DUNCAN

Published by Vineyard Books 2020

2 4 6 8 10 9 7 5 3 1

Copyright © Andrew Duncan 2020

Andrew Duncan has asserted his right under the Copyright, Designs and
Patents Act 1988 to be identified as the author of this work

ISBN (paperback) 978-1-5272-4450-4

Sold and distributed in the UK and worldwide by Vine House Distribution
Ltd, The Old Mill House, Mill Lane, Uckfield, East Sussex, TN22 5AA
sales@vinehouseuk.co.uk

Tel.+44 1825 767 396

Printed in India by Imprint Press

Foreword

Much of this story did happen, just as much did not. But most of what did not could have, only too easily.

It follows that all place names and all characters should be fictional. However, several are based on real places and real people. If you need to know more, refer at any time to the postscript on page 329.

Sumor Before about 900 AD, Old English noun meaning summer; or an adjective meaning friendly, warm, of a sunny disposition.

Somer After 900 AD, Middle English noun meaning summer, later spelt summer.

1

August 1940

It was as perfect as a day by the water can be. The sun shone on the muddy south coast estuary and it sparkled, reflecting the sailors' enjoyment. Little terns fed close, inshore, charming onlookers with their nervous, energetic dives.

The 19 dinghies out that day surged about the estuary in ideal conditions – an 8-knot south-easterly breeze. As usual, as he had done for the past decade, Brigadier Vivian Maxwell, Captain of the Somer River Sailing Club (the S.R.S.C.), was officer of the day, skilfully controlling the racing from the little platform on the hard. This was a community that liked continuity – and thought itself privileged. S.R.S.C. members, in fact everyone in Somerville, even Maxwell's children, called him the Brig, or just Brig. They accepted him and a few even liked him despite his manner, which was not merely shy but oddly withdrawn. The only sign of life inside was an occasional gleam of the eyes while the rest of his face was static. The gleam always came unexpectedly, its meaning rarely clear. Amusement? Disbelief? Irony?

Today was one of the few when you might detect something of the Brig's inner self: a serene equilibrium that mirrored the other members' own sense of well-being. A feeling that each and every element of this beautiful, remote place where the S.R.S.C. sailed was, right down to the sea pinks and the stunted maritime grass, just now, *right* – in its appointed place, despite the air battle that hung in the balance over Kent, Sussex and London. For now, the S.R.S.C.'s tenth annual regatta – perhaps the tenth and last – filled their heads with innocent preoccupations, helping them to forget the war and their obsessions.

A hundred yards away, hidden in a bird hide among gorse bushes, a young man lifted powerful binoculars to his face and fixed them on the hard. He was spying on the S.R.S.C. regatta not for intelligence but for other reasons.

'George Adams.' He repeated the words softly to himself, as if they were precious. Jerzy Adamski, or George Adams as he now chose to be called – he'd lost count of the times he'd said the name to himself – was a trainee agent at Somerville's recently set up spy school, SOE (Special Operations Executive) Somerville.

He would never tire, he told himself, of the name's reassuringly rhythmical Englishness, and of how it told so neatly of his respect for his adopted country, but above all his new identity: a freedom fighter, no less. 'George Adams.'

He'd been in the hide all night on a 24-hour outdoor survival exercise. His eyes were dry from lack of sleep, his body ached, but so what when the old, crushed Jerzy had been superseded by George? George had discovered the place on a previous exercise. It was marked Sailing Club Point on his map, a mile and half down a rutted gravel track, where the Somer River widened into its estuary. He liked it partly because of the hide's shelter, partly because it was so completely unlike his landlocked Polish village. But the main reason for his presence was a girl: *the* girl, with whom he felt he had fallen in love. One of the girls, outnumbered by men, who came to sail here some weekends.

As he scanned the hard, he saw Maxwell flanked by helpers on his platform, and noticed his withdrawn manner. He saw the queue of sailors wheeling boats on trolleys down the hard to launch at the waterline. Among them was the girl. Just seeing her form, the signature of her size, shape and posture, gave him a stab of longing, even if her face was turned away. Longing that turned to jealousy when he saw a young man helping her push her boat.

That he had fallen so completely – as he believed – in love at such a distance, through binoculars was, he recognized, a measure of his loneliness. He noticed how effortlessly the girl existed in her skin, and that everything she did was achieved in an idiosyncratic but practical way which looked as if it had been worked out just for her.

He kept checking her progress in the race through the binoculars, noticing how she concentrated for every part of every second, keeping the dinghy flatter than the other sailors, adjusting the tiller, sail and her body weight many times more often. For some of the race she was the leader but two other boats were pressing her all the way. In a tight finish she just kept her lead. After landing on the hard she went to kiss the man on the platform: a nimble kiss of carefully understated pleasure at winning, one which told Adamski that the man she was kissing could be her father.

The girl was indeed the Brig's daughter Leonora, always known as Leo, the middle of three children. The young man helping her push her boat was Henry Dunning-Green, heir to the Dunning-Green business empire, who had sailed with her on the Somer River since both were children and had loved her for as long as he could remember. Henry's life revolved around two goals: to get a transfer to active duties away from his present dull army posting, and to marry Leo.

Leo's obsession was to be a ferry pilot in the newly formed Air Transport Auxiliary. Getting into the ATA preoccupied her far more than her feelings for Henry. She liked his attention but was too young to cope with too much of it. She viewed him as part honorary brother, part friend. Somerville, however, thought it knew better: one day it would be in the scheme of things if

Leo and Henry got married – a marriage made not in heaven, but anyway in Somerville.

Now George turned his binoculars to the clubhouse. Members were starting their picnic lunches, and he could see that many of the adults were especially at ease with each other, as if the oldest of friends, except for one couple, perhaps in their mid-30s, who appeared to be newcomers. They hadn't claimed a plot for their own picnic, but moved instead, sandwich and glass in hand, from group to group, ingratiating themselves. The husband, with a poor posture and identikit features, was a very thorough and – by the look of it – practised networker, working his way round with a few words and a joke for almost everyone long after his wife had gone to find another glass of wine in the clubhouse. They were Kenneth Hodge and his wife Phyllida.

The regatta finished with a tug of war for the ladies, and rowing races for the deck hands of members' yachts. Several, including a beautiful ketch named *Shearwater* owned by the Brig, were moored downstream of the hard colourfully dressed with all the signal flags of the alphabet.

Next, the Earl of Taunton, hereditary Commodore of the S.R.S.C. and hereditary owner of 30,000 acres up and down the Somer River's banks, arrived to present the prizes. Leo Maxwell won the coveted Commodore's Trophy; Lord Taunton's eldest daughter Portia came second and Henry Dunning-Green third. Adamski watched it all with mixed feelings of amusement – and sadness when he compared the obvious spirits of these folk with the crushed, hopeless community he had left behind in Poland. He'd had enough of watching for now, and turned away to put them out of his mind.

The closing rituals of the regatta got under way. Lord Taunton's butler set up a picnic table and chairs, pouring tea into china cups. The Earl, Lady Taunton and Brigadier Maxwell sat down for tea while the rest of the members collected their cups from a table on the clubhouse veranda and strolled around socializing. Lady Taunton held forth. During a lull in one of her stories Kenneth Hodge went up to her and said:

'Countess, we all feel honoured to see our burgee flown in such a unique fashion.' Those within earshot cringed to hear him refer so directly to the glass eye. That was for Lady Taunton alone.

She had lost an eye in a car crash some years back (driving while drunk, Somerville assumed) and had ordered three glass replacements: one green, to match her remaining eye ('don't y'know, green's the colour of jealousy – the glass one is jealous of the real one'); one with a Union Jack worn for Conservative Party events; and one with an S.R.S.C. burgee, for regatta days.

Soon they all departed back up the gravel track in their cars.

An hour later George was still in the bird hide, bored. His 24-hour outdoor survival test ended at midnight. He would eat his supper of blackberries before setting back up the track. He didn't expect anyone else at the sailing club, but then he heard the crunch of a car on gravel. Two figures got out and entered the clubhouse, not by the front door, but through the sail locker door near the back. He couldn't see their faces.

Twenty minutes later, light fading, he again scanned the clubhouse's large windows, designed for broad views down the estuary, curious because of no signs of life within.

Then he saw the two backs. The male back was inside the window, close against it, naked. He was sitting facing inwards on a window seat. Someone else was sitting on his lap, also facing inwards, and this female's back was also naked. He could see her head, with medium length, straight blond hair, rising above his. In fact it was rising and falling – rhythmically rising and sinking as if to the trot of a horse.

After some minutes the man's head flipped back. Moments later she rose and vanished into the interior. All he saw was her naked figure from behind – the outline of a shapely woman, perhaps in her mid-20s. The man vanished. Soon after, the car left.

George, still laughing inwardly about this unexpected finale to the day, left a couple of hours later for the long trudge back to SOE Somerville and his bed at Brindley House. Like his fellow SOE trainees, he had found the 24-hour outdoor survival exercises pointless. They were meant to put into practice what his instructor had taught him about how to live off the land, undetected by locals, steal food and keep warm overnight in barns or outhouses. But the trainees knew there were already resistance networks on occupied mainland Europe into which agents were absorbed and sheltered in basements and attics.

He cheered himself with the thought that every tired step he now took was one nearer his return to Europe to kill Nazis. He had thought of little else, except the sailing girl, since September 1939 when he had fled his home near Lodz in Poland.

Escaping the German soldiers had been far more difficult than dodging the instructors, mostly slow, middle-aged army officers who would now be lying concealed beside the usual approach tracks to Brindley House in the woods behind Somerville. He must slip past unobserved, which he did simply by avoiding the usual tracks, arriving at 2 a.m. by a woodland path at the rear.

2

Next morning, Maxwell made his way from the garden door of The Rectory across the lawn to his riverside boathouse. On sunny mornings, he liked to have breakfast not in the main house, but in this quaint wooden structure put up by his father. It was his favourite place, more than just a boathouse. There was a living room, a bedroom, an open-air deck overlooking the water, big glass windows on three sides and a cavernous basement beneath for storing and maintaining boats.

His housekeeper, Mrs Renyard, was at work in the tiny boathouse kitchen, housed in little more than a cupboard. Laid out on the table were his binoculars for viewing birds down at the water's edge; a newspaper and a folder of papers. As the sun moved round, the brigadier, his breakfast things and papers moved with it. He liked to keep the sun on his back.

Mrs Renyard was employed at The Rectory because, unusually for Somerville locals, she didn't chatter. She was loyal, never joking in the village about his quirks. She considered them signs – proof in fact – that he was a real gentleman. She was innocent of exactly how suitable she was to be employed at The Rectory.

As he ate, absorbed in the newspaper, he stopped only to brood on how he would tell his children that their mother would not be returning from South Africa. Audrey had left three months before, her excuse for the trip, the third in 18 months, as usual the need to care for her ageing parents. Inside the folder, away from Mrs Renyard's gaze, was a letter from her saying she needed to delay returning for at least another month. But Maxwell knew that there was another reason: a polo pony trainer, 15 years younger than herself.

Leo came in as he was finishing the letter from Audrey. Unhurried, he closed the folder but left one hand resting on it.

'Brig, will you help me pay for more flying lessons? *Please*. I have decided *definitely* that I want to join the ATA. I need another 20 flying hours. They won't consider me with less than 45.'

He contemplated his daughter.

'Hello Brig, are you in there? You seem even further away than usual this morning. Right down the end of your cave. Couldn't you just come and stand at the entrance?'

Leo was the most difficult of his three children. Charles and Emily accepted that he was remote and worked around it. Leo couldn't. He didn't hold this against her, didn't love her any less, but she put him on edge by being direct, and asking him to be direct. He delivered his reply very slowly, littering it with agonizing pauses as if to say that it was painful to be talking at all. He seemed unaware of Leo struggling to control her impatience.

'What I am thinking, Leo, is that the Air Transport Auxiliary is a dangerous path for a young woman of 23… They insist you fly in all but the most impossible weather… Sometimes even in that, and with no radio contact with the ground… They'll stop at nothing to get fighters in place *on time* at the front line airfields. It's been making a difference to the air war… But they ask a great deal. Why don't you leave it to the men?'

'Daddy.' A word she never used except for serious business. 'You *know* why. The ATA has women pilots because they can fly as well as men. It's the one really useful thing I could do in this war. You *know* I want to help hurt the Nazis. I am *very* angry with them. You *know* that.'

Far within himself, Maxwell felt her aggression as if it was his own.

'Every time the ATA delivers a plane, it frees a combat pilot for action. It's the next best thing to pulling the trigger oneself.'

'So you've been saying… all round Somerville, I'm told. You shouldn't… It's… it's… Unladylike.'

'Brig, *really*. Who cares? Look. If you help me pay for the flying lessons, I'll stop saying it. Anyway, what's wrong with it? Makes people laugh.'

'Some think it's… artless.'

'Will you help pay?'

Another irritating pause. 'I will, but if you're accepted, expect fear, discomfort and exhaustion. D'you know what Beaverbrook said about the ATA pilots last week? He said they were fighting the war, just as surely as if they were in the front line. One of those young women has already been killed flying in low cloud – straight into a Welsh hillside.'

'I'm your awkward middle daughter. You can risk me. Charles is so brilliant at the Foreign Office, his job's reserved from call up. Emily's perfect too, ferrying admirals around Portsmouth harbour. You don't have to worry about her. The only one without a purpose is me. Isn't that shameful? Better risk than shame.'

'I know, Leo.' He sighed.

She saw, deep within, one of his gleams of approval. Leo stroked her spaniel, as if it was really her father who deserved to be stroked.

'Thank you Brig. You've made me very happy. If you'd said no, I would have borrowed the money from the Dunning-Greens, or someone.' Now her father looked truly horrified. Leo took no notice.

'I can't not do this. Did you know I am addicted to flying? Ever since the first lessons? I don't feel happy on the ground. I think of nothing else but being in the air. You don't know how happy it makes me just sitting in a cockpit.'

'I do, Leo. Now let's walk up to the house. Cobb is waiting to take me to the station.'

As they walked, Leo said 'I know about Mummy. If you like, I'll tell Charles and Emily.'

'How do you know? Oh don't tell me, Somerville gossip. But how do the locals know what's going on in South Africa, for heaven's sake?'

'Kenneth Hodge has friends who live in Cape Town. Apparently it's an open secret there.'

The Daimler was outside the front door, engine running, Cobb at the wheel. Maxwell knew that Leo's offer to tell Charles and Emily – a task he dreaded – was her way of thanking him for the flying lessons. For a change, he thought, she was doing something the Maxwell way – indirectly, dry of surface emotion. He turned to her and gave her another gleam.

'Yes, please tell them. *Thank you.* You get my vote for wanting to join the ATA. And I agree, women can obviously be as good as men at flying planes. I had to test your resolve – that's all.' The gleam vanished. 'One more thing. We're not going to win this war by getting cross with the Germans.'

Leo again took no notice, but savoured her good fortune. 'Brig, this is a special day. Usually you take all day to decide to spend money – whether it's five shillings or 500 pounds.'

The Daimler, 13th-18th Hussars pennant fluttering on the bonnet, made its way through the village high street. Locals were used to the sight of the uniformed Brig being driven to the local station on a Monday and back on a Friday. They understood that he spent the week working in Whitehall, lodging in The Cavalry Club.

Twenty minutes later the car reached the station. Cobb and Maxwell hadn't exchanged a word – like Mrs Renyard, the driver was chosen for his silent ways. Both felt deeply comfortable with each other: Cobb had never known the brigadier keep him waiting more than two minutes later than an agreed rendezvous and served him, partly as a result, with copper-bottomed loyalty. Instead of getting out to catch the London train, Maxwell stayed seated. Cobb scanned the forecourt for anyone who could be looking at the car, then said:

'Forecourt empty, sir, they must all be on the platform.'

At this the brigadier dipped out of sight, lying lengthwise on the back seat, covering himself with a rug. In seconds the car was turning out of the station, apparently without a passenger, and in another five it was off the main road down a gravel track, leading deep into woodland. Cobb got out to take a holdall from the boot. From it came a tweed jacket and tie for the brigadier and a sweater for himself. The brigadier exchanged his uniform coat for the jacket and tie. Cobb put the sweater on over his uniform. Next he clipped on false number plates, and took off the flag, all without a word exchanged.

Using a roundabout route through narrow lanes and farm tracks – Cobb varied the route every time – he drove the brigadier back towards Somerville.

Unseen, the car entered the woodland behind the village and

minutes later was approaching Woodland House, one of five taken over by the war office in 1939 for the SOE training schools. Maxwell had proposed the location, aware that SOE was the wild card of British intelligence, created by Churchill to mount showy, daring operations in occupied Europe. He still considered the choice inspired – Somerville was a community of individuals, if nothing else. Regular soldiers and ordinary spies – but not Maxwell – disapproved of SOE's free rein – its 'loud bangs', its explosions and its plain-clothes missions. They were jealous of its command structure. Independent of MI6, it was unencumbered by a top layer of spy chiefs. The head of SOE, Colonel Jeremy Gunn, reported directly to the Prime Minister and cabinet. Maxwell admitted to himself how much he enjoyed being directly connected via Gunn to the centre of power, yet not within its orbit, with maximum freedom to follow his own devices.

Not so enjoyable, he reminded himself, was having to mislead his Somerville neighbours. They remained convinced that Maxwell was a regular army officer.

He thought back, satisfied but not complacent, over the last 15 years, most of it spent in the secret world of intelligence. He was now one of the top layer – the four deputy chiefs – of SIS, the Secret Intelligence Service, also known as MI6, dealing with foreign rather than internal threats. Its employees almost never referred to it as MI6, preferring 'the Service' or 'C's organization' – C being the codename for its director. Maxwell's London office was an anonymous building in St James's Street, and his roving brief the envy of the other deputy chiefs: to understand and to observe the work of all branches of SIS and to report to the chief his views – a minister without portfolio. He knew everyone, and had exceptional influence, and now he told himself, again, never to be complacent about it. He'd heard that those inclined to be jealous described him as an interferer. In fact, Maxwell knew that he was the opposite, a worker.

'If I arrive in your office, asking what you would like to achieve but cannot because manpower is limited, things will change. My small team will deliver back-up, working all night and all weekend if necessary.'

People quickly found they could rely on his grasp of detail and concentration span. He didn't just apply himself, he ate work, and he told himself once more as they parked outside Woodland House that he would amount to nothing if he ever relaxed this austere commitment.

He'd pointed out to Gunn that Somerville was one of the few places in southern England that offered a group of neighbouring large houses, hidden down gravel tracks in woodland, invisible from roads and out of sight of each other.

'Few neighbourhoods are so upper-middle-class – so patriotic, or conservative.' Gunn had taken little persuading.

He'd asked Maxwell not only to find the houses, but to oversee the spy school's early months and first operations. The project had quickly caught Maxwell's imagination. He was all over it, spending almost every other week at Woodland House, unknown to his family or to Somerville.

Gleaming inwardly as he got out of the car, but his face as ever deadpan, he recalled how easy it had been getting the houses. They had been built as spacious country residences for friends of the old Lord Taunton in the early 1900s. Sold on long leases, over the intervening 40 years they had come back into the Somerville Estate as rental properties. He had asked Lord Taunton to make them available to SOE, and it was done. Gunn was duly grateful to Maxwell, and Maxwell gleamed again inwardly at the arrangement's secret bonus. He'd got to know Portia. Taunton had delegated to his eldest daughter the detailed work of writing the new leases. Contrary to her glacial reputation, Maxwell had found her delightfully accessible. She'd ignored his own reserved manner, as if to say 'Treat me the same'. He'd found her one of the easiest people he'd ever met to work with on detailed legal documents, her mind a steel trap, effortlessly cutting through the foliage to the consequences of every word, every comma. Audrey, by contrast (and now the gleam faded), was an uphill struggle when it came to any document longer than a few lines.

Woodland House was the officer's mess and headquarters, where Maxwell had a desk. Nearby Brindley House was where Polish and Czech trainee agents, including George Adams, were housed. Also in the same rhododendron and conifer woods was The Pines, which was mainly for English agents. A mile away, on the banks of the river, two more houses were for Norwegian and Free French agents.

Maxwell felt comfortable that Somerville residents were well aware of spies and saboteurs – hush-hush troops as they liked to call them – being trained in the houses, and luxuriated in the knowledge that SOE was one of Churchill's pet projects. They could only guess at the nature of the operations for which the agents were being prepared, and reckoned it their part of the war effort not to broadcast their presence.

Driving the establishment of SOE Somerville was the necessary realization that British intelligence, spies and special operations were amateurish (as Maxwell had realized on his first day in the Service) compared with their German counterparts – that they had hardly moved on since the First World War. There was a pressing need for training. British intelligence, he knew, could no longer rely so much on its senior officers' traditional weapon: their brilliance at judging character.

Lt. Colonel Robert MacDonald, commandant in day-to-day charge of SOE Somerville, was waiting for Maxwell inside the front door, tension in his face. He gestured Maxwell into his office, a tiny room with no space to move. Converted from a cloakroom, it still had a former occupant's sepia photos of yachts on the walls. Crammed in, they leant side by side on the desk – a piece of board mounted along one wall.

'Better not be heard.'

Forty-five years ago, MacDonald and Maxwell had arrived

at prep school as boys of eight, same day, same term. Both had gone to the same public school, and to the same Oxford college. Their near-absolute rapport was grounded in MacDonald being a natural communicator, and Maxwell the opposite. When alone, they still used their prep school nicknames, Viv for Vivian Maxwell and Robbo for Robert MacDonald. Robbo enjoyed the challenge of compressing his thoughts into clipped military language. Viv relied on Robbo's acute understanding of his sparse use of words and the subtleties of the nasal drawl he substituted for speech – when he could get away with it.

'Problem, Viv.'

'Oh?'

'Remember the O'Grady case? Two months back?'

'Indeed.'

'On the face of it, a respectable Isle of Wight landlady. Arrested for repeatedly trespassing on beaches near Ventnor. Walking her dog.'

'Ah… yes. The beaches were closed by the army – potential landing sites for a German amphibious force, as I remember.'

'Correct. And Ventnor Chain Home Station nearby.'

One of the chain of 21 south-coast radar posts, Ventnor relayed early warnings of German fighter and bomber formations to RAF fighter command when the enemy planes were still far out over the Channel. They were one of the RAF's critical advantages in the Battle of Britain.

'Yes… it was attacked by the Luftwaffe in August. Curious, eh

Robbo?'

'Maybe. But the point is, everyone thought she was innocent. She claimed she was walking her dog and hadn't noticed the 'keep out' signs. Police believed her. Press on her side. But she's still in jail, awaiting trial.'

'Oh?'

'The press weren't told what the police found in her bag: detailed drawings of the Ventnor radar site. Lists and map references of all the restricted beaches on the south side of the island. Plausible stuff, the work of someone who might have been trained.'

'How do you know?'

'MI5 have just sent us privileged sight of the notes of her interrogation. Take a look. They'll be used at the trial – private hearing's coming up.'

'Until now I've agreed with you that fifth columnists are unlikely. German agents have been dropped by parachute or landed by boat. None have admitted plans to work with agents already in place.'

'And this makes you think differently?'

'It's opened my mind. If German intelligence planted O'Grady, there could be others.'

'Hmm.'

'The question is not so much is there a fifth columnist in Somerville, but what should we do to cover ourselves?'

'Ah, yes.'

'SOE Somerville is vulnerable. Not on the inside, you know we've allowed for that. But outside? Different. Can't be controlled.'

'You really think it's possible a German sleeper might be in a place like Somerville, looking for a chance to turn one of our trainees?'

'Just possible if we got a bad egg. After all, they go all over the estate on exercises. Chance to meet, drop messages. If it happened, and we were shown to have taken no precautions – we wouldn't look good, Viv.'

Silence, then a sigh and a nod from Maxwell.

'I know you hate the idea, but I think we've got to start watching the local community. You know most of the residents personally or by repute. But more's needed. Active surveillance.'

MacDonald took Maxwell into a room across the hall, Woodland House's dining room, with its long polished table and views down the lawn to rhododendrons and azaleas. Seated at the table was Jerzy Adamski, who immediately recognized Maxwell as the man on the platform at Sailing Club Point. The father of the girl. Beneath his stubble, he turned pink.

'Brigadier, this is Adamski, codename Labrador. Adamski, Brigadier Maxwell is a senior colleague from London. Brigadier, I think Labrador could be ideal for our plan.'

No reply from Maxwell – he seemed to be withdrawing even further than usual. Then he issued some of his most curious sounds, between a drawl and a growl.

Labrador looked confused. MacDonald recognized them as strong disapproval. Maxwell explained:

'Churchill himself has ordered that agents' code names should never hint at the owner's identity.'

Everything about Labrador was dark, or black: dark brown eyes, darkened skin around the eyes, thick black eyebrows, deep black hair with a shine that made it even blacker. He was a black Labrador. The intervention gave him a little more time in which to compose himself. Again, he'd been surprised: MacDonald had referred to Maxwell as 'Brigadier'. The girl's father was a senior officer. MacDonald spoke.

'Well Brigadier, perhaps on this occasion Labrador is OK. It could mean a black dog or a province of Canada. And sometimes Labradors are yellow.'

'Ah. Very well.'

'Indeed, Brigadier, when you know Labrador better you may well conclude that his true character has little in common with that breed of dog.'

They sent Labrador out of the room while MacDonald showed Maxwell the Pole's file.

'He's one of our best current trainees. From a security perspective, as clean as a whistle. Told us that the Nazi atrocities near Lodz in September 1939 had claimed his family. We checked this out with other Poles who arrived in Britain at the same time. They're a fact. He never mentioned exactly what happened to his family during his debriefing, except indirectly. As if too hard to talk about.'

'So can you guess what happened?'

'He told us only that his family tried to escape – and that he got away.'

'What then?'

'He got to London via Spain. He was handed over to British intelligence within hours of his arrival, then sent to basic training school, then to Scotland for the physical stuff, then brought down to Somerville, where he's lived under the eyes of his instructors. His room's been searched regularly for any sign of outside contact – like them all.'

They called Labrador back into the dining room. Maxwell spoke, weightily.

'Labrador. Alongside training activities, in fact, as part of them, you will now keep the local community under surveillance. MacDonald will brief you in detail. Regard this as an honour, a sign we believe in your potential. Superb on-the-job training for any spy or saboteur.'

3

Maxwell stayed the week at Woodland House, returning to The Rectory on Friday using the reverse of the Monday morning routine, and arriving home in his uniform, as he had left. He couldn't remember when he had last come home to an empty house, and he didn't enjoy it. Leo was in lodgings near Eastleigh Aerodrome, on the edge of Southampton, absorbed in her flying hours. She and Charles would be back tomorrow for a brief visit. Emily, a recent recruit to the WRNS, had to stay in Portsmouth. Mrs Renyard had left his supper ready to put in the oven.

At least he had the Up River Race to distract him. It was usually held three weeks after the regatta, but the Brig had decided to bring it forward because he and his committee were embarrassed that the S.R.S.C., alone among south-coast sailing clubs, was still running races when the rest had wound themselves up after

Dunkirk. At the least he must get the dinghies away from Sailing Club Point, where they were conspicuous to passing craft. Lined up discreetly on his beach at the wooded top reach of the river, members could collect and take them home at their convenience.

Usually the Up River Race was followed by the Autumn Series of races, run from the Brig's jetty – a means of prolonging the charm of a Somerville summer. With the Battle of Britain raging over the Home Counties and Channel even more intensely, and more in the balance than a week ago, to carry on sailing would be inappropriate.

'Well Brigadier,' ventured Kenneth Hodge chummily, 'what rules are we following today?'

'Ehn?' The Brig's drawl irritated Hodge more than the Brig knew. Hodge was sitting in Maxwell's diesel launch as it followed the fleet up river. He had invited himself to join the Captain because he wasn't sailing – it was his wife's turn to use the boat they shared.

The launch was escort-and-rescue-boat for the long race, which was about three miles from the estuary to the top of the river, through numerous bends. The Brig was at the helm, staying silent if he could. His personal Captain's flag, the S.R.S.C. burgee modified by a large red blob, fluttered at the bow.

The bends and the trees lining the banks made the race uniquely difficult. Somerville sailors considered that if you could sail here, you could sail well anywhere. The wind's direction shifted, sometimes right round the compass, because the trees bounced the wind back and forth, or funnelled it. The race was always sailed on a rising tide, because if the wind died, the boats would be swept back down river on the ebb. Sailors had an advantage if they took the trouble to learn where the current was strongest. To the Brig and his fellow residents, the race was a near-sacred ritual – uniquely Somerville, they liked to say – in the way *terroir* defines the character of a wine.

The wind had turned since last weekend from a frivolous, dry, warm south-easterly to a business-like, moisture laden south-westerly. It smelt anxious: of going back to school, or to work, after the summer break. The dinghies heeled sharply in the first reach, exposed to the wind coming fresh off the sea, and the Brig was able to keep Hodge at a distance by staying close in at the rear and concentrating intensely on the boats, in case of a capsize.

He didn't want Hodge on his boat, but took pains – successfully – to conceal this. Yet someone who knew Maxwell better than Hodge might get wind of his feelings because he was drawling more than usual. After the first bend, when the wind had calmed, Hodge returned to his question. He didn't yet dare call this remotest of men by his nickname. Somehow – effortlessly – the Brig kept him from doing so, but with infinite politeness.

'Yes Brigadier... Normal sailing rules: first boat over the line wins, provided he or she hasn't infringed the rules of sailing, or if they have, made a penalty turn. Somerville rules: everyone holds back until the peerage – the Tauntons – have rounded the first mark, followed by younger sons and daughters, then baronets, then knights and afterwards commoners.'

'Ah. Yes. Very amusing.'

'That's what other sailing clubs joke about the S.R.S.C. Did you know that, Brigadier?'

'No. Yes. Yes, I did. Most amusing.' Silence.

In fact, Hodge did feel himself silenced, unarguably. His barometer measuring resentment against the brigadier specifically and Somerville attitudes in general, rose several points and the feeling was stored.

The Brig stayed silent, Hodge unable to read his face for any reaction. As they chugged among the dinghies, the Brig fell reluctantly to the odious task of pondering the possibility that someone on the river might be an *Abwehr* agent – a German intelligence agent – active or sleeping. He made himself consider the committee members one by one from the miserable perspective of an intelligence professional.

In fifth place, not too bad a position, was Portia St James, the club's Vice Commodore. Good sailor, but not among the best. The idea of her being a secret Nazi sympathizer was amusing: the Earldom of Taunton was one of the handful of British titles that could pass through the female line. The present Earl and Countess had five daughters, so Portia, the eldest, was the next Countess of Taunton in her own right. Somerville's acres would be hers; her eldest son or daughter would inherit the title and another smaller estate in Gloucestershire. And so on, probably forever. The family, staunch Roman Catholics, had been embedded in the fabric of Britain for 500 years.

And here, in third place, Henry Dunning-Green, the Sailing Secretary. A very good sailor, like his younger brother Freddie. Sometimes he could beat Leo. Good thing. Henry had almost as much to lose materially from Nazi occupation as Portia. Anyway, Maxwell could dismiss him: he had known almost every corner of his character since he was a boy.

Next he focussed on Patricia Selby-Pickforth, Club Secretary, and Colonel Mackworth, bosun, both as usual near the back of the fleet. They summed up Somerville gentry: too unimaginative, too settled in marriage, too comfortable financially and too content with life on the Somer River to have the motivation for treachery.

Then there was Lady Flavia, 23, youngest of the Taunton daughters, chasing Portia in sixth place. Somerville preferred not to think about the 17 years that separated them. Portia was unmarried, with not a suitor in sight. Flavia, the happy little afterthought, an outgoing creature, was very good indeed as Social Secretary. She loved organizing parties and Somerville loved her back. But now the Brig had to admit to himself that she could be a risk – vanishingly small, but still potentially a risk. She was the Taunton family's wild card, a Bohemian who spent time in London jazz clubs and was friendly with musicians.

Finally there was the newcomer, Hodge, the Treasurer, sitting uncomfortably close to him in his launch. In the two years since arriving at Somerville, the solicitor had ingratiated himself with the committee, determined to be accepted, to have a role. One of Maxwell's few prejudices was against lawyers, but he forced himself to balance out the evidence. On the one hand, Hodge had everything to gain from preserving the way of life for which he had worked hard. On the other, he could, just possibly, be a blackmail target. There was gossip that he'd left Hamble, another south-coast sailing village where he'd rented a cottage, because of an affair. Somerville was now used to observing how he reserved his charm for women, while not troubling with the men unless they could be useful. Enough for today. The rest of the community could wait for his scrutiny.

The following weekend, the Brig, still alone at The Rectory, held the final committee meeting of the year to formalize the winding up of the club. The committee members gathered before lunch. The Brig had turned the occasion into a modest celebration of ten golden years for the club, now coming to an end. The guests assembled on the boathouse deck, overlooking the river, Mrs Renyard handing round strips of smoked eel on toast while Cobb poured vintage champagne. 'Typical Brig', she muttered to herself approvingly. 'Expensive but not showy.'

The Brig suggested that there was time before lunch to go down to the first river bend to look at the godwits. Kenneth Hodge and Lady Flavia said they couldn't tell a godwit from a peewit and preferred to walk around the garden. As the godwit party chugged away from the jetty in the Brig's glossily varnished launch, Social Secretary and Treasurer were seen strolling across the lawn towards the rhododendron walk, a long, densely covered arbour.

The launch's diesel engine thumped reliably and the boat party was a contented group. The oaks overhanging the water's edge made a domesticating barrier between the salt of the river and the orderly gardens running down to the bank. This top reach was much gentler than Sailing Club Point. The Brig had another moment of serene awareness, of everything in its appointed place: the last for a long time. Portia interrupted his thoughts.

'Brig, what do you think about the air battle? Are we holding them off?'

'Possibly.' Long pause for thought. 'Our Spitfires and Hurricanes are outnumbered – no doubt about it. Of course you can't tell the truth about losses from the newspapers.' Another pause. 'But let's assume it's about the same on both sides – fair bet, don't you think? Then you're left with one factor the Germans can't overcome. They're operating at the limit of their range. As soon as they get into a dogfight this side of the Channel, fuel starts draining away double quick. All that climbing and turning. Time to turn tail comes very soon. Could well be a stalemate – but in our favour.'

'I read in my paper that some of the pilots are 19 years old.' Henry Dunning-Green intervened, sadly: 'And I'm 28, stuck on Pirbright ranges training the 19-year-olds.'

'Must try your patience, Henry. You shouldn't be such a brilliant shot.'

'My penance for all those happy times in the Eton shooting team. Whenever I meet someone who's on active service, or about to be posted, they seem... bigger than me. Actually larger, as if they occupy more space. It's unbearable, I'm so jealous, especially of the RAF pilots.'

Patricia Selby-Pickforth could not help herself. 'Our modern gladiators. Nobility personified. Must be so lonely and frightening up there in a cramped cockpit, knowing you're dead if you fly straight and level for more than 20 seconds. And most of them come from quite ordinary backgrounds – funny schools you've never heard of.'

'I'd have swapped Eton for a school you've never heard of if I'd known it would help me get into the RAF.'

'Can't you get transferred? Haven't you done your turn at Pirbright?'

'I'm trying to get into SOE, but it's taking months.' Maxwell silently took note. As they chugged back towards the jetty, Maxwell thought, once more, that the sea was not just a leveller of social class. Being afloat made people more candid than on land. And that Somerville was, on balance, a happy place, despite the petty snobberies, perhaps because the river life and the sailing were so useful for releasing locals from their everyday obsessions. There were endless gradations of wealth and status in the community, but not much jealousy, mainly acceptance. As for himself, he felt contented in his muted way, despite Audrey leaving. The marriage had not been happy, and his instincts told him that although he was in his 50s, life was far from over yet.

Around the dining table, the mood was unruffled, for a while. The white wine, a little known and subtle Loire, was perfect with the crab soufflé and the lemon soles that followed. Mrs Renyard brought the food to the sideboard, then retreated to the kitchen while the guests helped themselves. Cobb brought in the wine bottles, opened them and poured out the first glasses, then left them on the table.

'Brig, well done for getting things running smoothly despite Audrey being away. But do just ask me if you need help.' Patricia felt proprietorial about the Brig. Like him she had grown up at Somerville. Each other's foibles and faults no longer surprised them, their old friendship usually made them easier to overlook.

'Thank you, Patricia. By the way, Cobb is paid on a strictly private basis for help in the house. Don't want Somerville thinking the army funds my domestic arrangements.'

The trouble started when the main course was on the table. The Brig could be acutely aware of atmosphere. At the other end of the table, the talk had almost died, but only for a couple of heartbeats. Colonel Mackworth was observing Kenneth Hodge's right hand, which was holding his knife like a pencil. He had never sat down at a table with anyone who did this.

Nor had Patricia, who noticed it too, and was exchanging

looks with Mackworth. She shook her head briefly, as if to say 'Let it pass', which he did. This kind of incident was something to discuss later, at home. Hodge appeared innocent of the frisson he'd caused. If Patricia or Mackworth had made him aware, he would have ridiculed them, Maxwell suspected. In his imagination, Hodge's cutlery habit had rippled the gentle pool that was Somerville social life, and he would later think of the episode as an omen of trouble to come. He smoothed the moment's awkwardness by calling on Mackworth to fill the empty wine glasses. Lunch continued until the table was cleared and the committee meeting opened.

At the end of agenda item one, Hodge pulled his first deliberate stunt, as committee members would later describe it. There had been little argument about whether the club should disband. A war office regulation was in place requiring all small craft to be removed from waterways with sea access – in case they could help an invasion force. At least half the club's young and active members had been drafted into the forces or were doing compulsory war work.

Just before the Brig asked for a show of hands to confirm the decision to suspend sailing, Hodge cut in: 'Don't *you* have an opinion, Captain?' His tone was only half polite enquiry. Even Colonel Mackworth understood that this was a thinly veiled sneer at the Brig's taciturn style. The Brig took his time to reply, very quietly:

'Do I need one?' and again in his own time announced the

second item.

The Brig and Portia always dreaded the last but one item on the agenda – new membership applications. Their instinctive rapport, not noticed by the others – his reserve, and her poise – made sensing it impossible. Privately, they both wanted to relax the old guard's ban on anyone without good public school credentials. They thought the club could gradually admit a wider social range without spoiling its atmosphere. But they also knew that if there was to be change, it had to happen slowly. No one suspected they felt like this. Meanwhile they had to listen to Patricia Selby-Pickforth and Colonel Mackworth publicly scrutinising applicants' social standing. Three out of five new candidates were allowed in, and two rejected because they were in trade. They would get short messages telling them that the club was full. Then Hodge spoke again.

'I want the committee to know that at the AGM I will publicly ask for the S.R.S.C.'s membership rules to be examined by a subcommittee.'

'What *can* you mean?' Patricia Selby-Pickforth was profoundly shocked.

'I mean' – he spoke slowly, as if to child – 'that the rules are *outdated*, and that they *discriminate*.' Then, smoothly, and quietly, for maximum effect: 'You all need to move on. The world will be different after the war. You need to encourage all social classes to join the club.'

Hodge threw his final grenade towards the end of Any Other

Business, staring brazenly (as Patricia Selby-Pickforth would later say) at Portia:

'I propose that the *Viscountess* St James (intoning her name as if it was a pantomine part) be barred from attending future committee meetings as a so-called observer. She's not an observer. She influences outcomes, and she doesn't have a vote. It's a travesty of democracy.' Then, eyeballing The Brig:

'And don't fob me off with one of your subcommittees, Maxwell. This is simple stuff.'

So they were forced to vote on the unthinkable. The motion was defeated eight to one, but the worm had crawled out of the apple. No one lingered to chat as they usually did after meetings. By the front door, Hodge approached the Brig, who was trying to avoid him, and planted his business card in the Brig's hand.

'You might find this, erm… Useful, given… ' But now Hodge faltered. The Brig was gazing at him, and Hodge had never seen such frightening eyes. He had to squeeze it out.

'… Given what's happening in your private life.'

Several people saw and heard, and were too embarrassed to linger. The Brig opened the door showing Hodge out, silently handing back the card.

4

'Robbo? Are you alone?' Maxwell was on the phone to MacDonald next morning, from his London office. MacDonald sat up. Speech without pauses meant that Maxwell was agitated.

'Yes.'

'Something's rattled me. There's a Somerville character called Hodge. He had several outbursts during the sailing club meeting at the weekend. Most peculiar. I can't figure out the motive. He seems suspiciously like an agent under strain. Strange it happened so soon after our conversation about sleepers.'

'Go on.'

'He peppered our sailing club committee meeting with… with provocations – his behaviour seemed, well, contrived.'

'Give me some background.'

'His timing was odd, too. He's a newcomer to Somerville. Wants to be accepted. Maybe he's a private socialist with ambitions to reform the club – but why do it now when the club is about to hibernate for the war?'

Maxwell explained that since Hodge had bought his cottage at Somerville, despite working hard to be accepted, he hadn't made any real friends.

'Reforming the club would need lobbying to win a vote at the AGM. Can't be done without a power base of like-minded friends among the members. So what's he up to?'

'Seems like a warning. So soon after we talked about the O'Grady case. The answer's a full background report, Viv. If only to show London how thorough we are.'

'Oh God. Time consuming and expensive.'

'Don't be cheap. SOE Somerville's security is priceless.'

'Oh very well, Robbo. Do it.'

MacDonald immediately called MI5 to request a full confidential background report on Hodge covering every detail of his life, concentrating especially on friends at university and any foreign travel in the years leading up to 1939.

A team of three young MI5 staff, posing as journalists for the *London Professional Journal,* a bogus publication, began arranging interviews with anyone they could find who knew Hodge. They said they were researching a profile of Hodge and his successful legal practice, highlighting the impact of war on those men in their 30s left in the profession pending call-up. They talked to his teachers at school; to contemporaries at Cambridge; to professional contacts; and, for the personal angle and some colour, to former neighbours at Hamble.

Later in the day, MacDonald rang Maxwell again.

'Viv, I think we have to put Hodge under surveillance as well as doing the enquiry. What are his movements?'

'Arrives at his cottage after the week's work in London and leaves again Monday morning.'

'As good a place as any for Labrador to start. I think we should have an insurance policy too.'

'What d'you mean?'

'Have Labrador tailed too. Just to make sure he's clean. If he is, then we can use him long term without worrying.'

'I feel terrible about this, Robbo. It's fine for you, but I've lived in Somerville all my life. It's called littering the nest.'

As Maxwell walked from his St James's Street office to The Cavalry Club, he contemplated the leaves on the plane trees, now autumn yellow. In a week or two the branches would be bare. He had trained himself to react as little as possible to the changing of the seasons because the decline of summer into autumn always upset his aim of a dispassionate, balanced mind. But he couldn't ignore the changing season now – it mirrored the rising tide of his troubles. Audrey. Leo joining the ATA. The S.R.S.C. *status quo* challenged by an upstart. The dirty business of intelligence spilling over into Somerville. The unthinkable consequences of SOE Somerville penetrated by the *Abwehr*. The deaths of dozens of agents already sent, or soon to go, to occupied France.

*

Adrian Russell knew he was the best instructor at SOE, but he no longer took pride in it – if he ever had. His subject was psychological warfare and political subversion, which he had taught since June, when he had been transferred to Somerville from SOE's failed training establishment at Brackonbury in Hertfordshire. This morning he was at Brindley House, talking to a small group.

'Propaganda leaflets are a waste of time unless dropped from the air on a large population behind enemy lines. Using printing presses in Nazi-occupied countries is hopeless. The Germans will torture or imprison every printer until they confess who ordered the leaflets.

'The best way to undermine Nazi morale is to spend time in bars and eating places socializing with locals, introducing well-directed rumour at community level.'

Russell reckoned that Maxwell and MacDonald mostly thought well of him. It helped, probably, though he couldn't be sure, that he'd been at Westminster School, got a degree at Cambridge and was a reporter in Spain for *The Times* during the Spanish Civil War. He was vain enough to know that his good-looking, fleshy face and thick head of neatly parted hair were no handicap. To the instructors from less privileged backgrounds, he knew he appeared as a smoothly self-confident public school type, though unusually friendly and unassuming. For Maxwell and MacDonald he thought of himself as good company. He was well dressed, usually in pale, well-cut linen suits and light-coloured shoes. He didn't know that the shoes made Maxwell uneasy.

'Never claim you've heard something from a reliable source.' Russell went on. 'The best technique is to drop a rumour into conversation as a joke, saying you have no idea if it's true. For example, the prostitutes in the local brothel, used by Nazi officers, are riddled with venereal disease. Or that local Nazi officials were corruptly selling goods on the black market.

'You'll find it satisfying how quickly and effectively a rumour will travel if it's entertaining. Whether it's true hardly matters.'

It was pure pleasure that no one at SOE Somerville, or in SIS, suspected he was a Soviet agent who had been recruited in Spain by the Russian secret service in 1932. In 1940, The Nazi-Soviet Pact of August 1939 was still in place, so Russell was officially an enemy agent. 'But who cares if I contribute to the British war effort? Sooner rather than later the Nazis will have to be eradicated from Europe if communism is to flourish, and for this Britain and America are still useful. Plenty of time after that to damage British interests.' Meanwhile, he'd rise high in British intelligence, to where there was information worth passing to Moscow.

This interlude among the rhododendron woods of Somerville bored him. He longed to be nearer the centre. 'I need amusement.'

Which was why, soon after arriving, he had got in touch with his old Cambridge friend, Kenneth Hodge.

*

On a Friday soon after, Maxwell caught a late train from Paddington and got out at Hampton, a town 40 minutes up the railway line from Somerville. When Cobb and Mrs Renyard had Friday night off, he stayed overnight at the Admiral Collingwood, a coaching inn of character and charm opposite the station. It was a useful arrangement because he could use the Collingwood, or other discreet places in the city, for secret meetings. Cobb would pick him up next morning.

He ate quickly, alone in the dining room, then went to his room, settling down with a novel. The silence was broken soon after by soft sighs and murmurs, heard through the thin wall from the next room. Next there was the gentle, regular bump of a bedstead against the wall. Maxwell listened, feeling envy, fascination and irritation. The bumping went slowly, rhythmically on for minutes, and then he started to hear clear but more or less controlled female moans of pleasure. Whoever was making love with her was a stayer. The moans and the bumping mounted in volume and frequency for several minutes more until the bed was rattling fast against the wall and she abandoned herself to noisy gasps. Then the sounds ebbed away, and Maxwell had another thought to add to those already churning through his brain.

*

The following day, Hodge drove into Milton, the small town on the coast to the west of Somerville and after some shopping made his way on foot to the park, where he took from a litter bin a folded copy of *The Milton Times*. Starting on the inside pages, certain words had been underlined. Hodge wrote down in his notebook the third letter of each word. Soon he had a new word – c-h-e-q-u-e-r-s.

He walked to the station and bought a ticket to the next town along the coast, Streteford, a 15-minute ride. Labrador, who had been tracking Hodge since he left his cottage at Somerville, followed. Labrador's tails followed too, far enough behind not to alert Labrador. Once Hodge had gone in to The Chequers, Labrador loitered out of sight, checking the door regularly for Hodge's exit.

Adrian Russell was waiting for Hodge with a gin and tonic. One of Russell's little ways was to note what companions liked to drink, make a point of arriving at the bar first, and have it ready – a small thoughtfulness that had already won him friends in the Service.

Hodge and Russell had met in Streteford, at different pubs, on several weekends since Russell's arrival at Somerville in June. The secrecy of the meetings excited Hodge, and once inside their clandestine alcoholic bubble, the real world retreated. Russell always got very drunk, and Hodge relaxed, lapping up Russell's comic mockery of the SOE instructors, the army, the secret service and the British establishment.

Hodge's favourite subject, which chimed with Russell's mockery, was the absurdity and the outdated attitudes of the people he'd met at Somerville: Patricia Selby-Pickforth's obsession with genealogy – and her snobbery; Mackworth, the supreme colonel blimp; Portia St James's invincible breeding; and the strange brigadier.

'I'm going to admit something to you Adrian… I wouldn't say it to many people. Maxwell makes me feel small, without trying. Must be his effortless dignity. I far prefer the swagger of Sir Geoffrey Dunning-Green, even the dim arrogance of Colonel Mackworth.'

*

'Reggie, I want to hold a post-mortem dinner.'

'A what?'

'Don't be difficult, Reggie. I want to have people here to discuss the S.R.S.C. committee meeting. The one I told you about – when Hodge was so rude.'

Reggie Selby-Pickforth groaned.

'Somerville loves a post-mortem. Our friends get double value from social events by having a lunch or supper afterwards to discuss how it went.'

'You mean to pore over guests' behaviour and sift through the flotsam, looking for dirt.'

'*Reggie.* This is serious. I've told you, bad things happened at that meeting. We need to work out what to do.'

'Why must we do it here?'

'I'm the natural hostess for the event because I was the main victim of Hodge's rudeness.'

'Well, darling, I suppose you're not often called ridiculous to your face.'

'As I told you several times, the Brig was the second most important victim, and Portia St James the third, so they will be the top guests. But I also want to invite Colonel Mackworth and his wife.'

'Oh God.'

'And I want the Jenningses too, as independent observers. They will learn what happened and go out into Somerville to spread our version of events. Originating from this house, the gossip would give our little party a certain *cachet*. Think of it, Reggie, as a top-table council of war against change, with the biggest guns of old Somerville ranged against new and not yet understood forces. You're not against that, are you?'

Sir Reginald Selby-Pickforth had spent his life as a civil servant at the Home Office. He understood change, how to manage it, and how to resist it.

It was rare for one of the Tauntons to dine with a Somerville resident, and within a day or two, the village knew that Lady Selby-Pickforth had Lady St James coming to dinner. It was hard to know which was more to the point – that something major must be afoot, or that Patricia had never seemed happier, even when Reggie was knighted.

There was a final thrill for Patricia: under her roof she would have the two best family trees in Somerville – Portia's, and the Brig's.

Her set of social and genealogical reference books was legendary. Most Somerville residents had *Who's Who* on their shelves, and those with aristocratic connections also had *Burke's Peerage*. To these Patricia added *Debrett's Peerage, Burke's Landed Gentry, Kelly's Handbook of the Landed and Ruling Classes* and lastly, her favourite, *The Plantagenet Register*, a list of a few hundred individuals who were reasonably verifiable descendants, mainly in the male line, of the pre-Tudor kings of England. In other words, the surviving outposts of the real old nobility of Europe.

In Patricia's mind, Portia's pedigree was a Christmas tree lit up with the fairy lights – the names of all the great families with whom the Tauntons had intermarried over 500 years. Her books revealed that their founding father was a 15th-century abbot from humble origins, who had ended as a prince-bishop, raising and running a private army for the king.

She saw the Brig's tree as much less impressive, plainer but romantic: one of the oaks that lined the river banks. His father was the last of a line of Somerset landed gentry who had come south from lowland Scotland in the 1790s. The Brig was, as Patricia often told him, the only Somerville resident in *The Plantagenet Register*. She reminded herself once again of their pedigrees just before her guests arrived, accidentally leaving the books open on the piano. Reggie noticed, and put them away.

Patricia produced an acceptable dinner, even for October 1940. She had got venison from the Tauntons' keeper, and fish from local fishermen. Reggie still had some of The Wine Society's Claret in his cellar. Convention disallowed serious discussion of any topic until late in the first course. Colonel Mackworth burst out, as soon as he could:

'How about this Hodge fellow then, what?'

The discussion covered every viewpoint, from publicly demanding Hodge's immediate resignation from the club to inviting him to a private meeting to justify his views. The Brig and Portia listened closely, the Brig staying silent. Portia spoke:

'While there's a chance of it all going away, no one should be openly combative.' The Brig nodded.

The Jenningses didn't like the soft approach.

'If this kind of behaviour's allowed, what will happen next?'

Mackworth spluttered agreement.

'That Hodge fellow. Extremist. Wants to undo everything the club has achieved in its first ten years. Doesn't he realize we're the envy of every other sailing club on the South Coast? Why should we change? What's he up to? Wouldn't surprise me if he's a traitor – a German agent or what-have-you. Everything he said stank of treachery. Come on, Brigadier, speak up. You must have some friends in the spy world. Perhaps he's here spying on the hush-hush troops?'

The Brig sat up, keeping his hands out of sight and taking care to shift his gaze quickly from face to face as he spoke. No one had time to observe his eyes. Body language was a long way yet from a recognized study, but he knew that when you tell a lie, you cannot stop your pupils narrowing.

'I don't think he's an agent – that's just speculation. But if anything else suspicious happens, I might ask SIS to investigate.'

He went on slowly, in a low, forceful tone. Everyone listened. It was rare to hear him speak at this length without pauses.

'But... If you want to think of him as a Nazi agent, that's not a bad idea. Just don't assume it's true. And for heaven's sake, be professional. Don't *ever* let him think you suspect. Don't change your behaviour towards him. He's annoyed the community, so don't be too friendly – but don't cut him out, either. If he thinks he's suspected, he'll disappear. If he is an agent, he'll be working with someone else, and the intelligence people will want him to lead us to whoever that is.'

'Does that mean we have to let him meddle with the club membership rules?'

'Even that, Patricia. Let him meddle. We can always reverse it later.'

In the end, all of them, including Patricia, swallowed his plea but Maxwell went home deeply alarmed.

*

'Viv, the report's on my desk. Have you got a copy?'

Maxwell was in London again, MacDonald in his office at Woodland House.

'Yes. Will you summarize it for me?' MacDonald summarized brilliantly. Maxwell sometimes thought that Robbo was actually inhabiting the speech centre in his own left brain.

'Mostly it's starkly factual, relying on public and semi-private records. But combined with the anecdotes compiled by the *London Professional Journal* reporters, we get some colour. Reaches back into his grandfather's time. The man was a labourer in the London Docks, a loyal employee of the Queen Victoria Dock Company from the early 1860s to the late 1880s. His son, Norman, would have followed his father as a stevedore, but didn't have the physique for heavy manual labour. Instead, he was sponsored by the company charity to do an apprenticeship in the accounts office. The training was only available to families who'd served the company for more than 20 years.'

'Must have made the Hodges feel special.'

'Indeed. A pattern you'll see repeated. Norman did well in accounts, working there until 1920 but presumably outgrowing the job because he moved that year, aged 35, from Wapping to Chelmsford to start his own book keeping and accountancy practice, serving dentists and doctors.' MacDonald then sketched out how the practice had prospered, and when Norman's only son Kenneth was 13, with help from an inheritance from the sale of Mrs Hodge's father's hat shop, it was decided that Kenneth should have the best education possible.

'Mill Hill, in case you don't know, Viv, is a very minor public school in North London, just 45 minutes from the Hodge villa in Chelmsford. According to a master, Kenneth fitted in well. Teasing flowed off his back. He worked the system. Reached physical maturity early. Powerful frame at 15. He offered to carry prefects' rifles home at the end of corps exercises – in return for favours. Those of lesser status were turned away coldly. Then he found his way into the sailing world. Mersea, on the north bank of the Thames estuary, was an hour from Chelmsford. The family became members of the Mersea Sailing Club. The records show Kenneth had sailing lessons in the school holidays. He was competitive, a regular trophy winner.'

'How did he do at Mill Hill?'

'Well. In 1928 he was accepted by St John's College, Cambridge. Then, for the first time, things didn't go his way. Seems he had happy memories of club life at the Mersea Sailing Club, so he mistakenly decided that it would be in keeping with his new status as a Cambridge undergraduate to join the Pitt Club.'

'Oh dear.'

'Indeed. The records show that he was blackballed. In the new members' proposals book applicants have to name their school. Below where Hodge had put Mill Hill, a 20-year-old Lord MacNeith, committee member, wrote 'Mole Hill?' Someone else had scrawled 'Where's that?''

'Very public. How did he take it?'

'Friends in his college say he hid his disappointment well. My theory is he made use of the experience – helped him become an expert in the gradations of the middle- and upper-middle-class world where he'd landed and how to exploit them.'

MacDonald then sketched out the rest of the report's findings on his Cambridge years. Adrian Russell and Guy Burgess had arrived a year later, in 1929. Both were remembered as undergraduates whom Hodge knew – possibly they had met at a Union debate. Russell was soon a member of The Apostles, the fraternity whose meetings and aims were secret, but thought to be Christian and socialist. Russell invited Hodge to be an 'embryo' – a probationary member – and in due course got full membership.

'Well, well, our friend Adrian Russell. By the way he talks now, he's shrugged off socialism. That's Cambridge for you: cesspit of radicalism. Have you come across Guy Burgess?'

'Yes. In C's organization. Troublesome character. Very bright. Drinker.'

'Not the best company to keep.'

'All this comes from university records and reliable first-hand accounts. May I add my own theory? Fact that Burgess – Eton – and Russell – Westminster – were both from smart schools, yet happy to know Hodge, could have had an interesting effect on Hodge. Helped build his confidence. Seed bed for feelings of independent thought? Nursery school for treachery?'

'Hm.'

MacDonald continued. 'The rest was a simple story of early success. After leaving Cambridge, Hodge took over his father's accountancy practice, built it up to twice its size using his university contacts, got bored of it two years later, and sold his share of the partnership, remaining as a consultant. Next, he qualified as a solicitor. Speeding through the law exams, he joined Arbuthnots, the West End law firm. There he furiously sought new clients, landing wealthy ones, and becoming a junior partner at 26. Two years later he left, taking with him several clients, to start his own practice specializing in family law.

'Next bit will feed your hatred of lawyers, Viv.'

MacDonald told Maxwell how in the two years leading up to the war, Hodge developed a reputation for being one of the best young divorce lawyers in London. He worked his charm on male and female clients, but especially the women. He provided a round-the-clock service, calling distraught spouses late into the evening to dispense sympathy and ratchet up the billable hours. When the decree was delivered, he offered to sort out his clients' shattered finances.

'Finally the Hodge accountancy practice took over, milking yet more cash from the misery. As well as the house off the Brompton Road, he could now rent a place on the Hamble River for sailing at weekends.'

The report also noted that, unlike other men of his age, he didn't seem in a hurry to be called up. While others were pulling strings to join the forces, Hodge was letting the net reach him when it would.

'Lastly, we did some digging at Hamble. The secretary of the

Hamble Sailing Club gave our researcher the names of Hodge's main contacts there. One of them was a lonely 40-year-old war widow. Plied her with drinks, and found out that Hodge had had an affair with an older woman at the club. The Commodore's wife, no less. Kenneth's adventures were the not-so-private talk of Hamble.'

'Did the affair go public?'

'No. Locals liked Hodge's wife and wanted to spare her the truth. So the Commodore confronted Hodge, offering two choices: leave the neighbourhood; or he would make the affair public. Hodge gave up the lease on the cottage in a hurry and moved on: to the Somerville River.'

'So he's a blackmail target.'

'There's worse. Every year between 1934 and 1937, Hodge visited Germany for the Bayreuth Opera Festival. It's been hard finding out whom, if anyone, he met there. In the end, we persuaded a youngster from the station in Berlin, posing as a travel journalist, to visit hotels one by one in Bayreuth, discreetly checking the guest registers. He found Kenneth and Phyllida Hodge's names at the Hotel Ritterhof. Staying the same nights, coinciding with the Bayreuth Festival, for four years running, from 1934 to 1937, another couple had also registered: Rudolf and Ursula Hammel.'

Maxwell's cheeks reddened and his mouth went dry. Both knew of Rudolf Hammel. He was a card-carrying Nazi, who had joined the party in 1935 and was now a rising officer in the *Abwehr*.

5

October 1940

Adrian Russell felt narcissistically proud of being *the* supremely thorough spy, 'even in sleepy old Somerville' he laughed to himself, as he prepared for his next meeting with Hodge. To keep himself alert, he audited every contact he had with anyone, even his doctor. Could it conceivably be an opportunity for British intelligence to vet him? At every meeting with Kenneth Hodge, he had made it impossible for Hodge to give away the location beforehand and assumed, though he had no reason to think so, that Hodge could be tailed. So he also made it hard for a tail to see whom Hodge was meeting, unless the tail came inside the pub, in which case Russell would spot the tail.

To complete his protection he used one of the simplest tricks of 1940s spycraft: raincoat, hat and glasses. Arriving at a Hodge rendezvous, he entered the pub at least 20 minutes early, carrying a hat, a pair of glasses and a raincoat in a paper bag. After Hodge had gone, he would stay behind for another drink, chuckling to himself over the ugly mixture of resentment and desire to be accepted that was Kenneth Hodge. After half an hour he would go to the lavatory, put on the hat, raincoat and glasses, bin the paper bag and leave, if possible, by a back entrance. If the pub had no back entrance, he would watch for a group of fellow drinkers leaving by the main entrance and pretend to be one of them.

MacDonald reported to Maxwell after a couple of weekends' surveillance.

'Still no clue from Labrador's reports who Hodge is seeing.'

Over repeated meetings, the same contact going in and out of a pub at about the same times as Hodge, would have been observed. Here there was none.

'All we have is a pattern: Hodge is meeting someone in Streteford pubs some Saturdays, usually around lunchtime, sometimes in the evening. The only way to see whom he's meeting is for Labrador to enter the pub and watch from a nearby table. And as we know, that risks immediate exposure.'

As usual, Maxwell took his time to reply, speaking slowly and with long pauses. They heightened MacDonald's frustration and anxiety, but he suppressed his irritation.

'I'm afraid the London surveillance is even less conclusive… Hodge's tails have seen nothing… No sign of contacting a courier, no sign of a dead letter box… What about the tails you put on Labrador?'

'Nothing. Only that Labrador has a bicycle hidden in a shed at the back of the Somerville fire station. Sometimes takes time off to ride along the riverside path.'

They observed each other silently weighing up the factors for and against continuing the surveillance, then, as if inhabiting each other's minds, nodded. If the surveillance was to be done, it must be done properly. The remaining gaps would have to be plugged. The London tails on Hodge, now working Monday midday to Friday 4 p.m., would continue through Friday night to Saturday morning. The Somerville tails would carry on from Saturday morning to whenever Hodge returned to London – either Sunday night or Monday morning.

*

Lord Taunton rang MacDonald every week. 'I say, MacDonald, when are you going to do another exercise at the Castle? Us 70-year-olds like to be involved, you know. Awful not to have a job.'

'Moonless night coming up in a few days, Lord Taunton. I'll warn you the day before. It'll be the Norwegians.'

'Ah, brave sorts. I'll enjoy comparing their performance to the French.'

Trainees were dropped at the estate wall some time after 10 p.m. on dark nights. Instructors spread out through the woods and manned watching posts. The objective was to steal, avoiding interception by the instructors, any papers left on the desk in Lord Taunton's office at the top of the Castle's East Turret. From there, Taunton loved to watch the trainees as they squirmed out of the woods on to his lawn, dashing for the rhododendron arbour, which gave near-perfect cover the rest of the way to the turret.

It was the perfect excuse, he congratulated himself, not to go to bed at the same time as Griselda, who'd long since lost patience with his night-owl habits. 'How can I help needing three hours when she needs seven to sleep off the evening's bottled comfort?' On break-in nights, he could prowl the house until well past midnight, then climb the East Turret to his office, fiddle with the pens and pencils on his desk and if the moon came out, admire yet again – he loved views – the prospect of his little kingdom, the river a silver snake bending majestically down to the sea three miles away.

*

The Norwegian trainees fanned out through the wood inside the estate walls, crawling or squat-walking, never snapping a twig, avoiding the booby traps – tin cans threaded on string – set up by Lord Taunton's keeper under his close supervision.

One of them came to an obstacle midway through the wood: a clearing with a small pond, and a small single-storey timber building – a woodland teahouse – on the far side. In the window was a faint glimmer, candlelight perhaps.

The trainee worked his way round the pond extra carefully, worrying that he would be late for the rendezvous at the edge of the lawn. To warn the rest of the team he was lagging, he gave two owl hoots through his thumb knuckles. Standing beside the window, he leant far enough to see in.

There was a coal fire at the grate, two chairs and a table with the remains of supper. Soft mats were piled or scattered around the floor. A man and a woman were standing by the fire, methodically undressing each other. The trainee instinctively withdrew his face from the window, obeying his instinct not to pry, and not to be seen. He took several steps away from the teahouse, back into the darkness of the trees, then succumbed again to his curiosity. Just one more quick look. But now they'd disappeared. Were they on the floor? He climbed on to a tree stump to gain a view down through the window to the hearth. The man was lying there naked on his back. She was kneeling astride, mounting. He found that he didn't want to watch for long: it was surreal to witness this happening deep in the woods, and disturbing: an off-putting performance of joyless need.

*

Lord Taunton watched from the top of the turret as the Norwegians closed in. One of them broke into the ground-floor window, noiselessly, as he had been taught. Spreading treacle all over a pane, he then applied a sheet of brown paper. A slight tap broke the glass in one place, near the latch. Paper and treacle held the fractured pane in place: not even the briefest tinkle of glass breaking on the floor inside. Removing just enough glass to reach in, he released the latch. His companion trainee climbed through, while he removed the paper. The trainee on the inside took off his boots and padded up the spiral staircase. Lord Taunton slipped out of his office into the store room opposite and shut himself in, watching through the keyhole. The trainee glided into the office, picked up the folders on his desk and vanished.

Next day, Lord Taunton realized with a twinge of alarm that he'd left several folders, not just one, on the desk. Some were harmless estate correspondence, but one was his private bank file.

The Norwegians dispersed back through the woods. At the debriefing outside the estate wall, the folders were handed over to the instructor in charge.

'Congratulations: a faultless exercise. Any observations?'

'May I talk to you privately sir?' On the way home, the trainee who had seen inside the teahouse told the instructor what he'd witnessed.

'Odd: it looked mechanical – not one kiss. What do you make of that, sir?'

They allowed themselves to laugh.

'What do I make of it? Don't mention it to any other trainee or instructor. Leave it with me.'

*

Russell chose Sundays, when MacDonald was on leave, to snoop in the colonel's tiny office. As usual, the safe was locked. He wished he could discover the numbers needed to release the combination lock. Then he noticed the folders on MacDonald's desk. MacDonald had put them there to remind himself to return them to Lord Taunton first thing Monday morning. He hadn't looked inside. Russell did. He read for a few seconds, then took out a Minox sub-miniature camera and photographed every sheet in one of the folders. A few days later the negatives were processed by a photographer in Hampton. Russell read them with growing amusement. When through, he went straight to the phone.

'Kenneth, time we had another session. Next Saturday. Usual routine.'

*

Three weekends later, on a Sunday towards the end of October, Labrador finished his surveillance duties early. Hodge had recently changed his habit, arriving at Somerville on Saturday morning instead of Friday night, and spending the rest of Saturday and Sunday at home with his wife.

Labrador's tails decided to retire early too. Labrador's Sunday routine was now familiar. Surveillance work over, in the final hour of daylight he would pick up the bicycle behind the fire station to go for a ride down the riverside path.

They had followed him along it twice, satisfying themselves

that he was not making contact with anyone on the path. The only other person they saw regularly here, but recently less often, was a local girl they had traced to The Rectory, on the other side of the river. She used the path for walking her dog and never stopped to speak to Labrador.

It was no coincidence that Labrador and Leo Maxwell hadn't spoken: he was tongue tied. He dismounted his bike to follow her at a distance, still as rapt as when he had first seen her on the hard at Sailing Club Point, marvelling at her grace and her rapport with her dog, a brown cocker spaniel with a silky coat whose name was Brownie. The girl was shouting at her dog – she had a loud voice – telling him to get *out* of the mud. Something had attracted the dog down to the band of mud exposed by low tide. Now it was stuck in a soft spot, struggling to get out.

Labrador threw down his bike, tore off his shoes, rolled up his trousers and struck out across the soft mud towards the dog, quickly mastering the skill needed to glide across the soft surface without sinking too far in – something like cross-country skiing. He pulled Brownie clear and delivered her back to Leo, covered in black slime, looking ashamed.

'You didn't have to do that. I could have done it… Been skating that mud since I was a child. But how can I thank you?'

His reply slipped out. 'Let me buy you a drink next time you're here.' His Polish accent was thick even after ten months at SOE Somerville, but he had no trouble making himself understood.

'How do you mean, next time? How do you know I'm not here

all the time?' She spoke almost too fast for him to understand, but her aggressive undertone was clear enough. He stood his ground.

'I'm trained to be observant. I've noticed you on this path, only some weekends.'

'Are you from... one of those houses in the woods?'

'I'm not meant to say. But yes. My name's George Adams. What's yours?'

'Leo.' She wasn't sure. He looked at her in the same way as Henry Dunning-Green, but curiosity won. The accent was appealing, and his dark looks were the type she liked.

'Well. OK, George. I'm here again just for the weekend in mid-November.'

'How about the Saturday – six at the King's Head in Milton?'

She smiled and thanked him once more for rescuing Brownie.

*

As Leo settled into the train taking her to join the ATA at its headquarters, White Waltham Airfield near Maidenhead, it sank in that she was leaving home properly for the first time, and that it was miserable not to be more happy or excited. The last ten weeks spent at home after completing her flying hours at Eastleigh, waiting to hear if the ATA would admit her, had started well, but had gone downhill. At first it was pleasant to be at The Rectory for weeks on end – the first time since her school summer holidays.

Life was pleasantly regulated by the rise and fall of the tide every six hours. When the water was low she pottered around the house or garden, enjoying the peace but mildly looking forward to her father's return each Friday. When the river was full she would sail straight from the jetty two or three reaches downstream and back. The days had flowed effortlessly one into the next and the war seemed not to exist. The Brig had seemed genuinely pleased that she was at home: perhaps a peace offering, she thought, for all those times spent infuriating each other.

All too soon, the harmony had been spoiled by the letter that never arrived from the ATA. The Brig had silently borne her impatience at first, but later he'd started to be *awful*, just when she most needed sympathy. Worse, and thank goodness she hadn't told the Brig about it, she'd written a letter to the CO at White Waltham saying she thought it was 'lousy' they were keeping her waiting for so long. Lousy was a word she had heard used by the mechanics at Eastleigh Airfield to describe every grade of misfortune from the death of a brother in action to a sour pint of bitter.

Eventually, a reply from a Margot Grey had arrived. Yes, the ATA would be pleased to accept her application now she could prove more than 40 flying hours. However, she must accept that on arrival she would be 'required' to 'submit' to further training: stuffy words, which she instinctively hated. Finally, the worst bit of all: the letter had warned that colleagues and superiors would not tolerate the use of vocabulary such as 'lousy'. She felt ashamed and humiliated, but pleased that a single word had caused such a definite reaction.

Bad though, that there should already be a fly in the ointment of this, her first great adventure – her chance to really *do* something instead of being a cog. Driving an ambulance like the other girls was fine, but too safe, too far from the action; and driving wasn't flying – by a very long way.

What would they be like, these superiors who forbade her to say 'lousy'? She supposed, as the train rattled through the country stations between Basingstoke and Maidenhead, that they would be like the older generation of Somerville, which set her thinking about what she was leaving behind.

She found, with each station that passed, that her view of Somerville grew more distanced – and clearer. Somerville people, she thought, fell into two categories – real people and stuffy people. Or maybe three: there were those who were somewhere between the two.

The Mackworths, the Jenningses and the Somerville old guard were all, of course, stuffy. Patricia Selby-Pickforth was somewhere in between because although basically stuffy, her kindness sometimes made her real – a mirror unexpectedly catching and flashing the light. People might say something similar about the Brig. Alice Dunning-Green was definitely real; Sir Geoffrey: real, but mean – a bully in fact, like his younger son.

And Henry? Certainly not a bully, which made him without doubt the best of the men in that family, and which was possibly why she gave him any time at all. But he was all too different to the dark Pole, whose admiration had shone out of his eyes despite his nervousness on the river bank: that was real.

She supposed that Henry was also one of those who fell half way between the two, but he was *so* correct, his manners *so* far beyond criticism that it was hard to know exactly *what* he was. And yet… an attractive energy glowed inside him. She'd always wanted to see more of that potential, for him to be more spontaneous, more fun, and once or twice had hinted at her feeling, without results. Perhaps his correctness, like the Brig's remoteness, might be a way of keeping people at arm's length?

She needed to see who else there was out there in the real world, as opposed to Somerville's sheltered world, before thinking more about him.

*

'Too much courage for her own good', the Brig suddenly said. Then moments later, 'Physical, and moral.'

Alice Dunning-Green was taken aback by this unexpected – unsought – confidence. She'd never heard him speak his mind without pauses. What was he on about? They had walked together across Hardings's spreading lawns down to the river and along the jetty. The Brig had been his usual silent self – to be honest, awkward company – until they were at the end of the jetty. The tide was dead low, the inert, mid-November day dying already at four. The shallow channel of muddy water left at the centre of the river was a steel-grey ribbon, flat and sluggish. Even the waders, as the Brig had then remarked, seemed to be picking about without much enthusiasm: a scene of monochrome gloom that mirrored his own mood.

What had bought him to Hardings? It was clear to Alice now that he needed to talk, presumably about Leo. His excuse for the visit had been to discuss the church roof accounts – but that was now far from his mind.

'She's not cut out for service discipline', he continued, again without preamble, as if Alice was bound to catch up.

Since Leo had left for the ATA three days before, Maxwell had been in a sea of worry and foreboding about his daughter. The last fortnight had not gone well because he'd told her what she didn't want to hear – that all large organizations, especially military ones, proceed at their own pace. The ATA, a branch of the Air Ministry, was no different. Each time he'd mildly remade the point, she'd flashed anger and impatience. On the last occasion, he'd directed at her the same precisely focussed beam of disapproval, from an otherwise inert face, that had silenced Hodge after the committee meeting. It was the only thing that ever truly scared her. Her only defence, as Maxwell anticipated, was the female trump card: to try to make him feel guilty by being openly upset. 'I hate that look of yours,' Audrey had often said. 'There's only one good thing about it. Without it, Leo would be completely out of control.'

Now, if he tried to rationalize his intense foreboding, he supposed guilt about parting on bad terms might be playing a part, but only a part. His sense of something bad overhanging Leo was concrete. For one, she had too much courage. For another, he continued to Alice, 'When she feels something, it's never half measure.' Alice was leading him back indoors, adjusting willingly enough, now the cards were on the table, to a frank discussion about Leo and probably Henry too. 'In fact', he went on, 'she feels things far too strongly.' Then:

'I've always thought that Henry was the ideal foil to Leo's personality. Away from home, in a dangerous world, she needs his kind of stability.'

As Alice made sympathetic noises, the Brig reflected that he was lucky, and Leo too, that Alice was Henry's mother. She'd arrived in Somerville 20 years ago, the subdued and devoted bride of Geoffrey Dunning-Green. As Geoffrey had advanced from Mr Dunning-Green to Sir Geoffrey, as his money from his father's cloth business had turned into wealth, as he became yearly more convinced, with his growing economic power, that he was always right, Alice had evaded or outfaced his bullying and kept quiet her disappointment that Geoffrey was no longer the man who had needed her so much. Somerville saw this, and respected her aura of sadness threaded with resilience and kindness. She was almost universally liked, the person to whom one turned for advice and sympathy.

Griselda Taunton had been one of the first to see this, confessing to Alice her drink problem. Alice had been uncritical, but practical, firm in pointing out exactly where alcohol would lead. Soon Griselda was asking Alice to accompany her on county engagements. Alice would go, on condition that Alice kept the half bottle of gin in her own handbag, and that Griselda could approach her for sips, not swigs. Lady Taunton, with Alice as her minder, managed to perform most of her engagements without stumbling or slurring her words. On occasions when Griselda was too drunk to go out, Alice stood in for her. Alice was now known as the Deputy Countess.

She motioned the Brig to a sofa, pouring him a cup of tea, as she said:

'I don't think you should agonize over whether Leo will blow up at someone who gives her a silly order. For one thing, she'll carry out intelligent orders to the letter, with obsessive dedication. That's Leo: as you say, all or nothing. Her superiors will see it, and value her accordingly. For another, young women, even ones like Leo, tend to copy each other. If she's surrounded by obedient girls with strict upbringings, I'll be amazed if she doesn't mostly conform to the group mentality.'

'Thank you for trying to calm me down. Done me good. But you know how it is: middle children, so often the odd ones out. Audrey adored Charles, the perfect elder son. Emily was the enchanting baby. Well, we never actually showed it. But along the way, somehow Leo was left out.'

He was silent a few moments before asking her about the undercurrents in her own family.

'Simpler. Two boys, very different characters, both needing

different treatment. Freddie's as thick skinned as his father. He never rose to Geoffrey's bullying, never felt pressured. But Henry: until he left for the army, I had to tell him every day to keep calm and, when his father started bullying, gaze at his forehead. It usually worked. Henry's been toughened by the experience. Freddie's got away with murder.'

'You're a saint with Geoffrey.'

'I try to concentrate on his best side: he's a great doer. The world needs them, especially if they're generous, like Geoffrey. He wants to use his money to improve people's lives, as well as exert control.'

Maxwell had made an observation bordering on the intimate, so now she did the same.

'Why are you usually so remote, Vivian? You've amazed me today by being so much the opposite.'

'Possibly my father. I was born when he was 78. Never had a meaningful conversation with him – like talking to your grandfather. All he could say was how as a boy he'd watched the soldiers marching to Waterloo. What they wore, and so on. I never knew how to reply.'

Maxwell steered the conversation away from himself as fast as he could.

'May we talk about Henry and Leo?'

'Makes me feel shifty, Vivian – like an old Indian woman arranging a marriage.'

His next remark was carefully calculated.

'Leo's blind to status and money. Why? I don't know. Just is. It's not an intellectual position.'

'Well that's why I smile on Henry's feelings for her. My boys are such prey to fortune hunters. If Leo ever agrees to marry him, it'll be for himself... you know how important that is for a man of integrity.'

'In that case, I'll tell you why I approve so much of Henry. He's one of the few young men who's privileged, with leadership qualities, but a thoroughly good egg too. You know, cares about his fellow man – doesn't feel automatically entitled.'

'Well, thank you Vivian. I like to believe he's a good person.'

'Leo needs his moral qualities because she has them too. But she also needs his inner strength. Without that no one could ever manage her.'

'I think he's developed real confidence since he's been out of Geoffrey's orbit. It's unshowy confidence, though – perhaps not the sort that young women generally admire.'

A long sigh from the Brig. 'She's too young – and, to be honest, a bit silly to appreciate it... But at least she has the sense to value him as a friend.'

The Brig fell to brooding again, fidgeting mentally as if struggling to make up his mind to speak.

'Go on Vivian, what is it?'

'Well. Not my business. Entirely yours. No right to ask. But... do you think Henry fell in love too young? Will his early feelings fade, now he's a man, out there in the world?'

'Not Henry. He's curiously timeless. And stubborn. Once his mind is made up, count on him.'

'Timeless. Well said, Alice. That goes to the heart of why I like him.'

Another long silence, with the Brig once more struggling to resume. Then:

'Well, I may as well say it. Leo's work will put her in the way of many new potential admirers. Those women pilots have special glamour. Every day they fly into RAF airfields full of young men in need of distraction. I'm worried Henry will find out she's seeing other men, and that jealousy will wreck their friendship. There's no talking sense to Leo. Audrey tried once or twice. I'm far too embarrassed to talk about this – of all subjects.'

'Heavens, you're such a worrier. You simply can't calculate so many moves ahead. Anyway, there's something that might help you. But I can only tell you in strictest confidence.'

'I know how to keep secrets.'

'I think you do. Henry's been accepted by SOE. He's in training now, in the wilds of Scotland. Then he moves to SOE Somerville in the new year. Again, a monastic existence. Then he'll be sent directly to France on missions. He'll not hear news of Leo for months and months.'

6

Maxwell had a solitary Saturday lunch while Hodge was enjoying another alcoholic one with Adrian Russell. The brigadier fought the wasps in his head, trying to stop them taking over entirely. Spinning off his principal worries were dozens of linked suspicions. His mind was once again a corked bottle, unable to connect properly with the real world beyond. Reality would have made clear, if allowed to shine in, that his worries had a place but not an absolute right to dominate. He knew he needed to turn the telescope the wrong way round, view it all from a distance, but the wasps won.

Hodge's mind was more subtly infested. His pride stopped him admitting to himself that he was starting to need Russell, perhaps even to love him, though not in a sexual way. Russell's charm was a drug. He looked at Hodge through mild blue eyes, under an untidy flop of hair, and asked, as usual:

'How's everything going?' Not just a passing courtesy. 'How are you getting on with Phyllida?'

'Things aren't great in the bedroom.'

'Don't be so middle-class Ken.' Said teasingly – but kindly. 'You mean the sex is boring.' Hodge lapped up the frankness. He could discuss this sort of thing with no one else. Everything seemed to *matter* to Russell. Next Russell spiced the mix with a choice morsel.

'Good news from London. I've lined up that introduction to the Service. Just need to wait until the time is right. My colleague's been told he's getting funds to recruit extra staff – just a question of when.' Hodge basked. Joining MI6 was the golden option, compared with a dull regular army desk job.

Most of all, Russell wanted to know about the S.R.S.C. meeting. 'So did you manage to rock the boat?'

'The old buffers – the Selby-Pickforth woman and Colonel Mackworth – were seriously annoyed. Banning Lady St James from further meetings was outvoted of course. Blasphemy even to raise it.'

Gusts of laughter from Russell. Amusing this delightful man, thought Hodge, was the most gratifying thing in the world.

'And what about our main idea – altering the membership rules at the AGM?'

'The old buffers were apoplectic but Lady St James and Maxwell kept their counsel. Deadpan. Couldn't tell what they thought. Both of them use inscrutability as a means of control.'

'Well, they'll have no choice but to accept it… If you're right about the club rules allowing anyone to propose anything at the AGM. Will you check that again?'

'Of course.' Next Hodge launched into another riff of dislike, this time directed at Portia and Maxwell together.

'She's not really a woman. Handsome, possibly, but not pretty. And she's well past her best – must be the wrong side of 40. Natural authority, too – like a man's. And she's practical – hard to beat in a sailing dinghy. Don't you think women should be feminine?'

'Aristocrats don't follow middle-class gender rules. They have huge inner confidence, propped up by centuries of controlling the system. If Portia's on the masculine end of the gender spectrum, she's not going to hide it.'

'Whereas Maxwell is on the female end. He completely lacks masculine energy – just sits there, withdrawn, never *initiating*. And why does she have to call herself St James?'

'Ever heard of the St James's Way?

'No.'

'It's a pilgrim route – actually several routes – into Northern Spain and along the coast to Santiago de Compestella. Portia's medieval forbears were famous for using their ill-earned cash to buy off local landowners who blocked the way. St James is the saint associated with Santiago's cathedral.'

'But why not just use James?'

'They were – are – Roman Catholics. They believed – literally –

in his sainthood. Using the name in full was a way of announcing they'd done their noble act of charity... Toffs need to soothe their conscience when they make excessive amounts of money from the system – without doing any work.'

Hodge's concealed, ingrained resentment of social superiors flared into life. He was where Russell wanted him. What followed was presented as an item of casual gossip, not as a bidding.

'Well there's something else that m-m-might interest you about that family.' Russell's stammer, which added to his appeal, surfaced when he most needed people to relax their critical faculties. He produced a folder containing the photographed copies of the letters in MacDonald's office.

Hodge flicked through with the accustomed speed of a lawyer mastering the essentials.

'So Lord Taunton has money troubles? Like ordinary beings? He gives the impression of being above money.' Ripples of laughter from Russell.

'Landed estates are in trouble everywhere. He probably needs cash to pay off his father's death duties.'

'And now the bank is giving them five years to reduce their borrowings – or find other security because the bank deems the land value insufficient.'

They wound up soon after. Russell liked Hodge to go back to normal life with his latest piece of subversion buzzing loudly in his head.

On his way back to Woodland House, Russell reflected that his experiment on the S.R.S.C. committee had started well. They couldn't organize a response to the challenge because they were caught in their own democratic web. There had to be a vote to resolve an issue, and votes were by definition public. Public discussion leads to questioning of the status quo. With deft manipulation, he might even get Hodge to precipitate the self-destruction of the S.R.S.C. at the AGM in January. At least an ugly public row.

Meanwhile, he calculated, another ingredient was required for his cocktail. Soon Hodge would leak the news about the Taunton's mortgage into the Somerville grapevine. With the backdrop of Somerville troubled that the exclusive character of the river would be lost forever if the Tauntons had to sell, something else, more personal, undermining Maxwell, would maximize the subversive effect.

He didn't dislike Maxwell, he told himself. He respected his dignity, and recognized him as one of the few competent deputy chiefs in the Service. What he must do would not be driven by animosity. In any case, feelings were irrelevant to his cause. Subverting Somerville and Maxwell might be a nursery school prank, but it would still be useful practice for things to come. 'Everything I do, even the most trivial, must be for communism.'

He thought fondly of George Kohn, who had converted him to communism at 23 in Vienna. 'From now on, Adrian, all of you will be invested in the Soviet dream. The ideal deserves nothing less.' And so it had been.

Russell hadn't flinched when Kohn perished in Stalin's purges, together with at least two of his subsequent handlers, as well as millions of innocent Russians. But he missed Kohn and the old handlers: they had been his surrogate family, now replaced by codenames at Moscow Central.

Nonetheless, his creed still dominated a place in his mind where it lodged in privileged isolation, guarded by gatekeepers. Not actual gatekeepers, but the equivalent: highly inhibited connections back out to the real world – so inhibited, in fact, as to be useless.

Hours later Labrador went to The King's Head for the second time that day, for his rendezvous with Leo. As he drove the six miles, he was aware of his tail – just one today, following as closely as he dared – while Labrador considered the increasing farce of his surveillance duties.

He was posing, on MacDonald's instructions, as a casual labourer taken on by the Somerville Estate. Not a bad cover story: labour was short, because of the war, so short-term workers brought in from outside were familiar in the neighbourhood. A long section of fencing on the western boundary of the estate needed replacing. Labrador delivered new posts and rails piled in a small truck, from the estate yard next to the Castle to the fence workers. Driving there and back gave Labrador the chance to build up a picture of the comings and goings of Somerville. 'Try to see patterns,' MacDonald had said. 'Even if they're just dog-walking patterns. Then watch for alterations in those patterns. Anyone who varies their habits. Could they be diverting to a dead letter box location? Keep a special watch on the beaches. Who goes there regularly?'

Some nights, with a radio instructor, he would help monitor corners of the estate and surrounding villages for radio transmissions. Always nothing.

Labrador had pondered the phenomenon of dead letter boxes and planned to make use of his conclusions. Apart from that, the long hours were pointless. Nothing out of the ordinary was happening in and around Somerville, except Hodge's meetings in pubs in Milton and Streteford. Probably a woman friend. He couldn't understand why MacDonald didn't stop this ridiculous procession of Hodge followed by Labrador, followed by Labrador's tails.

Labrador reached The King's Head an hour before the meeting, and sat at a corner table he favoured because of the mirror hanging above – he could see most of the bar without turning round. His tail came in five minutes later, bought a drink and pretended to read a newspaper. Labrador sipped his beer slowly, sometimes looking up to glance around for a pretty girl, for about 20 minutes. He folded up the paper as if in no hurry, finished his pint and strolled to the door. Outside, he sprinted 30 yards along the High Street to a men's outfitters, slid in, took a pair of trousers from a rail and entered a changing cubicle, pulling the curtain. His tail would be in the street by now, frantically scanning it for a sign of a disappearing Labrador. Labrador stayed in the shop another 15 minutes, trying on different clothes, then left and walked up and down the street searching in shop window reflections for his tail.

Certain he was no longer being followed, he went back to the pub five minutes ahead of his meeting with Leo, pitying the plight of his tails. Doing nothing but surveillance must drain their will to live. MI5's surveillance section was manned by people who did nothing else. Its bosses must be skilled at hiring people with the mindless patience to do it well. The opposite to Labrador.

Leo was coming into the pub, wearing her ATA uniform, with Brownie on a lead. She went straight to the bar and beamed at the barman:

'Don't *suppose* you could *consider* allowing Brownie in here?'

'Dogs are not allowed.'

'Are you *sure?*' Enchanting smile. That and the uniform prevailed.

'This once, miss. If he sits by your feet.'

To Labrador's relief, she led the conversation. 'Sorry about the uniform. I'm straight off the train.' Then without missing a beat: 'Tell me as much as you're allowed'.

Despite the distraction of sitting within reach of her, he managed to say haltingly, his accent thickening, 'Been in England almost a year now. Had to escape Poland. Long journey. Left my family behind. Difficult... Impossible to talk about.'

'What did those *swine* do?'

'Imagine the worst things. How you never want to see your family.'

Her eyes glistened briefly, making her face, a subtle combination of boyish good looks and female grace, all the more irresistible.

'So I'm here to take revenge.'

'I'm *very* angry with them too.'

She told him about her first weeks in the ATA, eyes alight, occasionally flashing with strong feeling. She was an entry-level pilot, cleared to fly 'boring' planes such as Lysanders, Tiger Moths and the Walrus. 'More exams, more instruction before I get to the next level. Then more again before I can fly Spitfires, Hurricanes and Wellington bombers. *Then* I'll feel as if I'm fighting. Every time I get into a fighter, it will free a combat pilot for action... Next best to firing at the Nazis myself.'

Labrador mumbled admiration. 'I believe you will fly Spitfires.' To Leo, his accent made it sound all the more heartfelt. Labrador thought, 'this is an odd way to tell a girl that she's the loveliest creature I've ever seen.' Leo lapped it up.

'Oh I can't be sure. I'm no good at the written stuff. I'm practical. The flying itself isn't a problem... Sailing a dinghy is quite like it, and I've done that all my life.'

'I know, I've seen you win most of the races on the river.'

'You've seen *what?*' Eyes flashing, body instantly stiff with anger.

'Er... I... Er... '

'How do you know I win races?'

Silence.

'No need to tell me. I can work it out. Same reason you knew I walked Brownie by the river. You're a spy... and you've been stalking me.'

'Sorry. I can explain. Let me explain.'

Seeing how hard she found it to control her impatience unnerved him.

'Several weekends... I was sent on outdoor survival exercises. Best place I found – prettiest, most comfortable – was that hut at Sailing Club Point – the birdwatcher's hut. I couldn't help seeing the sailing races. Three or four weekends.'

Silence again, while she considered.

'People don't like being spied on.'

'I understand. But I was on duty.'

'You mustn't do it again.'

'That's why I asked you to meet properly.'

'OK. OK. But *please* don't get ideas. Most of my time is away from Somerville now. There'd be very few times we can meet. If that's OK, we can be friends. *Just* friends.'

Leo was being honest. She didn't mind seeing the dark man again. He *was* good looking, as black as a black Labrador.

'I suppose you've got a code name?'

'Yes.'

'Tell me.'

'Against orders.'

'But not against orders to stalk innocent local girls.'

He changed the subject. 'If we're to meet again, you would have to learn some spycraft.'

'*Definitely.*'

Labrador produced two aluminium cigar tubes – Romeo and Juliets. They were the largest size, seven inches long and nearly three-quarters of an inch thick.

'They're on sale in the Somerville newspaper shop.'

'Are you saying the newspaper shop is where we should have – what do you call it – a place to leave messages?'

'A dead letter box.'

'But everyone goes there, including my father. It's public. It's where you go for the gossip.'

'Much more secure than a hollow tree stump by a woodland path. No one would ask why either of us went into the newspaper shop.'

'Go on then.'

He explained that at the back of the shop there was a shelf displaying packets of cigarettes, and a couple of boxes of cigars. 'Stand with your back to the shop, and no one can see you remove a cigar and put a message in its protective tube. Don't try to hide the message between the tube liner and wall. Needs to seem innocent.'

'Then you put the tube back in the box with the other cigars?'

'No, behind the box. Wait until no one is looking, then slide the tube with the message behind the box, out of sight.'

'And if someone finds one of our tubes there?'

Enjoying Leo's beguilement, he told her that it was a small

risk – that he'd left a tube with a message inside for ten days and that it hadn't been disturbed. Then he added the icing: they would make the messages seem innocent, with a code: 'Wonderful smoke, try again' would mean meet me here, same place, same time, on Saturday at six. 'Too strong, try another brand' would mean meeting not possible, look for next message. To show the message had been read, it should be folded inside out, writing visible, then put back.

Leo was sold. 'So now I'm a spy.'

'A trainee spy, like me.' He let himself gaze into her eyes and they gazed back, sparkling with delight at the prospect of the game.

'I'm back on leave in two or three weekends. I'll keep looking on Saturday mornings.' She got up to leave.

'Tell me your code name, George. *Please.*' Long silence.

'*Only* for you, yes? *Promise* never to repeat?'

'Promise.'

'Labrador.'

He bathed in her delight, mixed with approval, all the way back to Brindley House.

*

'It's smoky in here,' Diana announced as she entered the kitchen for breakfast. She tried to sound casual, but it was still an announcement, and had the result she wanted: giggles from Daisy and Margot, who shared the cottage with her. The fourth and newest ATA girl in the cottage was Leo. She remained deadpan, saying:

'Must be the coal fire, Diana. It always does that when newly lit.'

But as breakfast went on, Diana wouldn't let go, seizing any opportunity to mention smoke. 'The toaster is always smoking, they must get it mended'; 'perhaps there was time to smoke a cigarette before the airfield car came to collect them,' and so on.

Leo still refused to be drawn. She liked Diana, but was determined not to share any information, until absolutely necessary, about Flight Commander Alastair Mackenzie-Cole, otherwise known as Smokey. Gossip about the Spitfire ace's interest in Leo had reached the Hatfield Ferry Pool within days of Leo first meeting him, and she sensed that Diana was a shade too interested in the subject. Diana was not only pretty, with an artful tongue, but had had the most fashionable, cosmopolitan upbringing of the four – her father was a wealthy playboy and amateur racing driver. Leo had been run-of-the-mill at school, not one of the clever, knowing girls, such as Diana, but she knew how to deal with their remarks.

Although any ATA girl would kill for a fighter pilot, Leo's instincts told her that Margot and Daisy were not the type to steal a boyfriend. Diana's attitude, on the other hand, was 'all's fair in love and war' and she often said so. Smokey was too new, too exciting, to share with anyone, except possibly Margot Duhalde, a newcomer from Chile.

Besides, the subject of Smokey made Leo dislike herself, or as she preferred to put it, not like herself very much. Part of her saw having a third admirer alongside Henry and Labrador as greedy and ungrateful – especially to Henry. But safety in numbers – sitting on the fence – was convenient. It allowed her to postpone serious thought about any of them, yet she could still hear her father saying that this was 'all very well, but not what the nicest girls do.'

She'd enjoyed her first proper encounter with the Pole in the pub at Milton, but had found him mysterious and unsettling. Highly attractive physically, of course, and even more frank in his admiration than at their first meeting on the river bank. Possibly a little *too* frank? She'd noticed him undressing her with his eyes – quite a contrast to Henry's steady devotion that never crossed a boundary.

Smokey versus Labrador? Definitely Smokey. He was not as handsome as Labrador, but more of a challenge, real in a more interesting way because while making clear he was smitten with her, he was also his own man. He had a fascinating aura of aggression mixed, intriguingly, with lively, kindly *bonhomie* in company. Smokey first, then; second Labrador; Henry third.

Diana and Daisy were the first to be collected for ferry duty at the airfield; Leo and Margot were picked up later. Alone with Leo in the car, Margot said:

'Go on Leo, you can trust me. How did you meet? I bet you want to talk about it really.'

Leo was drawn to Chile, as Margot had quickly been renamed:

she was understanding about people, rather than bitchily knowing, and she was one of a handful of ATA girls to have travelled half way across the world to join Britain's war effort, much respected for their enterprise and loyalty.

'I've met him four times now – just drinks in the pub with the other pilots at RAF Kenley. It was special being invited into their group, they're so close knit, doing what they do… It's so important, but they're all so modest.' She tailed off, but Chile drew her out again.

'How did he make his first move? He must have done it the right way, otherwise you wouldn't have seen him again.'

'I was delivering a Magister to Kenley. He was watching me taxi to a halt – didn't know I was a girl 'til I took my headgear off.' 'Ah, ATA, keeping the wheels rolling nicely' was all he said. Nothing patronising like 'Good landing'. He took that for granted. Then he pointed to the row of Spitfires, and said 'Come and have a drink with the boys… we can talk about flying those. Maybe you will, one day.'

Before reaching the airfield they had a few moments left to swap feelings about how thrilled they were with their new life. Not just because of meeting Spitfire and Hurricane pilots at RAF bases, but because this was a first taste of freedom and the adult world, made digestible by demanding but sensible routines and discipline, as if in a grown-up boarding school. There was little time to be lonely, all the time they could want to savour being high on flying, and a novel feeling: a sense of purpose.

'It's our element,' Chile said as they parted.

*

Labrador sat, desperate with boredom, in one of Adrian Russell's lectures on subversion. The man was just about words... why did he never talk of action? He was young and fit, so why was he here teaching instead of fighting? Labrador could teach him more about subversion than he could ever know. *Nothing* is as subversive as a girl who fills your mind – day and night – for months on end. If not for her, Labrador would have escaped Somerville long ago. He'd been here more than six months already, far longer than the other trainees. Why had they picked on him for the extra surveillance duties? He still couldn't work out why, but at least the work allowed him to see Leo, occasionally.

Now that he'd met her twice, his longing was not so intense. After the summer spent in distant worship, the first meeting had, naturally, made him feel like a rabbit dazzled by headlights. Not only because of her looks, but because of her fascinatingly foreign, poised Englishness: she was a racehorse, on the surface so assured, almost serene, yet sending out signals that underneath she was ready, any time, to prance.

If he was being honest with Labrador, he hadn't liked the way she'd accused him so aggressively of spying on her.

There: he was referring to himself as Labrador yet again, as if Jerzy or George no longer existed, as if Labrador was the real person, not Jerzy-George. Leo's delight in his codename had disturbed him too: as if this code person might be better than George, better than *him*. What right did she have to think that?

What harm had his watching done her? Could she have felt his eyes on her body? Of course not. So how could it affect her so deeply? He had never met someone who reacted so much against a simple thought.

The women in his life so far had all been essentially submissive, outwardly anyway. Dealing with someone so different stretched him uncomfortably. Could she be tamed? He'd heard men talking about strong women: how they could only be handled, never tamed; that you have to ignore some of their vagaries, but occasionally stand firm. Could Labrador rise to that? Probably not. Not when there was her social assurance to deal with, as well as her temperament: all a little too much for a farmer's boy. Admitting this now made the longing more bearable – but only a little.

A shame, perhaps, for Labrador that he never saw her interacting with her dog. It would have revealed her softest, easiest side. But Brownie always sat quietly alert at her feet, as if waiting for her slightest command. If her dog was so well behaved, Labrador reasoned, how could her boyfriend ever relax? Yet however sternly he told himself she was beyond his reach, the more he wanted her. If by some extraordinary chance their paths really could join... if the opportunity to share her bed could miraculously arise... then Labrador wouldn't say no.

As Russell talked on and on, Labrador felt less and less committed to SOE Somerville. It was a waste of his time. His life had moved beyond words. Words could never describe the emptiness of his emotion about what had happened in Poland. It was so bad, he couldn't feel it. Words were traps. The Germans had trapped his sister with words. Never trust them. 'Stay in the village, don't try to escape, and you will come to no harm,' the German officer had said to the entire village, assembled in the barn that doubled as its meeting place. As they filed towards the door, one of his men, at a signal from him, had fired his gun into the air. Several terrified villagers, including his sister, had bolted for the door. They were marched back into the barn and hanged with wire in front of everyone. It hadn't been a tragedy: words could have expressed a tragedy, and there were no words for what he had witnessed. It had been a void – a thing beyond words, beyond horror, beyond even emptiness.

*

Two fresh Friday evening tails got on to Hodge's train at Waterloo and sat in the same carriage. Hodge was so absorbed in his work that he was oblivious of being followed. He got off at Hampton, three stops short of Somerville: a new development for the Friday night tails.

It was a four-minute walk to the Admiral Collingwood. One tail, estimating it safe because he was a new face, went in with

Hodge. He sat in the reception area, glancing at his watch as if waiting for a friend, close enough to the desk to hear Hodge checking in as a Mr Robert Williams. The other tail went round to the back of the inn, watching the rear exit. Hodge went up to his room, having ordered supper for two. 'Mrs Williams will be here in half an hour.'

Thirty minutes later a woman in her 20s with straight, flimsy blond hair walked in.

'Hello Mrs Williams – good to see you back.' The receptionist's face was dutifully deadpan. 'Your husband's already gone up – room six.'

'No need to show me up.'

Twenty minutes later, the tail slipped upstairs to listen at the door of room six. The sounds he heard were unmistakeable.

*

At the same time as Hodge was heading for his assignation in the Admiral Collingwood, Russell was in London for a secret meeting. To put himself in the mood, he dropped by the Traveller's Club and bought double whiskies for a couple of MI6 friends, then walked to Brown's Hotel in Mayfair, going in by the Dover Street entrance. In a cubicle of the ground-floor gentleman's lavatory, he put on a brown wig, a false moustache and glasses, one of several sets he owned, chosen because it had not been used in London before. He swapped his pale blue linen suit for a grey pinstripe, and his fawn-coloured raincoat for a dark blue one, packing the unwanted items tightly in a collapsible overnight bag, which was green – the original brown one was stuffed inside the green along with the discarded clothes.

Leaving by the Albemarle Street entrance, he made for Piccadilly tube station, and from there jinked across London, reversing and re-reversing direction every four stations, three times, until convinced he was clean of tails. He got out at Islington and made his way to the KGB safe house in a street off the Caledonian Road, from which he routinely forwarded messages to his handlers in Moscow. He announced himself at the door using his codename, Agent Sonny. The radio operator encoded Sonny's report, sending it while he waited.

> *Comrades: I apologise once again for the lack of new intelligence, a result of my continuing exile at Somerville. I confirm that I am still doing all I can to get transferred back to London.*
>
> *P.S. I am staying in practice by subverting the local community and its sailing club – a pernicious bourgeois organization of no consequence to my comrades in Moscow, but nonetheless a soft target that will help keep my mind focussed.*

He added some sharp character sketches of the 'grand-bourgeois' Colonel Mackworth and Lady Selby-Pickforth; also of the 'authoritarian aristocrat,' Viscountess St James. A reply from the Moscow duty handler came back within an hour. Russell's new

Moscow controllers' ingrained paranoia made them unsure of his loyalty or his usefulness, but they hedged their bets.

Comrade Sonny: your report is appreciated. We continue to trust your value as a long-term investment. Payments will be kept up as usual. Your dedication is noted.

Long live Stalin.

P.S. Please record the names of the most reactionary sailing club committee members. They can be re-educated at a correctional institution after the revolution reaches Britain. The Party is continuously improving its techniques for curing bourgeois confusions. The female aristocrat sounds dangerous, and may require a more radical approach.

As Russell left, he collected his monthly retainer, £200 in cash, just over double his monthly salary from the Service, and returned to Somerville next day, freshly motivated for the next stage of his S.R.S.C. experiment. If it amused Moscow, it amused him.

*

Russell now calculated that his next meeting with Hodge could be the clincher, and planned his moves in detail. But when they next met it soon came clear that Hodge was not interested in talking about the S.R.S.C. He wanted to talk about Phyllida again, 'or rather, not exactly about Phyllida.'

Russell suppressed his impatience. His eyes switched to sympathy mode, and he cocked his head into rapt attention.

'Of course.'

'Have you ever strayed? I mean... outside your marriage?'

Russell had, frequently, but chose not to tell Hodge. Both men found it as hard as each other to be truly candid about relationships with women, but Russell was better at pretending to be frank.

'I know people who have. Main thing, apart from not getting caught, is to have a positive attitude. Tell yourself that playing away could improve the marriage. Can't have a man frustrated in his own house. A little light relief might do everyone good in the long run.'

In a series of hints and half-statements, Hodge managed to tell Russell that he hadn't gone out looking – that *she* had approached *him*. 'You wouldn't believe how direct she was.' And that she was interested not in a relationship, in fact not especially in Hodge, but in sex.

'Doesn't want to chat before or after.' Hodge tried not to sound plaintive. 'She's like a man. I mean, afterwards, she just seems, well, neutral. Just wants me to recover so we can... Do it again.'

Russell stopped himself telling Hodge to enjoy it while he could.

'It's dull when there's no feeling of possession. I'm getting tired of it. Worried it might put me off women for good. I feel exploited... Like a Somerville estate worker. She told me she had been through most of the attractive ones by the time she was 20.'

'She's one of the Tauntons?'

'Lady St James's youngest sister. Lady Flavia Somer.' His tone was nonchalant, but Russell heard in it a trace of pride.

Four gin and tonics later, Russell steered the conversation back to Flavia.

'I say Ken, crafty of you to get away with meeting your sexpot in Somerville. Everyone must know everyone else's business. Where d'you go?'

'Careful planning. In the summer our favourite spot was the sailing club – miles down a bumpy track. It's deserted when no one's sailing.'

'Romantic. Nothing but the sounds of gulls, wind and tide. A midsummer night's dream. Come to think of it, Somerville is a sort of fairy kingdom. Exists alongside, but apart from the real world – like in the play.'

'It was a dream – then. Now it's colder we use two other places. A teahouse in Somerville Castle's woods and the Admiral Collingwood in Hampton for Friday nights. Phyllida gets a call from the office saying I'm held up with a client and to expect me on the Saturday morning train.'

'Sure Phyllida doesn't suspect?'

'Sure.'

'I still think you're a lucky chap.'

'At first, it seemed like an achievement. Kenneth Hodge and the daughter of an earl. Now it feels as if I'm doing a job.'

'I daresay you can put up with it a while longer.'

To build up Hodge's mood, Russell mentioned the date, now confirmed, ten days ahead, when Hodge would meet his contact in the Service. Hodge's spirits lifted, so Russell made his move.

First he lowered the temperature by asking a few run-of-the-mill questions about life in Somerville. Then, disguising his intense interest in Hodge's response to his next question, he asked it as if it was an afterthought. Before Hodge could answer he sloped off to the bar for more drinks, reinforcing the impression that he was in no hurry for an answer.

'I suppose rumours circulate quickly in fairy land?'

'True. I mentioned the Tauntons' money troubles – vaguely of course – to some old boys in the paper shop. Did the rounds in a week. Got back to Phyllida when she was collecting the papers on Sunday.'

'Talking of fairies, something occurred to me. Maybe your friend Maxwell is – well – a-a-a-a f-f-f-fairy.'

'*What?*' But Hodge got there quickly enough, despite being three-quarters drunk.

'Maybe that's why he's so withdrawn. Repressing the love that dares not say its name?'

'People in his position often have a faithful retainer who provides – well – s-s-s-services.'

Hodge lit up.

'His driver. Cobb.'

'Oh yes?'

'Cobb's just been given a flat over The Rectory's garage. Helps Maxwell around the house and garden. Pops up every other minute.'

'Could explain the divorce.'

7

Late November 1940

Sir Geoffrey Dunning-Green looked at his face in the shaving mirror and, as almost always, liked what he saw. It made him feel so cheerful that he allowed himself what he considered a little imaginative word play – for which generally he had no time.

'Dunning-Somer-Green.' Bit clumsy. And maybe the Tauntons wouldn't care for Somer being sandwiched between Dunning and Green.

'Dunning-Green-Somer.' Still not right. Somer needs more emphasis.

'Somer-Dunning-Green.' Ah yes. Proper emphasis on Somer. And people would think me, well, gentlemanly, for letting Somer come first.

Sir Geoffrey's principal ambition in 1940 was to bring about the marriage between Portia St James and Henry. His wife had told him countless times that Henry had been in love with Leo Maxwell as long as anyone could remember. Sir Geoffrey ignored her. Henry and Freddie had been diverted by the war from joining the family business. That would have to wait, so all the more important to push on with this other dynastic project.

On the death of the present Earl of Taunton, Portia would become the new Countess of Taunton. If she was married to Henry, their eldest child – Sir Geoffrey's grandchild – would inherit the courtesy title of Viscount or Viscountess St James. But he (or she) and his or her younger siblings would still need a surname. Naturally, they would inherit Dunning-Green from the male side, but it would be only right to preserve their mother's great surname alongside it. Somer-Dunning-Green. Give them something to think about in Whites.

Sir Geoffrey strode into the dining room, where breakfast had been placed by the kitchen staff on the sideboard. Henry, Alice and Freddie were already seated not at the long dining table, but at a beautiful rosewood circular breakfast table in the bow window with its views to the river.

'Henry, what's this I hear about you trying to get a transfer to some secret job?'

'Secret. Not allowed to discuss it.'

'Either you've asked for a transfer, or they're not happy with you. Neither's acceptable. Your colonel is a personal friend. I lunched him endlessly to get you into The Rifle Brigade. We need to talk about this privately in my study. Straight after breakfast.'

'There's nothing to discuss. It's done.'

Furious, only just controlling himself, Sir Geoffrey tried a new tack. 'I suppose you've heard the gossip about the Tauntons' finances? You ought to see an opportunity here. My businesses are flush with cash. If a certain event took place, lending to the Tauntons, or providing security, would be the natural consequence. Understand me?'

Henry had heard the gossip too. He understood only too well what his father meant, and so did his younger brother Freddie who was staying quiet, but amused by Henry's disgust. For 18 months, Sir Geoffrey had engineered every opportunity to get Henry and Portia together, even a family Mediterranean cruise on the Dunning-Green yacht, with Portia as the sole non-family guest. Henry avoided Freddie's eye, but exchanged glances with his mother. No point, her expression made clear, in confronting his father.

'So Henry, how about seeing Portia this afternoon? Everyone knows you youngsters don't procrastinate in wartime. Take the opportunity to propose, or there may never be another. I tell you, the timing's perfect.'

'I'll drop round at her house before lunch.'

But not to do what his father wanted. He would go to Portia, explain his father's obsession, and beg her to make clear that *she* didn't want to marry *him*. Henry knew Portia well enough to ask for an un-proposal. They were friends, no more, and comfortable with that.

At the same time – it was the final weekend in November, the one closest to St Andrew's Day – Charles, Leo and Emily Maxwell were also having breakfast at home in Somerville. For them, the Dunning-Greens, and most other Somerville families, it was the last weekend to be together before a brief or non-existent Christmas leave. The Brig was down in the boathouse, being looked after by Mrs Renyard.

'As soon as we've finished, we should go and join him,' said Charles. 'Ask him what birds he's seen.'

Leo and Emily knew what he really meant. Last night Leo had told them both separately the news about their mother. She had merely confirmed their suspicions. Even so, Leo had raised her eyebrows when Charles simply replied 'Oh,' trailing off into a Maxwellian drawl. Emily said 'Poor Brig,' but nothing more.

'So what have you seen, Brig?'

'Red-breasted merganser... Rather special. A winter visitor rarely seen this far up the river.'

Of Maxwell's children, only Emily enjoyed listening to her father identifying the wildfowl on the river below the boathouse, but today all three took turns with the binoculars, expressing interest, patiently taking in what their father had to say about the birds. They knew it made him happy. He knew they knew, and he gleamed at them all. Conversation about Audrey was not necessary.

Afterwards, Leo went to the newspaper shop and found a message from Labrador. She went to meet him at six, stayed 45 minutes, and enjoyed his attention, before joining the rest of her family for dinner with the Dunning-Greens at Hardings, their house on the banks of the Somer River.

Earlier, Portia had met Henry in the drive of Somerville Lodge, her gracious Regency house at the west end of the village. She preferred its unassuming elegance to the grandeur and discomfort of the Castle, and didn't look forward to the time when, as Countess of Somerville, she would have to live there.

'Let me make it easy for you, Henry. Your father sent you?'

'Yes. Whatever I say, he's still determined I ask you to marry me.'

Portia was amused, graceful, and a little aloof.

'Of course, you're eligible. And our age difference doesn't matter to me – I find you perfectly mature. In fact, I'm honoured by the *idea* of the offer. But I could never marry someone so obviously in love with someone else.'

'What shall I say to him then, Portia? You always have the answer.'

'Say that I thanked you for the offer.'

'Nothing else?'

'Nothing. That's the way I deal with my father. Shove him into limbo. As soon as you give these old bullies a scrap of information, they worry it like terriers. Let them chew on air.'

Henry went back to Hardings and avoided his father, determined to tell him about Portia tomorrow. This evening was for Leo.

His mother, always Henry's ally, helped calm down Sir Geoffrey, now apoplectic because Henry refused to report on his meeting with Portia. She sat at her desk in the hall, pretending to catch up on paperwork. Seeing Alice at the delicate 18th-century French bureau he'd given her for their 30th wedding anniversary had a magically soothing effect. His own desk, facing hers the other end of the impressively panelled hall, was a vast Victorian kneehole. Some of his happiest moments were spent there, getting on with arrangements with Alice under his gaze at her own desk, as he imagined, being industrious too.

By the time the Maxwells – the Brig, Charles, Leo and Emily – had arrived for dinner, plus the Tauntons with Portia and Flavia (Portia for the eldest Dunning-Green, of course, but possibly Flavia might do for Freddie?), he was in a serviceable mood. After dinner he took Lord Taunton into the smoking room for port, cigars and unsubtle hints. Lord Taunton pretended not to understand. Not being sure of what Portia had said to Henry, Sir Geoffrey couldn't press the topic further.

Henry, by contrast, did make his move. He lured Leo out on to the terrace, with its view of a particularly lovely reach of the river. The night was warm, for late November. He told her his 'problem' with Portia was finally out of the way.

'Now my father could never expect me to marry Portia – not that it had ever been anything I've considered *at all*, not for a *moment*.' Before Leo could reply, he moved on.

'There's only one person I've ever wanted to marry… If I should be so lucky. You've always known it, haven't you?'

The timing was no surprise to Leo. Her ATA girlfriends joked daily about how the war made the men so decisive. She thanked him, simply and sincerely. 'I'm not against it, but nor am I ready yet. Things are so uncertain for both of us. Please may we put it on hold?' Delighted to have got even this far, Henry agreed.

*

For Hodge, the day after his latest meeting with Russell was a boring Sunday at home with Phyllida. As it got dark, she settled herself on the sofa with her tapestry, irritatingly self contained, neutral towards the world, and to Hodge. Hodge generally rationed his impulse to shock her, but this evening it won.

'I learned something interesting about Maxwell recently.'

She raised her head, wary of his tone.

'Only a theory, but a good one. Maybe he's homosexual.'

The word exploded on Phyllida. Such people, such words, had not existed during her church-going childhood in Pinner. They were part of the alarming, bigger world – Kenneth's world – which at first had drawn her to him.

'How can you possibly know?'

'Oh, just signs, but they might explain his divorce. And why Cobb is always there now. He's been given a flat over the garage.'

Hodge had succeeded, as usual, in making her feel narrow, unworthy, incapable of a worldly reply.

*

In the newspaper shop two days later, Kenneth back in London, Phyllida met Cynthia Jennings. She felt the other woman's bright 'Hello', and the coolness behind it. For weeks now, Phyllida had been sensing a change in the way Somerville reacted to her and to Kenneth. Breezy on the surface, inert below. Conversations always just a little short lived.

'Very jolly lunch at The Rectory the other day. Maxwell and his daughters on cracking form. Both girls doing amazing war work.' Phyllida took this as a reference to Hodge doing no war work at all. 'By the way, will we see you at the Selby-Pickforths' cocktail party next Friday?'

Two invitations the Hodges hadn't received, mentioned in the same breath: Cynthia clearly wanted to give her pause for thought. Phyllida, still fragile after Kenneth's bullying on Sunday evening, needed a release. If Cynthia wants to give me something to think about, I can do the same for her. So out it slipped.

'The Maxwells? Notice anything funny about the Brig's relationship with Cobb?'

Cynthia Jennings's eyes widened. 'You're not suggesting...'

Phyllida shrugged.

'Cobb's just moved into that flat above the garage. Maxwell's marriage is on the rocks. Apparently Cobb is always around now.'

As soon as she'd spoken, she wished she hadn't. Phyllida had nothing against Maxwell. In fact, she could sense that behind his reserve he was mostly benign. Why did Kenneth dislike him so much? But Cynthia Jennings had hurried on before she could limit the damage by saying it was probably only one of Ken's crackpot theories.

8

MacDonald rang Maxwell.

'Discovered something. Not from Labrador's surveillance, though.'

'Oh?'

'Hodge is having an affair. But not with the contact he's meeting in Streteford and Milton.'

'Well?'

'Lady Flavia Somer.'

Maxwell hardly reacted. MacDonald grew suspicous, but masked his concern.

'How did you find out?'

'The noiseless break-in exercise. One of the Norwegian trainees saw them at it – and I mean at it – the description was detailed. They were in the teahouse in the woods below the Castle.'

'Detailed?'

'The trainee watched them long enough to memorize a full description of them both. Told his instructor afterwards, who swore him to silence. Instructor came to me. I've never met Hodge, but the description matched the one we got from the woman at Hamble. I've met Lady Flavia – dinner at the Castle – so no doubt at all there.'

'How d'you know Flavia isn't the person meeting him on Saturdays?'

'Solid alibis. Every time Hodge has had a pub session, Flavia was doing Somerville Estate duties. The Manor Office keeps a diary. Mostly the WI, followed by lunch at the Castle. Anyway, unless she's had training, she wouldn't know how to enter and leave the meetings unrecognized. It's beyond me why Labrador hasn't identified whom Hodge is meeting. Whoever it is must be not just a professional, but superbly inventive with disguise. Last time, the tail had followed Hodge to a park in Milton, watched him take a newspaper out of a litter bin, scan the pages and note the third letter of underlined words. Gave the name of the pub.'

'Doesn't even trust Hodge. That means we've got to stick at it, and keep pressing Berlin.'

'Flavia could still be working with Hodge and the third person. Maybe she's a courier. Goes to London quite regularly. Maybe she's dropping messages for Berlin there, or has access to a transmitter.'

A silence from Maxwell, then:

'Robbo, I have a confession. I've done some checking up on

112

Flavia independently. You know, the Tauntons, Somerville and all that. Close to home, so extra discretion needed. I've had her investigated – don't ask me how. Trust me, she's clean.'

The tension was obvious in MacDonald's face, unlike Maxwell's, and now Maxwell was pleased to see his features relax. They agreed it was a small relief they could eliminate Flavia, though it didn't solve the mystery. They would have to keep tailing Hodge, yet they couldn't continue indefinitely. MacDonald asked,

'Anything from our agent in Berlin?'

'Only that Hammel's understood to run agents in Poland, trying to destroy the underground resistance there. Let's give it until January. If there's still no result, I have one other idea, but it's risky.'

The Brig's Sunday morning trips to the paper shop were a Somerville institution. Instead of walking 20 minutes along the river bank and across the village green, which marked the end of the final salt water reach of the river, he chugged from his jetty direct to the green in his launch, pipe in mouth. It was the third weekend before Christmas, but mild. The gentlest of airs carried the spicy smell of his tobacco into his neighbours' gardens. The Brig standing in his launch, the unhurried rhythm of the engine, the delicious smell of pipe tobacco, spread ripples of contentment.

Approaching the green's landing stage, he slowed down to

a crawl – not just good seamanship – anyone watching would expect flawless boat handling from the Captain of the S.R.S.C. – but to give the two boys who lived in the Mill House, next to the landing stage, time to come out. The brothers, aged six and seven, delighted in catching the ropes thrown to them by the Brig and in tying them to the iron rings. He scrutinized their performance minutely, but constructively. After patient coaching, they could tie a bowline, a clove hitch or a round turn and two half hitches. The Brig tested them with a different knot each time, leaving his choice to the last minute. 'Need to do it without thinking, boys.' If they did well, they got a generous shilling each. Today, they weren't there.

He tied the boat up himself and walked towards the village high street, past the Mill House's garden, where the boys' mother was digging. She didn't look up.

'Morning, Mrs Howlett. How are the boys?'

'Got colds.' Usually, she grabbed at any chance to talk to the brigadier. Several residents were collecting papers from the newsagent as he walked in. He sensed the subtlest alteration in the rhythm of their Sunday morning small talk.

Colonel Mackworth said 'Good morning, Brigadier,' with curious emphasis. The couple behind the counter served him pipe tobacco, *The Sunday Times* and Swan Vesta matches. 'Anything else, sir?' No eye contact. None of their usual enquiries, not even about Leo. Last time, they'd ask him to bring a photograph of her in her ATA uniform. He left it in his pocket.

*

Since her first meeting with Smokey, Leo's deliveries to RAF Kenley, typically one a week, had developed a delightful pattern: first, taxi to a halt opposite the hangar where they'd first met – but he wouldn't be waiting for her there – far too public; then a short walk to the station office, where she would hand over the delivery paperwork; once it was signed, the sergeant behind the desk would say in a deadpan voice, adding the subtlest of winks:

'Car waiting for you outside, Second Officer Maxwell.' There, engine running, would be the station commander's car and driver. It was highly irregular to use RAF transport for private purposes, but Smokey, on best of terms with his CO, had charmed him into allowing occasional use of the car to transport Leo off the airfield and half a mile down the approach road, where Smokey would be waiting in his MG.

Leo would transfer to Smokey's car, the CO's would head back to the airfield, and he and Leo would drive to whichever local pub was in favour.

Today, Smokey detoured through some unfamiliar lanes, stopping outside a new pub. Politely, but clearly not expecting 'no' for an answer, he said:

'Would you mind waiting in the car? Just for ten minutes? I've promised to meet some old friends from Tangmere. Can't let them down.'

Ten minutes passed, and another ten, and another. Leo passed through mild impatience, to indignation, to anger and soon full-throttle fury.

Who *does* he think he is? We've met all of four times and already he thinks he can keep me waiting... as if I'm his driver.

When he arrived back minutes later she managed to contain her anger, but not to hide it. Smokey mumbled some apologies and rode out Leo's frost by telling her anecdotes about his former pilots at Tangmere, stories he knew she loved to hear. By the time they joined his Kenley friends at the next pub, she had given way to finding him as attractive as ever.

*

Maxwell admitted to himself that he was finding it hard to let SOE Somerville go. Having found the houses and overseen the first few months, he knew he should have let MacDonald get on with it himself. But he needed to have his fingers in more than one pie, and so he kept up his visits. Besides, he valued MacDonald's company. SOE's potential interested him as much as any of his regular work in MI6, and he had gone out of his way to cultivate Jeremy Gunn. He'd let drop to Gunn that he had some ideas for operations. Would Gunn like him to develop them? 'Bit of moonlighting.' Gunn had easily agreed over lunch in The Cavalry Club. Now, on yet another visit to Woodland House, MacDonald told Maxwell:

'We need to start matching trainees to missions. After six

months of training, personalities are starting to emerge. Not all of them will work well together, but the right combinations could be highly effective.'

Then, after a particularly irritating pause: 'Gunn tells me Churchill calls him most weeks about Henrietta and Jane. One of them will have to happen, sooner rather than later.'

'Remind me about Henrietta, Robbo.'

'It's the type of high-profile raids that Churchill craves. An attack on the electric transformer station at Pessac in South West France. Disable it and there's no power for the German submarine base at Bordeaux and, for a while, fewer attacks on the Atlantic convoys.'

He didn't have to remind Maxwell about Jane – they'd often discussed its objective: to disable Meucon airfield in Brittany, where the Luftwaffe's target-marking squadron was based. Its planes, equipped with radio direction-finding equipment, flew ahead of bombers directing them on to targets with radio beams. Attempts to jam the radio beams from the ground in Britain had failed. Maxwell liked the idea of disabling Meucon but thought it was flawed in practice.

'Disabling airfields in Northern France is perfectly suited to SOE, Robbo. It sends the discomforting message that after amphibious landings on the French coast, the Germans could be deprived for weeks of local airpower. But Jane is flawed. Too much left to chance. The answer, Robbo, is Zodiac. I've been on it since January, with Gunn's approval. Ground work's done: we've rebuilt the Normandy network that was destroyed last year. Fortunately, it's easier now to collaborate with the French resistance. Gunn and Churchill have placated De Gaulle. He no longer insists that he alone control the Free French. Understands at last that SOE and his people will be more effective if they work together.'

Next he told MacDonald how, helped by the Free French, Maxwell and his staff had gone some way to creating a new, highly compact Free French *reseau* or network, centred on a safe house near Caen. 'I've sworn Gunn not to mention Zodiac to Churchill. He'd insist SOE press ahead with it straight away, without completing the preparation.'

MacDonald observed: 'We've got an interesting new trainee coming in after Christmas. Could be ideal for Zodiac. Local fellow. Henry Dunning-Green. Suppose you know the family?'

'Indeed.' Maxwell had been expecting the question since Henry had told him at Christmas that his transfer to SOE was finally complete.

'What's he like? Apart from being a superb shot – we know about that. He was modest about his marksmanship when we interviewed him. When we checked with his CO, he said that he's extraordinary.'

'That's Henry. Modest, and unflappable – takes after his mother. The father's different – he'd sell his children to the Bosch if he thought he could make a profit. Could say the same for the younger brother. Sir Geoffrey is very successful, he built up a small business he inherited from his father into a huge concern. But he's also a bully.'

'Did he bully Henry?'

'Yes, but Henry stood up to him. He kept his head down, and came out toughened. He's a team player, and a good organizer – I've watched him run our Somerville regatta – endless threads to hold together, fielding stupid questions from the inexperienced sailors. He does it all effortlessly, and creates a relaxed atmosphere. He doesn't say much, seems a bit dull, but if you scratch beneath the surface, there's humour.' Maxwell delivered this speech with the usual maddening pauses, but MacDonald was as patient as ever.

'Sounds like top-class material.'

'You know why I'm asking?'

'Yes, you're looking out for someone to work with Labrador.'

'We might make them join Henrietta in March. See how they work together. If it goes well, they could be the pair for Zodiac.'

'Good idea.' Long pause. 'Viv, it'll be odd for Henry being here at Somerville, where he grew up, separated from his community. Strange feeling.'

And strange for me, thought Maxwell. Henry joining SOE Somerville was a conflict of interest with which he had tried to come to terms with – and not entirely succeeded. Applying to SOE had been Henry's decision, his alone, and it would have been more than dishonourable to intervene – even if he could have influenced the outcome.

So it was strange and uncomfortable sitting here plotting to send Henry on dangerous missions. Controlled as Maxwell was, a small corner of his mind entertained a superstition: that his current woes, crowned by the slow torture of being forced to stand by while Leo and Henry put themselves in the way of danger, were punishment, just or otherwise, for keeping the world at arm's length

*

'Brig? It's Flavia Somer.'

'Morning Flavia.'

'I'm doing the seating plan for the dance. Odd thing. You're not on any table.' Flavia had heard the rumours about Maxwell and Cobb. She had a Bohemian attitude to homosexuality – couldn't understand the disapproval – and wanted to ease the Brig's embarrassment, should he feel any.

The S.R.S.C. dance, in a medieval hall adjacent to the Castle, was yet another Somerville ritual, always held two Saturdays before Christmas: a warm up for the rash of end-of-year parties. Usually residents competed for the honour of inviting the S.R.S.C.'s Captain and his wife to join their table, taking it strictly in turns. Maxwell had noticed the absence of his invitation and toyed with the possibility that it was late because without Audrey he was more difficult to accommodate. Then, after the coolness he'd met on the green and in the paper shop, he had begun to suppose that it might be connected with Hodge's antipathy.

'Well, best thing is for you to join our table. We've at least one single woman staying at the Castle. Hope you don't mind taking a chance?'

Entering the hall on the night of the dance, Maxwell was immediately aware of invisible walls. Usually, knots of Somerville small talk loosened automatically to include him. Lacking small talk, he now found it impossible to insert himself. Disturbing, for the first time in his life at Somerville, to feel like an outsider – but his face revealed nothing.

To his relief, Patricia Selby-Pickforth appeared beside him. 'Can we talk privately downstairs? Outside the entrance lobby?'

'See you there.'

'This is difficult.'

'Go on, Pat. I know something's afoot. I wasn't invited to join a table. Some people aren't talking to me, and those that are seem reluctant. The atmosphere is... Brittle. And it's not just about the uncertainties... The war, the future of Somerville.'

'True. It's about you. Someone's put it about that you and Cobb are... Well... I don't know how to say it. It's so shocking. You know. You and Cobb. They're connecting Audrey's absence and Cobb being given the flat over your garage.'

Maxwell stayed impassive, in no hurry to speak.

'Amusing. Yes, amusing. Thank you for telling me. You're a true friend.'

'What shall we do?'

'Nothing. I beg you, nothing. Go along with it.'

'But I know it's not true. So unfair. Must be Hodge, I suppose. How can he have that much of a grudge against you?'

The Brig went back in to dinner, sitting between Portia and the spare house guest, who forever after marked him down as the heaviest going dinner companion of her life. Still his face revealed nothing of his feelings. The Tauntons were the same as ever towards him, but as he rose to toast the Commodore, the rest of the room was staring at its plates.

After coffee, dancing began, to the strains of an amateurish string quintet. Maxwell strolled unhurriedly to the lavatory, then slid away home when he was sure no one would notice. Maxwell, like many of his kind, fancied himself immune to serious misery. He believed he'd survived the worst when uprooted and sent to boarding school, a child of eight. Now, he was unsure. After he had gone, the party didn't take off. Few people danced, and most left early, too.

Two days later, Patricia went to see Maxwell.

'You must confront Hodge, Brig, or someone will do it for you. Better the truth's out than in.'

'I'm sorry, but we've got to carry on with the waiting game.'

'Every day that passes damages you more.'

'These things simmer down after a while. People get over the shock and look for something else to complain about.'

'If it's not true, why not go to Hodge and ask him to retract?'

'The same reason I gave you at dinner after that S.R.S.C. meeting. If you swear not to discuss it with anyone, even Reggie, I'll tell you a little more.'

'Swear.'

'There's a chance that someone is putting pressure on Hodge. Can't give you details, but the security of SOE Somerville might be at risk. We have to wait patiently until he leads us to whomever he's seeing. That overrides *everything*.'

'Have you thought about what he might do at the AGM? It's coming up, soon as Christmas is over.'

'Yes, I'm prepared.'

Russell rang Hodge. 'How did the dance go?'

'Somerville's split down the middle. Half of them outraged by Maxwell. Half of them outraged because the other half is outraged.'

'Doesn't take much, does it?'

'I suppose you'd call their horror of homosexuality a middle-class confusion.'

'Something like that. No actual confrontations?'

'No, just simmering disquiet. Whispering behind turned backs. Awful, to be honest. It was a terrible party. No fun.'

'Maybe there'll be real fisticuffs at the AGM.'

'Maybe. About my starting date in the Service... '

'Sorry, there's been another postponement. Should be very soon after the AGM. Let's meet then.'

'Flavia? It's Ken.'

'Hello.'

'Can we talk?'

'Of course.'

'Friday evenings are soon going to be difficult. I've got a job at the MOD, most likely starting next month. I'm putting my practice in mothballs, so excuses about clients to visit on Friday nights won't work.'

'Oh dear. That leaves the teahouse on Saturday or Sunday.'

'I suppose so.'

'Don't worry, I'll fit you in. We're both busy at weekends, I know, so it'll have to be quickies. Nothing wrong with a quickie.'

Kenneth stayed silent.

'Ken, where's your sense of humour?'

Maxwell was mostly alone and depressed at Christmas and New Year, relieved by a fleeting visit from Charles. Leo and Emily were offered twelve hours' leave – not long enough to justify the journey to Somerville. Apart from lunch with the Selby-Pickforths, where there were no Somerville folk, only a couple down from London, he kept to The Rectory. Cobb, unaware of the rumours circulating about him and his employer, had gone back to London for Christmas with his wife and family.

The last Saturday in December was balmy, warm enough for breakfast in the boathouse. Two letters were waiting for him on the table. The first was from Shaw, Ackroyd, Tanner and Burn, Hampton solicitors.

Dear Brigadier Maxwell,

We act for your wife, Audrey Louise Maxwell.

She has instructed us to initiate divorce proceedings.

She requires your prompt recognition that your marriage has broken down irretrievably. She is minded to remain in South Africa, and has no plans to return to England.

She assumes that you will not wish to contest the divorce. That being so, it remains to achieve the quickest possible resolution. Our client proposes that your dignity, and her interests, i.e. the quickest possible outcome, are best served by our client suing yourself on grounds of adultery. Whether or not you have committed adultery during the course of your marriage is not at issue here.

We have advised Mrs Maxwell, and she instructs us to advise you, to take advantage of a local agency that specializes in such

125

matters. Its name is shown at the foot of this letter. They will arrange a meeting, and a photographer, at a hotel of your choosing to record the necessary evidence.

Yours sincerely

James Shaw
Partner

CC Askews Private Investigations, 36 Castle Street, Hampton.

The second letter was much longer. It came from Armstrong Ward, Maidstone General Hospital, Kent.

Dear Brig,

I am all right, but I have had a pile-up. Only three broken ribs and some burns, not serious but boring because the ribs hurt like anything when anyone makes me laugh.

I thought the best way to tell you was a letter because you don't like the phone, especially for things like this. I'll try to make it a good letter. You were right. The ATA is dangerous, but this time it was not the weather. It was a Walrus, an unattractive aeroplane to fly, like flying several sacks of coal. An unstable, wallowing thing, and it makes a dreadful noise.

I was trying to take off at Tangmere in a crosswind, I couldn't get an angle into the wind. As soon as I opened up, it felt to me as if it wanted to turn over on its back, I simply could not hold it. I concluded that the controls might have been crossed, something that can happen, so I throttled back. But the minute I throttled back, it righted itself, so I quickly realized it wasn't the controls, it must be able to take off, but by this time, since I had left the ground, the aircraft had swung even further across wind.

It was a silly thing, looking back, to have opened up again, but I did. I thought I could make it, but it clearly was not to be so. I didn't want to crash into the hangar, and managed to keep clear. I had throttled back again by this time and could see I was going to crash, we hit a shed at the side of the airfield. That's the last thing I remember, the aeroplane tipping forwards. I apparently ended up straggled across a road near a bungalow. I think one of the wings hit the bungalow. Luckily for me, I was not strapped in.

In a Walrus, you can't reach the peddles if you are strapped in — you need to be able to reach forwards. My short legs make it worse, so that's why I was unstrapped. When the aeroplane came to rest it burst into flames immediately, but I was thrown half out of the cockpit. The baker's man was just delivering his bread at that particular moment, and had to dive out of the way, but when he saw what had happened he came rushing over and pulled me away from the flames. I was burnt, along with my clothes, and was unconscious — but he managed to pull me clear.

So there you are. I know you like all the details, so I have tried to put them down for you. Putting it down like this may help

127

me write my own report, which I am dreading. As soon as I am out of the hospital I've got take it to White Waltham to show my commanding officer, Margot Grey. I am terribly worried she's going to find me at fault and stop me flying, or keep me on these boring Type 1 aircraft, so I'll never move up to flying fighters. This is far worse than a bit of pain in my ribs.

No need to visit me. I'll be out in about ten days, anyway I have had some visitors, including Chile from the Hatfield Ferry Pool and some of the Spitfire pilots at Kenley that I met. I am quite friendly with one of them. He's called Smokey because his surname is Cole – well, MacKenzie-Cole in fact. To cheer me up I made him talk to me about dogfights. He's like all of them, hates talking shop, tried to say no, but this time he couldn't because I told him I wouldn't be cheered up otherwise!! It's fascinating, all about tailing and being tailed. I'll tell you when I see you.

Please show this letter to friends at Somerville, and to Charles and Emily. Mummy too if you think that would be right.

Love from Leo.
P.S. Don't worry about me.

Despite the narrowness of Leo's escape, Maxwell found her letter comforting. Its poor, hurried punctuation made it seem the more honest, evidence of a humble struggle to connect words directly with reality. It was a reassuring contrast to the solicitor's well-turned but stale circumlocutions, language smugly content with itself. Leo's language showed her living a life; the lawyer's, a proxy-life.

Leo and her aeroplane were 'we.' Touching, and truthful. A mistake was a 'silly thing': an admission that she was still half girl, half adult, and despite such a harsh encounter with flying's dangers, still lit up with it. And still not ready to settle down with Henry.

He'd read newspaper reports of Mackenzie-Cole's exploits as a Battle of Britain pilot after each of his two visits to the Palace, first to collect a DFC then its bar. He'd already shot down five ME109s. He and Leo were only too glamorously suited – on the face of it.

As for Audrey: nothing new in her selfishness, nothing new about her expecting him to do the dirty work.

*

The ambulance had delivered Leo to hospital breathing but unconscious. While her broken ribs were being strapped, she had drifted in and out of consciousness, feeling no pain, luxuriating in morphine nirvana. Everything would be alright. She loved everyone, even the Brig when he radiated that awful look of his; even Emily and Charles when they teased her for losing her temper; even Freddie Dunning-Green when he cheated on the river. As for Henry, Labrador and Smokey, that would work out too. They would end up liking each other enormously and she wouldn't even have to make a choice – it would just happen, without any ghastly decision to make.

Later, the morphine wore off and she became aware, step by excruciating step, of her body – or rather not Leo's body, but an assembly of terrible stiffness, aches and shafting pains. Knives, buried in her chest, tweaked with every breath; her eyes felt puffy and leaden. Unasked, the nurse had brought a mirror to reassure her that the only injuries to her face were the black eyes. 'Quite a jolt you had, Miss Maxwell. Nothing made contact with your face, but the impact threw you so hard against the instrument panel that besides the broken ribs you got two black eyes.'

Now everything was *not* going to be alright. How could she have been so stupid? The ATA would probably stop her flying – anyway there would be an enquiry, and worse, a report to write. This, and the guilt she felt for not making up her mind between Labrador, Henry and Smokey, barged every other thought out of her head. She may as well have had no other existence except her two problems. She wrestled with them in turn obsessively for the next 24 hours, until Chile turned up.

'I've just come from the wreckage – burnt to a cinder.'

'I'm only here because I wasn't wearing the seat straps. I'll never wear them again. Will you do something for me? Thank the baker's boy who pulled me out?'

'Of course.'

'Don't go yet. I need to ask you some things.'

Without a pause she plunged into a black peroration on her

guilt for sitting on the fence, and especially how terrible she felt about Henry. Had Chile guessed? No, she supposed not, she spoke about him so little. Well, Henry had proposed to her just before she joined the ATA, and she had put him on hold. 'It was flattering. I liked him asking. For some funny reason it deepened our friendship. And now I feel ungrateful and spoilt for making him wait. I don't know what to do.'

'You've had a shock – it's no time to torture yourself with things like that. Come on Leo, you know that if a girl's unsure, she should never say yes. Stores up trouble in the long run.'

'The problem's his correctness, Chile. He's no fun. Maybe it's because he's moulded by privilege. I don't mind privilege, but I like men's eyes to shine with confidence – don't you? Because of who they are, not because they're rich.'

'You're right Leo. But give it time.'

'I wish you could meet all three and tell me which you think is best.'

'Describe them to me.'

'If they were all in the same room, you'd think Henry was the most substantial, but not much else. Labrador is irresistible. Have you read *Wuthering Heights*? He broods, like Heathcliff. And Smokey? Fearless, fearsome, but kind. Marvellous. But would I trust my future to Smokey? Can't tell. Same with Labrador. He's so mysterious that sometimes I can't imagine he has a future at all. And Henry? Life would be secure and comfortable with him – he already has a big private income, enough to run a family.'

'But you still put more value on sparkling eyes... and raw masculinity? You want a man who makes your knees go weak?'

Leo's laughter turned into a gasp of pain. Serious again, she said:

'After 20 years of marriage, when I'm past my best, would Henry just change me for someone younger? That's what men do when they've always had everything they want.'

Chile left soon after, liking this paradoxical English girl even more than before: fierce, sensitive, naughty and moral in bewildering succession. Leo's parting words were about how much she was looking forward to Smokey's visit next day.

9

January 1941

MacDonald's opening address to the newest batch of trainees lasted more than an hour – too long. It analysed, for their benefit, every one of SOE's objectives. Henry Dunning-Green lost concentration early on, only waking up when he heard MacDonald's sobering conclusion.

'Some agents, when they get into the field, find it much easier than they expected, and relax their precautions. That is the moment to beware of. Never relax and never fool yourself by thinking that the enemy are asleep. They're probably watching you, directly or indirectly, all the time.'

As the trainees left Woodland House, one of the instructors took Henry aside. 'Colonel MacDonald wants to see you in half an hour.'

'Captain Dunning-Green, sir. You asked to see me.'

'Ah yes. David. Sit down.'

'David, sir?'

'Yes. Your code name. Can't resist being the first to tell you. Not strictly regular, I suppose. Agents' names are meant to be completely disconnected with anything.'

'But David, sir?'

'As in David and Goliath. SOE Somerville is all about sending out Davids to challenge Goliath the other side of the Channel. As you're a Somerville boy, born and bred, we're giving you our flagship code name. *And* David was a good shot. Amusing, don't you think?'

'Yes sir. Thank you, sir.'

'Mind you live up to it. By the way, this is not the regular army, thank God. Less form, more content. No need to call me sir every time. Now, your family still have a place round here?'

'Yes. House on the river for weekends and holidays. Otherwise London.'

'Do they know you're here?'

'No.'

'Local friends and acquaintances? Girlfriends?'

'None have any idea.'

'I can't stress enough that the security of these training schools could be compromised, fatally, if anyone – I mean anyone – in Somerville heard that you're here. We'll have to disguise you whenever you go outside the campus for training exercises.'

'If I get leave, I'll go to London.'

'Good. You've had military training, so we're going to push you through the courses quickly. You'll be excused the parachute course, because you've done it already and subversion, because you won't need it. Shame that, because it's done by our best lecturer. But you'll do the rest – outdoor survival, noiseless break-in, tailing, communications – radio and secret messaging, resistance to interrogation.'

'I will apply myself.'

'Good. If you do, you might find yourself in the field sooner than you expected.'

Formalities over, MacDonald set about scrutinizing David. He gave him a whisky and soda and invited him to talk about his life to date – 'anything that paints a picture of who you really are, not what society made you.'

The open-endedness of the question almost always worked on would-be agents, especially the self-centred, garrulous types. With Henry, it was not so easy. He spoke not unwillingly, but as if to make clear that he was talking about himself only because he must.

Long enough, though, for MacDonald to focus intensely on what the exterior David might reveal about the interior. There was the clean, well-cared for appearance of his clothes, and the way they hung naturally on his frame – medium height, medium build, medium colouring: everything medium, nothing memorable – all to the good for undercover work. His facial features were symmetrical, but not handsome, or plain. His hair was brown, his eyes a nondescript hazel. The most noticeable feature was his balance – more than that, his poise. He was not a man you could imagine sweating or shaking with anger or fear – or for that matter, defecating.

His economical hand movements suggested a calm metabolism, an athlete's slow pulse. Above all, he noticed how each eye had the same intensity of gaze. Over the years, MacDonald had developed a theory that people with one eye obviously more dominant than the other could, potentially, be unstable, even fanatic. Time and again, do-or-die risk takers were those with a starey, seemingly disconnected right eye.

Henry was the opposite. His eyes were in harmony, suggesting equilibrium, while his unhurried, accurate choice of words implied intelligence, determination, deep-down energy.

*

It was below zero in the basement storage area of The Rectory's boathouse. David struggled not to shiver uncontrollably as he lay fully clothed under two thickly folded cotton sails, wedged into a small wooden rowing dinghy, half sitting, half lying. The January night outside was foul, a north-east gale blowing drifts of snow, but inside the boathouse, though cold, he was happy with thoughts of Leo. To him the untidy concrete cavern was a shrine: only a few feet away was her sailing dinghy, laid up for the duration of the war.

His instructor had almost let him off the outdoor survival exercises, knowing that at Sandhurst he would have coped with worse. 'On the other hand, David, they're useful because you're forced to slip in and out unseen.' So after dark, face blackened with burnt cork, wearing two sweaters and a duffel coat, hood up, David had silently made his way though the rhododendron bushes, down through the monastery ruins, across the village green and on to a path that led through two small fields bordering the river and past The Rectory's garden. He'd climbed through the iron fence and located the key to the basement in its hiding place known only to the Maxwells and S.R.S.C. committee members. The cavern provided perfect cover, it was much nearer home than Sailing Club Point and it made him feel connected with Leo: a bitter-sweet feeling, but still sweeter than bitter. He visualized her in her dinghy, well ahead of the fleet, her shoulders bare in a sleeveless blouse on a glorious August day. Those shoulders... so weakly built, so endearingly vulnerable, yet with such power over him... they were the only bit of her he'd seen naked – like all the other women, she wore trousers for sailing. He didn't want to consider the rest of her. It was too sacred even to think about.

He smiled at the thought of her flare-ups, mostly against Freddie, but others too if she thought they'd broken the racing rules. The flare-ups had never unsettled him – only made him feel he wanted to protect her from herself.

He shivered, adjusted the bulky life jackets he'd found to cushion his back from the ribs and planks of the dinghy and pondered yet again the marvel of her energy: how it vitalized him, made his life seem worth living, no less. He said to himself: 'I have energy to match hers. I wonder if she's noticed it? Maybe not. My father has driven it underground.'

He didn't know, yet, enough about the human heart to understand that the love that burns slowly for years is as worthy as the love that flares up suddenly and turns you inside out. But he did know he'd been toughened by his strong, stubborn feeling for Leo, which had survived the torture of watching others trying to court her favour.

He relived once again the dread he'd felt at the approach of the day they would part for the war, soon after the dinner at Hardings. But: she hadn't said yes, and she hadn't said no, and he was strong enough to wait.

Lord Taunton strolled into the village hall and sat down at the table, facing his audience, flanked either side by the Vice Commodore and committee of the S.R.S.C. Portia, Maxwell, Hodge, Patricia Selby-Pickforth, Flavia and Colonel Mackworth. Henry Dunning-Green was absent. Taunton glanced benignly at his audience – only 20 or so members had turned up – and they fell silent.

'I declare the tenth annual general meeting of the S.R.S.C. now open. And, as usual, I am happy to hand over the running of the meeting to my daughter Portia, Vice Commodore, who as you know, commands –' the merest hint of emphasis on this last word raised a politely subdued titter '– every detail.'

Portia stood up quickly. 'Thank you, Commodore.' Then, in her calmest, most business-like voice she said,

'I have decided not to follow the written agenda for this AGM. This is because we find ourselves, without warning, in a highly unusual situation.' Theatrical pause.

'This morning I had a letter of resignation.' Another minutely judged pause. 'From our Captain.' Murmurs from the floor.

'With the greatest regret, I have had to accept his resignation. Pressure of work in London now makes it impossible for Brigadier Maxwell to discharge even the lightest of S.R.S.C. duties, even if the club is dormant for the war. I hardly need to add that the brigadier's devotion to the S.R.S.C. is unquestionable. I take this opportunity to thank him on behalf of the membership for almost a decade of service to the club, first as Sailing Secretary then in recent years as Captain.'

A short pause while more murmurs died down.

'In fact, I think it's safe to say that in many senses he *is* the S.R.S.C.' More murmurs of approval, mixed with surprise. Clearly visible to everyone on the floor, Kenneth Hodge was rising to his feet, signalling his intention to speak, frustration mixed with anger blackening his face.

'Mr Treasurer, I'll call on you shortly.' Hodge had to sit down.

Maxwell then left the committee table, his face beyond inscrutable, and made his way to an empty seat in the audience. Silence re-established, Portia sailed on:

'So, as the current committee was assembled by Brigadier Maxwell, and as there will be no sailing and no social events, it now makes sense for the Sailing Secretary and Social Secretary both to stand down too. I've already had agreement from Henry Dunning-Green, Sailing Secretary, who apologises for his absence. Flavia, are you also happy to stand down as Social Secretary?'

Flavia murmured yes and made her way to another empty seat in the audience. Her sister repeated the same procedure for the rest of the committee, except Hodge.

'You will notice, members, that one committee member is left with myself and the Commodore at the committee table – our Treasurer, Kenneth Hodge.'

Hodge tried to speak again, but Portia continued, suppressing him effortlessly, no need even to raise her voice.

'Mr Hodge, I would like to propose to the meeting that you become acting Captain for the duration of the war, but to face re-election when the club reconvenes. Meanwhile, I propose that you combine the roles of Captain and Treasurer.'

Hodge nodded mechanically, so piqued that he was briefly without words.

'Good. Then may I take a vote? Who is for my proposal to elect Kenneth Hodge acting Captain?'

No hands were raised.

'Then may I have a show of hands from those against?'

No hands were raised. Without missing a beat, Portia rolled on.

'In that case, the proposal is neither carried nor rejected. I am therefore obliged to invoke rule 24 of the S.R.S.C.'s constitution. Allow me to quote: 'In the event of no agreement on a matter critical to the club, and in the absence of a vote at the AGM, the Vice Commodore shall exercise a casting vote.'

'Congratulations Kenneth, you are hereby appointed acting Captain of the S.R.S.C.'

Silence from the audience.

'Kenneth, would you care to say a few words to the members?'

Hodge could only just mask his fury. They had handed him the empty honour of running a dormant club; and they had combined it with a public snub. Not one member had supported his appointment.

'I... I... I suppose so. I came to this meeting with two proposals. The first is now redundant – but I think that members know what it would have been.'

More murmurs.

'The second is to form a subcommittee to examine our membership rules. The findings to be put to the members if the club reconvenes. I feel that this is as good a time as any to reform our outdated membership criteria. Who will volunteer to join this subcommittee?'

Silence.

'Then I will prepare a report and make the proposals myself.'

To avoid further embarassment Lord Taunton quickly declared the meeting closed. Normally members stayed gossiping over a glass of wine, but now they streamed out of the door as fast as they could.

Outside the hall, Portia asked the Brig to join her for supper at Somerville House, as she had done after every AGM since Maxwell had been Captain. In Audrey's absence, the meaning of the invitation was different, but no one heard her except Maxwell and no one else saw the gleam deep behind his eyes. Patricia Selby-Pickforth came up behind them.

'Vivian…' Patricia hadn't used his Christian name for years. 'What *have* you allowed him to do to you?'

'He doesn't know *what* he's doing.'

Hodge reported the AGM to Russell straight afterwards.

'It didn't go as expected. Portia certainly knows how to manage a meeting. No chance to humiliate Maxwell.'

'Shame.'

'He and the rest of the committee stood down voluntarily before I had a chance to speak. I'm left running a virtually non-existent club without a committee. Just a dogsbody.'

'Hard luck, Ken. *Very* annoying when a peach turns out tasteless. On the other hand, you can't make an omelette without breaking eggs. At least you've taken the club a step or two forwards into the 20th century.'

'I'd be surprised.'

'Well, there's good news to compensate. Meet me at the Service's Baker Street office on Monday week. That's your confirmed starting date. Can you sort out things at your office by then? If not, the Service will give you the odd day off to complete arrangements.'

Comrade Sonny to Moscow Central

I am pleased to report that my colleagues in London have now agreed to confine my time at Somerville to 12 months. I can return to London in June — just five months away.

Long live Stalin.

P.S. Somerville has been successfully destabilized. The community is unhappy, divided. The sailing club leader has been forced to resign. A new, progressive leader of my choosing — with working class origins — has taken his place. In a deeply reactionary community such as Somerville, this amounts to revolutionary change. The new leader has bourgeois confusions, but his principles will be more acceptable to my comrades in Moscow than his predecessor's.

10

Slinking away from unpleasantness was foreign to Maxwell, but the day after the meeting he left Somerville. A taxi took him to the station. No one noticed him go. He controlled his misery – his sense of exile from the place that made him happiest – by a mixture of inbred stoicism and by boxing it off into a compartment of his mind. By concentrating on the better parts of his life, especially Operation Zodiac.

Ensuring Zodiac's success was his newest obsession. Its well-crafted ruthlessness would dazzle the Service and SOE. And, he admitted freely to himself, it was more than comforting to have a personal channel for his aggression. If he was inclined to associate his mystery tormentor at Somerville with Nazi Germany, objectifying them as one and the same enemy, then so be it. Anyway, it was entirely possible that they were.

Cobb was never seen in Somerville again, in fact he hadn't

been there, nor had the army car, since the weekend before the sailing club meeting. Maxwell had knocked on the door of the garage flat.

'Am I disturbing you?'

'No, sir.'

'Remember we talked of five months at Somerville?'

'Yes, sir.'

'It's turned out shorter. I'm back to London next weekend – indefinitely. The training schools are running smoothly, so I'm needed in London.'

'Very well, sir. I can leave tomorrow. Mrs Cobb will be pleased to have me back.'

Maxwell broke his journey at Hampton, walking purposefully through the town centre to The Queen Anne, a less congenial inn than the Collingwood – and on this occasion, to be used for uncongenial business. A Miss Gilbert, dressed as if for a smart lunch date, was waiting for Maxwell in reception. He bought her a drink at the bar while a private detective sat in the corner taking notes. Miss Gilbert slipped Maxwell a folded piece of paper, on it written 'room 9'. She went up first. Maxwell followed, then the detective, at a discreet distance, arriving in the corridor just in time to see Maxwell and the young woman enter the room.

The detective took more notes, and left. Fifteen minutes later, Maxwell and Miss Gilbert left too. Maxwell had said nothing to her inside the bedroom except 'Do you mind if I read the paper?'

Maxwell continued his journey to London, went to The Cavalry

Club and installed himself in a new room – not just a bedroom, but a bedroom with bathroom and sitting room attached – one of a handful of suites the club reserved for visiting VIPs. This was to be his home for as far ahead as he could plan. He enjoyed its simplicity.

'Robbo? Are you sitting down?'

'What's happened?'

'Hodge has turned up in C's organization. Working on the North Africa Desk, analysing intelligence from an observer in Tripoli docks. He writes reports on how much equipment is unloaded for the Afrika Corps.'

'Who got him in?'

'No one's telling. It's a new post, only advertised internally. His section head told me he couldn't possibly name the man who made the introduction. Too valuable a contact.'

'At every turn, there's a guardian angel at Hodge's side.'

'Bad fairy, you mean.'

'Guiding his moves. Ensuring he can't be linked to whoever he's meeting. Pulling his strings.'

'Helping him avoid call-up to a regular army unit.'

'And whoever is doing it is superb, otherwise we would have got him by now.'

'If this angel is someone inside the training schools, Hodge is still dangerous, even in London. Imagine what he can still pass on to Germany. Wouldn't be surprised if they know the name of Lord Taunton's dog by now.'

'There's no sign the Germans are acting on intelligence from Somerville.'

'We still have to do something about him. Henrietta is only eight weeks away.'

'Do you remember I mentioned a back-up plan?'

Ultimately, MacDonald saw his job at SOE Somerville as about dealing with the trainees' uncertainties. He had to be sure that the instructors taught to the highest standards, but alleviating their tensions, keeping them hoping for a mission, was more important.

They all looked forward, some in desperation, to release from the limbo of the training schools. Every day, a trainee described to him how corrosive it was not knowing when. Speculation and rumour ran round the schools, merging to produce deadly, morale-sapping theories and countertheories. The trainees craved scraps of information.

To offset a little of the uncertainty, MacDonald reminded trainees individually, as often as he could, that they were in the queue for an operation. Now it was Labrador's and David's turn. MacDonald introduced them in the dining room of Woodland House.

They appraised each other acutely. David tried to hide his interest behind a relaxed smile and a warm handshake. Labrador, immediately recognizing David as the man who'd helped Leo push her boat, was doubly guarded. David noticed Labrador's implacable, deep brown eyes.

'We have something in mind for you two. Late March. I can't tell you the name of the operation, but I can say it's in South West France. Not so dangerous as the North-east and Paris. Many fewer Bosch.'

'Can you say anything about the work?'

'Not at this stage. Your briefing will be the day before departure. Even then, you'll be told as little as possible.'

'Knowing something is better than nothing.'

'Yes, but don't raise your expectations. You'll be understudies in a small team of experienced saboteurs. Learning the ropes for something bigger – much bigger. You'll have to obey orders, to the letter.'

Labrador and David went back to their training marginally happier. MacDonald told their instructors to watch them closely when together in the same classroom. Maxwell was pleased to be told that they never gave anyone a clue that they had a common mission.

*

Five weeks after the crash, Leo was back on ATA duty. The Fairey Swordfish was the navy's new torpedo aircraft, technically ahead of its time yet so draughty that she was wearing two pairs of socks, woollen underwear, two sweaters, her ATA overalls and over them a leather flying jacket lined with fur half an inch thick. The canvas flying boots were fur lined too, but her feet were still so numb that, as she lined up the plane on the runway at Sherburn Airfield, she could have been pushing the rudder pedals with prosthetic limbs. Sherburn was on the top of the North Yorkshire Moors, close to the East Coast. An east wind was blowing in uninterrupted from the Urals.

She landed, handed in the paperwork and was assigned to a curtained-off section of a Nissen hut for her overnight quarters. She had a cup of tea in the mess, went for a walk and then back to the hut to cook baked beans on toast for supper, to be followed by an early night.

The hut was heated by an anthracite stove but almost as freezing as the Swordfish. This was her fourth night away from the comfortable cottage at Hatfield, shuttling planes between airfields in Scotland and Yorkshire, once more climbing into bed, piling the flying jacket on top of the thin blankets. She thought how pleasantly warm it would be to have a man in her bed. Later she dozed... or did she?

Next day, she would ask herself if she had been half asleep, or asleep and dreaming. Perhaps it didn't matter. The fantasies had amounted to reality.

Her first visitor was Labrador, dressed only in a shirt. Circles of sweat showed dark under the arms, and as he advanced on her bed his need was only too obvious. He smelt a little of sweat, but that hadn't been especially unattractive. He was a dark, hairy thing, a force of nature, crawling all over her. No part of her was left unexplored by his hands, lips and tongue. Giving way to him was easy – he was a delicious mixture of urgency and self control, determined she should have her equal share of the pleasure. It had been everything she could have hoped for, twice.

Soon after, Smokey appeared, in uniform, gold braid glinting – he was now a Squadron Leader. By contrast, his was an elegant performance. He made love without undressing, taking his time, with impressive staying power. It too had been delightful, but had she felt a touch controlled? When he'd reached orgasm, was there in his gasps a hint of a fanfare for Smokey? A sense that if Leo happened to enjoy it too, that was a bonus, for which she should be grateful?

And if she had to choose? Labrador? To be honest, a little too animal. Smokey? A little pleased with himself.

And Henry? He hadn't even had a turn, and she couldn't begin to imagine what he would be like.

*

Stanley Judd was not looking forward to his meeting with Brigadier Maxwell. The former detective inspector, before the war a plodder with the Surrey Constabulary, found his new colleagues in MI5 a different breed: hard bitten and ambitious. To face a top man in MI6, the foreign intelligence service, was all the more terrifying.

MI6 was thought of – thought of itself – as a privileged caste. He felt jittery as he waited in the anteroom of Maxwell's office.

Maxwell's order had been easy but time consuming. He'd asked for a shortlist of category C individuals from the huge list of German citizens who were living in Britain at the outbreak of war in 1939 – people who should, in theory, be interned. The 60,000 category C names were thought to carry no risk to Britain, and remained free, but would, if they aroused suspicion, be moved up to category B. Category B individuals were supervised, and could be moved up to Category A. Category A meant prison – being interned, as the Home Office preferred to call it.

Compiled and double checked by a team of clerks overseen by Judd, the shortlist ended up with just six names.

Maxwell had asked for women in their 20s, with a German father or mother, working either in the Foreign Office, in the War Office or in journalism. In other words, any young woman who could engineer meetings with men with access, or potential access, to sensitive information. Maxwell had not given his reasons, but it was obvious to Stanley Judd that the brigadier was looking for an attractive young woman, because he'd asked for a photograph of each.

True, thought Judd, the brigadier was distant – and dignified – but there was none of the superiority, none of the impatience he'd been led to expect. This man treated him respectfully, as an expert, and the very few words he used were spoken softly. Not the tones of a man who wanted to make him feel small.

'Are you sure, Judd, that the parentage information is a hundred per cent accurate?'

'Every one double checked against the birth certificates.'

'And this young woman here – Clare Nicholson...' He picked out one of the six folders, all with photographs attached.

'Has she ever been spoken to by MI5, or been monitored by the Service?'

'Definitely not. Like the rest, we let them go about their business, assuming innocence, until asked to investigate.'

'That's right. We've bet that the aliens who stayed here in 1939 did so because they liked our way of life. If we approach her, will it be a complete surprise?'

'Yes. May I ask you, Brigadier, why you have picked out Clare Nicholson, rather than any of the others?'

'Sorry, can't say. But I think she'll do.'

Days later, a letter arrived at the house in Wimbledon where Clare Nicholson lived with her mother. It ordered Miss Nicholson to report to a suite at the Dorchester on Wednesday the following week. The reason given for the order was 'national security'. The recipient was 'advised', meaning ordered, under pain of prosecution under the Wartime Official Secrets Act, not to mention the letter to anyone, even close relations. Her employer would be given orders to allow her the morning off work, again under the same requirement of secrecy. It was signed Brigadier V. G. Maxwell, CBE.

The letter terrified Clare. She assumed it could only be to

do with her true identity, and scarcely slept from the fear that this mysterious brigadier would send her back to her father in Germany.

She'd done her best to forget whom she once was. She was Jutta Blessing, the daughter of a German diplomat posted to Germany's London embassy soon after the 1918 armistice. Eighteen months later he had met and married an English girl. At first, the relationship was happy, but soured when he had an affair with his secretary. Jutta was then three years old.

When Johannes Blessing was posted back to Germany a year later, Jutta's mother stayed in London. She changed her daughter's name to Clare Nicholson, as solidly, unobtrusively English a name as she could invent, and gave her, helped by Blessing and by a timely grandparent's will, an expensive private education at a London day school, followed by Roedean. 'English public school girl to her fingertips' was how her boss, the Foreign Editor of *The Times*, described her to Maxwell. 'Perfect secretary, capable of better things. Might make a good journalist if the paper were prepared to give a bright girl a chance – but they won't.'

'So, Miss Nicholson, or rather, Fraulein Blessing.'

Maxwell switched on his most inscrutable gaze as he gauged her likely reaction to what was to come, and decided to dive straight in.

'I want you to write a letter.'

'You mean I'm not here because I'm in trouble for having a German father?'

'You're here because you have a German father. But not because you're in trouble.'

'Can I count on that?'

Maxwell's reply was rehearsed and fluent – none of the usual pauses.

'The only trouble you could possibly count on is if you tell anyone of your visit here, or if you won't co-operate. What I want you to do is easy, won't put you in any danger, and in three months or less will be forgotten. It will be as if I – all this –' he gestured to the plush furnishings of the Dorchester suite '– never existed.'

Still frightened, she asked exactly what she had to do.

'Read this letter to me out loud. Stop at anything you don't understand and ask me to explain. Forgive me if we haven't captured your prose style – but that's hardly likely to be noticed by a German reader.'

She read with increasing alarm.

'Dear Admiral Canaris,

You have never heard of me. I am a German citizen, a loyal daughter of the Third Reich. My father, Johannes Blessing, is a diplomat in the Auswartiges Amt.'

Maxwell interrupted. 'That's the German Foreign Office, in case you didn't know.' She carried on.

'My father lives in Germany, while I am stranded here in England with my mother. It is very dull. He has told me in his letters of the wonderful transformation of Germany as a result of National Socialism.

I am most unhappy and restless here in England. Evening after evening it is just my mother and me. I never meet people of my own age. At work I spend the day in a room in Fleet Street with a middle-aged man – he is the Foreign Editor of *The Times*. I tried to improve myself by taking an evening course in journalism. I applied for a junior reporter's post in the newsroom, but they rejected me.

I am desperate for some excitement in my life – to do something that counts. I feel a strong loyalty to the Third Reich, but dare not say so to my mother.

On the outside I am a privileged young English woman. I speak perfect English. Inside, I am German, and very frustrated by the stalemate in the war. I badly want to make a contribution to the Fatherland's war effort.'

She stopped reading. 'How do you know I'm bored living with my mother?'

'We guessed.'

'It's private.'

'It will remain private – this letter excepted. Please read on.'
She continued, grudgingly:

'My post as the secretary to the Foreign Editor of *The Times* has given me access to diplomatic and intelligence circles in London. Only last week I went to an after-work gathering of MI6 personnel. My boss took me with him. I think he appreciates my company. In fact, I think I can say without exaggeration that men generally find me agreeable. I have enclosed a recent photograph.'

One of the MI6 personnel at the party, the letter went on, was named Kenneth Hodge. He had made it clear that he would like to meet her again. He was surprisingly loose-tongued about his work, and she had quickly got the impression that she could lead him into an affair, and that as he was married, she would then be in a position to blackmail him: her silence in return for information.

Next she mentioned other MI6 people she had met at the gathering, a certain George Dowding, an Eastern European expert, and an Edward Hale. They too had given her their numbers, and if required she would try to lure them into a honey trap too.

Then she gave way to tears. 'You want me to seduce a man I've never met... and to send this letterful of lies.'

Was Maxwell aware that not long ago he would have handled the situation differently? Then, profoundly embarrassed, he would have effortlessly disengaged his feelings and left the room, pausing to invite the young lady to compose herself for his return in five minutes. Now, he asked his secretary, on duty in the entrance lobby, to help him 'calm the young lady down.' Armed with a cup of tea for her, and for him, they both went back into the room. His secretary sat next to Clare, held her hand briefly and said:

'You can trust the brigadier.'

Maxwell continued.

'Miss Nicholson, please look me directly in the eye. I am not, I repeat, emphatically not asking you to seduce and then blackmail these men. I know that is what you think – understandably – but it isn't true. You have my word.' The secretary spoke again.

'The brigadier has never broken his word to me, not once, in 25 years, even on the smallest matter.'

'Then why must I write this letter?'

Maxwell explained patiently that although he couldn't give reasons in full, it might help her to see the letter as an identity parade. That he needed to discover whether any of these men were already known to German intelligence. That he needed her only to send the letter, and bring him the reply – if there was one.

'After that, you will never hear from me again. All records will be destroyed.'

Clare asked herself what she felt – rather than what she thought – about this strange, remote man, and quickly realized that she could risk trusting him. That though he was distant and inscrutable, he was himself, no more or less – however intricate that self might be. There was something profoundly straight and benign in the gaze he now directed at her, waiting unhurriedly for her answer.

'I'll carry on reading.'

'Please, there's only a little more.'

The letter ended with a contact address for the reply and a suggestion that any response was made secure by using invisible ink. It was signed 'Clare Georgina Nicholson, aka Jutta Blessing.'

'Have you heard of Admiral Canaris?'

'No.'

'He's the head of the German secret service. By sending the letter straight to him, your offer will reach the highest level. Canaris may not read it himself, but the letter will be circulated to all his most senior staff. They will be asked to give their view on the sender's reliability, and whether they are interested in Hodge, Dowding or Hale. Then, with luck, someone will reply.'

'What shall I do next?'

'Take this copy home. Type it on your own typewriter. Bring it back to me for posting tomorrow. My secretary will tell you where to go. She will meet you there to take the letter from you. Your boss will give you a couple of hours off tomorrow afternoon – I've spoken to him.'

'How can you post a letter to Germany in war time?'

'Through our embassy in neutral Switzerland.'

*

Leo was in further training, learning to fly more sophisticated aircraft than those of her first few months. Smokey was delighted: it was an excuse to lure her as often as possible to Kenley, where he'd fixed, again through his friendship with his CO, use of the station's training aircraft. Today he and Leo were circling above the Surrey countryside on the edge of London, partly for the joy of it, partly to build up Leo's flying hours. They both had their dogs aboard, mostly dozing in their laps, though at take off or landing they sat up to gaze rapt through the windscreen. The animals seemed to love flying, in fact they also seemed to like each other, perhaps as much as their owners. The flight was romantic, and useful – for Leo, what could be more seductive? When they landed she was bubbling. Smokey said casually:

'I've booked dinner and a room at the Fisherman's Arms. Let's make it our first night together.'

Taken by surprise, Leo wasn't ready. Did a memory of her feeling about the fantasy in the Sherburn Nissen hut cross her mind?

She prevaricated. 'That would be wonderful Smokey, but we have all the time in the world for *that*, don't we? I'd love to stay for dinner, but I must get back to Hatfield tonight – I'm on duty at seven tomorrow.'

Smokey looked annoyed, shrugging his shoulders as if she was at fault for indecision.

She flashed a bolt of anger at him.

'If *you're* allowed to ask, why don't *I* have a right to say no?'

11

April 1941

As David and Labrador left a secret communications class, an instructor discreetly handed each a note telling them to report immediately to Woodland House. In the drive of Woodland House, engine running, was MacDonald's car, in its boot two canvas holdalls, ready packed. MacDonald gestured them into the back seat and drove away at speed. There was no chance to say goodbye to fellow trainees. They had evaporated.

The car headed through country lanes towards the sea. MacDonald spoke.

'We're going to Estuary House, at the mouth of the Somerville River, opposite Sailing Club Point. It's where the Norwegian and Free French agents live and train.'

David noticed a bird feeding on the ground, head cocked to one side. He felt like the bird. Its left eye, looking upwards, took in the big picture, wary for the outline of a predator. The other eye was fixed on the ground, focussed sharply on the seeds it was eating, oblivious to the world at large. This was his own mind. One part receiving the world as it is, seeing the big picture. Another analysing scraps of information that could give some clue about the mission. The Norwegians and the French? Then these could be the other members of the group. Or perhaps only the French, as the mission was to be in France?

Labrador, he recognized, was different: a cheetah, only just held by his leash, straining to get at his prey. His obsession with revenge swamped every part of his mind. He didn't see a big picture. He didn't notice, as Henry did, the landscape bathed in golden evening light.

David remembered the time – he must have been 16 or 17 – when the exceptional variety of his Somerville surroundings had first got under his skin: the acid heath, the woodland, the placid pasture of the river banks, and near the sea, the maritime habitats of marsh, mud and shingle beach. The countryside that slipped past didn't care if he lived or died, but its neutrality was at least soothing. When part of his mind, as now, was in turmoil, thoughts of never seeing Leo again buzzing like wasps in a corked bottle, the landscape's calm presence helped to remind another part of his mind – but never fully persuaded it – that love of Leo and the burning need to come home safely, to be with her, were pieces of a *much* larger reality.

MacDonald, Labrador, David and another man introduced as Cabard sat down in the dining room of Estuary House. Its owners were a branch of a legendary and patriotic Anglo-Jewish family that had made it available to the War Office in 1939. The furnishings were in store except for some cabinets lining the walls, stuffed with fine porcelain and *objets d'art*, witness to the family's taste, wealth and to their love of colourful, elaborate ornament.

Cabard did most of the talking, in the thickest of French accents.

'You are lucky,' he announced haughtily, 'not to be dining on the disgusting food served at Woodland House. Our chef is French, chosen by me. Tonight we have hare from the fields, cooked in red wine, some of its own blood and with – how do you call them – *ceps? chanterelles?* – wild mushrooms – from the woods. Chef spent hours in the autumn drying the mushrooms for us to enjoy them now. This may be the last edible food you eat for two months.'

Afterwards they were joined by three Free French agents. Over glasses of cognac, MacDonald briefed them.

'Labrador, David. *Never* forget that you are numbers four and five in this group. General de Gaulle has personally authorized the operation, and your place on it. Usually he insists on all-French sabotage teams. It's a privilege for you to be sent to France with three such experienced agents. You are there to help if you can, but mainly to gain experience in moving around occupied France.

You won't even share in their pre-operation briefing – you're not important enough.'

'Can't you tell us just the bare essentials of the operation?'

'No. Only one of your French colleagues will know all the details. What you don't know you cannot give way under… pressure.'

'How will we get to France?'

'Tonight you'll sleep here. At 6.30 a.m. tomorrow you'll be driven to the station to catch the 7.15 to London. You'll have a whole day and a night to amuse yourselves in London while Cabard and his colleagues get their final briefing at SOE's London safe house.' He paused to allow the information to settle.

'The day after tomorrow you will all meet, 11 a.m. sharp, at the ticket office of Liverpool Station. Hand these requests for rail passes to any ticket clerk. Make your way to platform five to catch the 11.30 to Newmarket. At Newmarket a car will meet you. You'll be driven to Newmarket Airfield. Around six you'll take off in a Lysander for South West France – a cold, noisy journey I'm afraid. Provided it's cloudy, your pilot will be over the drop zone after midnight. You will jump at the co-pilot's order. After landing, reassemble as quickly as you can and hand your parachutes to the local reception group, who will reveal their presence with flashing torches. Cabard will then take over.'

David had time to study Labrador during the train journey to London – the French had gone to another carriage. He saw the Pole's humility: Labrador thought himself nothing unless he could succeed in this mission. By David's standards, he was unspoilt, still marvelling at the depth of flavour in last night's glass of cognac – to him, a wonderful new experience.

'Have you anywhere to stay in London?'

'The Polish Club.'

'My parents have a house in London. Come and stay with me. We'll have supper with my mother – my father's bound to be out at his club – then we'll go to the Café de Paris and listen to some jazz.'

'I don't have the money to buy drinks.'

'I do.'

David liked Labrador even more when he saw that he was neither intimidated nor impressed by the grandeur of the Dunning-Green's house in Chester Square. On the train, Labrador had asked a few questions about David's circumstances. David had replied honestly, but without pretension. Labrador had shrugged and said: 'We're simple folk. Farmers. But tough.'

Sir Geoffrey was indeed having dinner at White's. Alice was overjoyed to see her son, but also welcoming to the dark Pole, whose presence meant that she would not have Henry to herself. She put him in the best guest bedroom, and told her cook to have something special – as far as rations would allow – on the table at 8.45. She put as much effort into putting the Pole at his ease as she did into talking to Henry.

'I know enough not to ask you where you're going or what you must do, but at least tell me how long you'll be away.'

'We've been told very little ourselves. Some weeks.'

To fill the pause, overflowing with unanswered questions, she said:

'Most people are playing their part in this war, but a few are playing more than just a part. They give all of themselves. I wonder what makes people do that? I believe you're both among those few. Going out of your way. I'm proud of you. The only other person I know who's going out of their way is Leo Maxwell. By the way, Henry, she's just been cleared to fly ATA group two aircraft. Only one more hurdle before she can fly everything – including Lancasters and Spitfires. Such a slip of a girl, such violent machines.'

Labrador was no longer at his ease.

Later, they went to the Café de Paris, Labrador wearing David's spare dinner jacket, which the butler had laid out on the bed, with white shirt and black tie.

'Robbo? Things to tell. Come to London, tomorrow. Cobb'll meet the 6.45 – breakfast at The Cavalry Club.'

Here was Viv at his most demanding, but MacDonald took no offence. He lacked ambition compared with his friend. Happy to lead a relatively quiet life at Somerville. Viv was only demanding when necessary. A next-day summons to London meant gold.

'I'll be there.' And to remind Viv that despite his rank he thought of him as an equal, he put the phone down a fraction of second early, cutting short Maxwell's parting drawl.

At breakfast in The Cavalry Club they talked in subdued voices, even though the tables were out of earshot. Maxwell, perhaps drawling less incontinently than usual, gave some sketchy details of the latest moves in the divorce. Secret business only began when they were in the anteroom of Maxwell's office, fifth cup of tea in hand, poured by the same reassuring middle-aged secretary who had helped rescue Maxwell's interview with Clare Nicholson.

'Let's start with Labrador and David. They've dropped safely, but the operation is postponed while they all go to Paris.'

'Why?'

'Maybe Cabard has a girlfriend there. Maybe they all have. Frogs, Robbo.'

'Ha ha. So no excitement for a while.'

'Now for Kenneth Hodge. Look at this.'

Maxwell produced a letter, written in German, in widely spaced type. The address was a government office in Berlin. The gist of the letter was that in response to Frau Blessing's enquiry, she would acquire pension rights in Germany if she contributed for a minimum of 30 years, and that she could begin contributions at any time, even from abroad.

Between the lines, handwritten, with small neat lettering in pale brown ink, was a very different message, still in German. Maxwell translated fluently.

'As for Frau Blessing's offer, I am instructed to reply on

behalf of Admiral Canaris. Your devotion to the country of your father's birth, and to the struggle in which the Third Reich is engaged, is noted and appreciated, and will be useful to us in due course.'

Next, the brown ink gave details of a German agent, living in London, whom she could contact if ordered to do so in future.

'Ah yes. Agent Cold Store. We turned him last year.'

'Concentrate, Robbo. The meaty bit comes next.'

'Unfortunately, the three targets you mention in your letter are of no current interest to the *Abwehr*. Dowding's and Hale's areas of expertise are not needed at present. The third man, Kenneth Hodge is, by coincidence, known to me personally. We met before the war at Bayreuth. Our wives were friends. *Er gefallt mir nicht* – I don't like him. He took an inappropriate interest in my wife. You will conclude, *ewige Fraulein Blessing* – most respected Miss Blessing – that Kenneth Hodge *ist nich zu vertrauen* – is not to be trusted. *Unter keinen Umstanden* – under no circumstances – is he to be involved in secret work. *Auch* – also – and *nicht weniger wichtig* – no less important – his political principles do not coincide with those of National Socialism. I would describe his politics, in fact, as leaning towards Bolshevism.

For your own good, and ours, steer clear of the man

Hodge. Please await further instructions about more appropriate targets, which will be sent to the mailbox. No reply to this communication is required.

Yours sincerely,
Rudolph Hammel

'How about that? Hodge caught with his trousers down – or up – whichever way you prefer.'

'Who's this Fraulein Blessing?'

While Maxwell explained, MacDonald reflected yet again on the worldly cunning of his old friend, a man who seemed often not to be of this world.

'I suppose the poor girl was terrified at the thought of having to seduce *and* blackmail Hodge?'

Both indulged in a short professional chuckle. 'In fact, Robbo, I was kind. I made clear she would never have to bed the man. She wrote the letter because she was terrified we might send her back to Germany. Wrong about that of course, but I allowed her to think it.'

'And now you have Hodge on a skewer.'

'Kebabbed.'

'Whatever he is or isn't, whoever his guardian angel might be, we can be rid of him now there's proof he's not been in touch with Hammel since 1937. True, one more unresolved suspicion remains, so we have grounds to remove him as far from the

Service as possible. We'll write a report alerting the Service he might still be a blackmail target. Then let others worry about him.'

They spent the rest of the morning discussing SOE Somerville matters, then went to celebrate on rare roast beef carved from the trolley at Simpsons in the Strand. Returning, they found Maxwell's usually neat, sparse office transformed by his secretary into a military operations centre. The long meeting table was covered with neat rows of photographs of French country inns. On the wall behind was a map of Northern France with roads highlighted – mostly to the west of Caen. Six large box files occupied Maxwell's desk. Dozens more stood on the floor, lining the walls.

'Zodiac.'

Anyone but Macdonald would have bridled at the prospect of teasing out of Maxwell the meaning of the maps and photographs, but for MacDonald it was fun – like being back in a classroom at Winchester, expected not only to answer the question, but to test the underlying basis of the question. He scrutinized the wall map, especially the area just to the west of Caen, looked at the photographs and examined the labels on some of the box files.

'Carpiquet Airfield.'

'Yes.'

'ME109s.'

'Indeed. Eight kept serviced, and three more spares – a squadron plus back ups.'

'Fuel dumps?'

'Yes. Good, Robbo. For the airfield and for surrounding military units.'

'Blow them up and the squadron is crippled – anyway for a while?'

'True.'

'And these,' MacDonald walked to the long table, 'are safe houses where the saboteurs might stay. Assuming that an operation of this complexity needs agents on the ground for at least three weeks?'

'More than just stay. I am contriving the ultimate safe house. A base where agents can live in some comfort, in fact be looked after, eat tolerably well even in wartime and can come and go indefinitely. And escape if by some extraordinary chance it's compromised.'

'This road', MacDonald pointed to the highlighted main road leading south-west out of Caen, to Avranches. 'The escape route?'

'Yes. It carries on from Avranches along the North Coast of Brittany past Dinard – nice town. German troops get scarcer by the mile. It ends at Tréguier, a lovely little yachting and fishing port. Agents can leave freely, on a French fishing boat manned by Free French agents.'

'So how does an agent get from Caen to Tréguier in a hurry? Must be 150 miles.'

'You're jumping ahead, but very well. In this small furniture removal van.' Maxwell produced a photograph.

'So. The airfield. The ME109s. The fuel dumps. Somewhere

agents can stay for a lengthy operation.'

'Bit more, Robbo.' Maxwell was gleaming. MacDonald was at a loss.

'ME109s don't fly on their own.'

'The pilots?'

'Yes.'

'You're going to kill eight German fighter pilots in cold blood?'

'Yes.'

'When will you get them all together? In the airfield mess? That would be instant capture for whoever dispatches them.' He paused, reflecting that both of them knew only too well who would be doing the work. 'The airfield must be guarded by at least a battalion.'

'In a bus.' Maxwell produced a photograph of a small bus parked outside a town house with a uniformed German pilot stepping inside. 'The bus collects the pilots each day at 5.30 a.m., from their various lodgings in Caen. It takes different routes to the airfield, but by 6.15 they've all been picked up and are on their way to Carpiquet. All eight, cooped up in a tin box.'

'You plan to murder eight German pilots in a bus and blow up Carpiquet Airfield at the same time?'

'Not quite at the same time. About 30 minutes apart.'

'How did you figure all this out?'

Maxwell told him of the months of patient observation by Free French agents since January, and of the time he'd spent schmoozing De Gaulle – the most trying work of all. 'He keeps giving long speeches about nothing. But I suppose it kept my mind off the divorce.'

MacDonald considered the implications.

'How many different routes does the bus driver use to get from Caen centre to the airfield?'

'Six.' Maxwell pointed to the map, where all six routes were marked. They began on one suburban road leading west from the centre, and soon diverged on the outskirts of the city on to country lanes, to meet again, circuitously, at the main entrance to the airfield. 'These are the only variations possible.'

'Where's best to ambush the bus?'

Maxwell pointed to the map. 'This isolated farmhouse, nothing but fields for a mile in every direction. Plenty of lanes leading away from the scene, and it's right on the road.'

'So David and Labrador have to wait there a maximum of six mornings?'

'Maximum. And before leaving for work at five, a good night's sleep at the safe house.'

Discussing the merits of the various inns in the photographs lasted well into the afternoon. Eventually Maxwell got MacDonald's agreement on one which stood at the western edge of Verson, a large village on the old Roman road leading more or less south-west out of Caen, south of and parallel to the N25, the modern main road leading west from the city to Northern Brittany – the same escape route just described earlier by Maxwell.

Before Maxwell left, MacDonald put a direct question to him, not expecting an answer. 'How do you feel about killing eight off-duty pilots in cold blood?'

'Not quite off duty. They're on service as soon as they step aboard the bus. But of course I don't like it at all, and my regular army colleagues are horrified. They want our people to be wearing uniforms – otherwise they won't be associated with it.'

'David won't like it either.'

'He will hate it, but he will do it if he has to. Labrador, on the other hand, would be happiest if he could kill 16 – or preferably 32 – in cold blood.'

'That's why you're so keen for them to work together?'

Maxwell described, dispassionately, as if reading from a training manual, how David would kill four or five with rapid head shots, achieving surprise. That would be all he could stomach. By then, the survivors would, anyway, have ducked below the line of fire. Labrador would finish them off at close quarters, as they crawled from the bus's front door. To minimize the noise from more gunshots, he would slit their throats, probably muttering Polish curses as he went. Maxwell went on:

'The only justification for this bloodbath is a credible long-term gain… a number of lives potentially saved by shortening the war. The physical damage to the airfield is easily repaired, and the pilots, though in short supply, will be replaced. But the psychological damage will be longer lived. Imagine being a German pilot in Northern France after Zodiac. Would you sleep in your bed?'

'Adrian Russell would give it ten out of ten. He would say, ensure that every agent in Normandy and Pas de Calais keeps spreading rumours that similar operations are imminent.'

'If Zodiac succeeds, we'll take his advice.'

Maxwell, even now, didn't trouble himself with personal dislike for Hodge. He felt neutral towards him, but he profoundly disapproved of the man's assumption that progressive politics conferred the moral high ground. He loathed his mischief making, especially when it damaged Somerville. He would take no personal pleasure in exiling Hodge, but to give the experience an appropriate chill, he would delegate it to Hodge's section head.

Within 24 hours, Hodge was striding confidently into his section head's office, expecting praise for good work, perhaps a transfer to a better desk; possibly even a promotion. He knew he had been effective in his first weeks, outperforming colleagues.

'Sit down, Hodge. Bad news.'

'You can't be dissatisfied with my work.'

'Your work is fine, but we've been running some routine background checks on you. Same as for all new personnel.'

'I'm clean, of course.'

'Not sure, Hodge. Some odd things have cropped up.'

'You can't mean Cambridge, can you? The Apostles?'

'We know about the Apostles: a socialist fraternity, and it's produced some communists. We try to keep an eye on them. Possibly harmless, possibly not. But for now, we look mainly at links with fascism. In your case, that's the problem.'

Hodge's face darkened.

'What else could you possibly have? This is outrageous. Sorry, I don't have time for this.' He made as if to leave.

'You're going to have all the time in the world to reflect on this, Hodge. May as well sit calmly now.'

'What?'

'Try not to be emotional, Hodge. Makes it more difficult for both of us.'

Silence.

'I have here a report from our people in Berlin. Take a look.'

Hodge stared in disbelief at the typewritten memo, complete with secret filing code and the names of several spies responsible for compiling the information. It chronicled each of his and Phyllida's three trips to Berlin in 1935, 1936 and 1937 to join the Hammels at Bayreuth. Photographs were attached of his and Hammel's entries in the Ritterhof's guest register.

'Evidence doesn't come much harder than this, Hodge. We prefer not to rely on tittle-tattle round here. Just the facts.'

'You listen to me, I know the facts. The visits were entirely for pleasure. Ursula Hammel is my wife's old school friend who had the misfortune to marry a humourless Kraut.'

'The humourless Kraut was a Nazi when you met him. A party member.'

'I didn't know that.'

'And now he's a Nazi spy – a senior officer in the *Abwehr*.'

'So what? How can I possibly be a security risk? Haven't seen him since 1937. You know my politics. Can't stand the far right. If anything, knowing Hammel makes me useful. If he ever approached me, I'd run him as a double agent.'

'Listen old boy. You need to understand some facts about how bureaucracies work. We don't always make intelligent assessments. We make steel traps. And you are caught in one. Anyone with any kind of previous contact with a Nazi cannot work in the Service. Sorry, but I have no alternative but to follow the rules. Innocence doesn't come into it. The Service has to have its insurance policy. You're a bad risk.'

'You're going to dismiss me because of this?'

'Not just this. You're a blackmail target.'

'Do you realize who you're talking to? In civilian life I'm a respected lawyer. An officer of the court.'

'You're also a serial adulterer. Look at these.'

He placed in front of Hodge first an extract from the background report commissioned by MacDonald and Maxwell, describing his affair with the wife of the Commodore of the Hamble Sailing Club. Then a statement from the Norwegian agent who had witnessed Hodge and Flavia in the teahouse.

'Even if true, and I'm admitting nothing – these reports would have to be corroborated to stand up in court – they don't mean I'm a security risk.'

'They mean you're potentially a blackmail target. That's enough for us. The *Abwehr* has attractive female agents all over London

177

angling to meet men like you. Wouldn't be surprised if you'd had an approach already.'

Hodge felt, for the first time, the sinister sensation of an unseen figure moving against him.

'Someone has taken against me. Someone is plotting against me.'

'All I can tell you is that the order to dismiss you comes from the highest level. So yes, Hodge, someone up there doesn't like you.'

Hodge's impotent rage dwarfed anything he had known at the S.R.S.C. meeting. His section head talked calmly on.

'As you now have to be called up for war service, we have consulted our colleagues in the regular army. They've found a comfortable job for you. Far from London. You'll be nowhere near a secret, ever again.'

'Where?'

'Yorkshire. They need an extra pair of hands in the pay office at Catterick Camp.'

'That's an accountant's job. I moved on from that years ago.' His voice crumpled.

'Useful to polish up old skills, Hodge.'

*

Labrador, David and the three French agents dropped blind after four miserable hours in the air, bumping through turbulence.

The reception party hadn't received London's radio messages confirming incoming agents. There were no flashing torches to guide the plane to the drop zone, so the pilot worked on dead reckoning and all five tumbled queasily into the night in hope rather than expectation.

They drifted down under a half moon into ploughed fields, hid their parachutes in scrub and trekked three miles to the edge of Pessac, where they easily located their target, the electrical transformer station. A quick survey by Cabard revealed that out of reach, just inside the perimeter fence, nine feet above ground, was a high-voltage electric wire.

It was 4 a.m. They heard people moving around inside, which alarmed Cabard so much that he ordered them away from the fence. To Labrador's and David's well-concealed amazement, and disapproval, he then gave up. They trudged back to the field where they had hidden their parachutes and containers, buried them in shallow graves, then walked to Pessac's station and, exhausted, caught the early morning train to Paris. Struggling against feelings of disappointment with the French, the novices' mood lifted temporarily when they found how freely they could travel under the noses of the German security forces and the French *gendarmes*. Their faked papers passed without comment.

Approaching Paris, their French companions, brightening by the minute, began boasting about the old girlfriends they would look up – and, if unavailable, the *putains* they knew by name in Place Pigalle.

Labrador and David soon got bored of the novel sensation of playing truant, knuckling down to the dull smear of routine

179

vigilance when walking the city's streets. They could only relax once inside the seedy room they shared on rue M. le Prince, in the university quarter. While the French amused themselves, Labrador and David went to bed early, six feet apart, with their own separate and very private thoughts – of Leo.

After seven depressing days, Cabard summoned them to meet a senior figure in the French resistance. 'Return to Pessac immediately. The transformer station isn't patrolled regularly at night. I guarantee that my local people will provide getaway bicycles.'

By now, Labrador and David had moved beyond approving of each other: they were building trust. They realized that, unlike their French companions, who were out for swagger, for *gloire*, they were there for the job alone. That allowing anything, especially their personalities, to come between them and the task was pointless, perhaps dangerous. Labrador hadn't expected the privileged Englishman to have such a professional attitude, and respected him even more.

The French, behind the *rosbif's* backs, described them as boring. Now boarding the return train to Pessac, Labrador and David were quietly content to be back at work, while the French raucously swapped stories of night operations that had not been taught at SOE Somerville.

12

May 1941

Four weeks later, news of Henrietta reached SOE HQ in Baker Street. Major Fuller, head of the French section, passed it around. Maxwell called MacDonald.

'Six out of eight transformers were blown up.'

The report that circulated around SOE and MI6 some days later described the operation in detail. When the group had got back to Pessac, they found that the transformer station was patrolled at random – just as they had been told in Paris. After dark that evening they had dug up their container, recut the detonators, some of which were damp, and rode their bicycles to the main gates. One of the French had climbed the wall, jumped over the high-tension wire and dropped to the ground on the other side. He went to the main gate, secured by a catch on the inside, and let in the other four. Within 15 minutes, the three-

and-a-half pound magnetic charges were in place. They went off a couple of minutes after the five had cycled away into the darkness. Search lights criss-crossed the sky, looking hopelessly for enemy bombers.

'Just as we hoped, Labrador and David co-operated perfectly with the French and with each other. The French noticed no desire to compete for important tasks.'

MacDonald asked if there were reprisals.

'The Germans shot 12 of their own men for failing to patrol the station properly.'

After a sober pause, Maxwell went on. 'Only one problem. They haven't come back directly – a submarine was waiting for them, but they missed it. Don't know why – the French never say. They're travelling home via Spain and Portugal, then a boat from Lisbon. They won't be home until July.' Maxwell finished reluctantly.

'It means postponing Zodiac.'

As spring weather came to London in May, Maxwell, confined to his office and club, reliant on male company, struggled more than usual not to miss Somerville. This time last year, the sailing season had been well under way, keeping him busy and distracting the community with its rituals. First the spring series of races in the top reach of the river, overlooked by The Rectory, then the Downriver Race on the last weekend of May, when the entire fleet sailed in reverse the course of the Up River Race, ending at the

182

Sailing Club Point clubhouse for yet another party.

He no longer had to think about Hodge, or the threat he might pose to Zodiac and to Somerville. He felt his former equilibrium beginning to rebuild, but behind the calm façade, he still felt restless because of Labrador's and David's prolonged absence, and because of self-questioning prompted by the recurring memory of that appalling moment at the S.R.S.C. dance. Seeing *his* S.R.S.C. members staring at their plates – withdrawing out of disapproval, embarrassment and distaste – made him ask himself how his own permanently withdrawn manner might affect others.

To distract himself, he arranged a small lunch party at the Connaught. His table there was the most discreetly placed in a dining room famous for wide spaces between tables. Waiters in white ties ushered Portia and Flavia into their chairs. A nod from Maxwell, and the waiters slid away. Maxwell poured the champagne himself. Like Portia, he didn't care to be fussed over, and he was going to control the pouring of a bottle for which he had paid.

Portia took control of the conversation. 'Well Brig, you're not back in favour *yet*, but things are simmering down. Patricia has been a brick – telling everyone how much you liked the girls in your youth. It'll take time, but we'll overcome it.'

'How can I thank you?'

Flavia replied for her sister. 'Lunch at the Connaught is a good start. Wish my friends would bring me here.'

'That is unlikely,' said Portia regally, but with a hint of humour.

'I don't think your musical types would be comfortable. Especially not the saxophone player – what's his name? Moses Oka-Ngubwe? Have I pronounced it right?'

Flavia lapped up Portia's mock disapproval, affecting indifference. Her sister accepted her as she was – had harboured her endless 'secrets' since her first teenage encounter with one of the stable boys. Maxwell, mildly uncomfortable, tried to move them on with an emission of extraordinary, drawling laughter. Portia knew how to tease Maxwell into coherent speech using the shortest of quizzical looks.

'I don't think we'll be seeing Hodge at Somerville again. He's been dismissed from his post at the War Office – banished to a regular army job – in Yorkshire.'

The two women knew better than to ask for details. They said nothing, looked serious, and raised their glasses a fraction higher than normal. Maxwell copied their gesture precisely: a toast so devoid of triumphalism that it was scarcely a toast at all.

'That *is* good news, Brig. But I suspected something of the sort. I met Phyllida at the weekend.'

'Did she say she'd follow him to Catterick?'

'No. She seemed in a hurry to go to their house in London. Implied she'd stay there. She asked me how soon the Estate could wind up the lease on their farmhouse. I said yes, as soon as we can, and no penalty.'

'I must say, the AGM went off better than I dared hope. How did you manage to brief all 20 in the audience?'

'Me and Flavia. A bit of telephoning, a bit of taking people aside after church. The message was simple: turn up, don't vote on anything, and you'll get an amusing spectacle. They love an intrigue.'

'Masterful.'

'I'll write to Hodge asking for his resignation as Captain. Should be able to take over his bits and pieces myself.'

'That's ideal, Portia…' He began drawling again. Portia stifled her amusement, and impatience, throwing him the merest spark of eye contact, but enough.

'By the way, another bit of news. My divorce from Audrey should be final in six months.'

Flavia glanced sideways at her sister. Portia smiled and said in her softest, rarely heard voice, 'That's made me very happy, Vivian.'

This time, glasses were clinked.

Later, when the atmosphere had mellowed still further, Maxwell asked Flavia whether Hodge had ever seemed close to answering her questions about whom he was meeting in Streteford and Milton.

'Never. I tried and tried. But I couldn't keep on suggesting we meet on Saturday evenings or lunchtimes when he was always unavailable. He'd have got suspicious. Whoever it was couldn't be cancelled. Even for me.'

'Thank you for trying Flavia. Portia told me you'd had enough of Hodge by September.'

'True.'

'But you did it for England,' said Portia. 'War work.'

*

Labrador and David returned to Somerville as soon as their boat docked in Portsmouth. The training schools were essentially unchanged, cocooned in their parallel world in the woods, though the instructors found the mess at Woodland House less noisy, and less amusing, now that Adrian Russell had completed his posting and returned to London.

The barman complained to MacDonald that without Russell's extraordinary consumption he could no longer get bulk purchase discounts. He feared the bar would no longer make its modest profit. 'I might have to put the prices up, sir. It would help if some of the other officers had decent private incomes, like Mr Russell, sir. Then they might drink like him, and we'd all be better off.'

Without congratulating David and Labrador on the success of Henrietta, MacDonald sent them straight back into training. It was as if they had a deadline. While Labrador spent hours each day with the close combat trainer, David was on the shooting range, and in French lessons, where he read and re-read the short stories of Guy de Maupassant out loud, in French, until his accent was flawless.

Both learned by heart more than a hundred and fifty questions and answers until their responses were automatic. 'What brings you to Normandy?' 'What is your home address?' 'When was your wife born?' Both were pushed to perform at much higher levels than in basic training, and before long they were introduced to the new identities that had been painstakingly created for them in SOE's D section at Baker Street.

David was to be a water inspector, sent from Paris to make an audit of Normandy's water supplies. Labrador was a Polish civil engineer, with a special knowledge of the load-bearing capacity of bridges.

One day at the end of July, MacDonald summoned them without warning to Woodland House.

'You're to be sent on a new operation in a fortnight.' Asked details, he said 'It's major. Supreme teamwork, needed. You'll be attacking a bus. In fact, I've got a derelict bus for you to practise on.'

They walked to a remote corner of the grounds with their personal instructors. David's asked him to climb a pine tree, stationing himself about 20 feet from the ground. Labrador's told him to lie in wait at the edge of the track. 'When the bus appears, walk calmly out on to the track as if you're a policeman, and flag it down. As soon as you hear the first shots, drop to the ground.'

David's instructor continued: 'As soon as the bus has stopped, shoot out five windows, starting at the rear – you don't want to hit Labrador. No more. Seated behind each window will be a dummy. Shoot at least four in the head, five if possible. Show us how fast you can kill – cleanly.'

'Labrador. During the shooting, work your way along the ground

187

to the bus's front door. When the shooting stops, four instructors will crawl out, one by one. Don't actually cut their throats, but act out how fast you can do it.'

Two hours later they were still rehearsing as the light was fading. By now, the dummies' heads were riddled with neat holes, all within a small circle on the left temple.

*

Catterick was worse than the newly called-up Captain Hodge had feared. The bleak Yorkshire town and its garrison stood at the edge of the Vale of York, with the ground rising modestly to the west, anticipating the grander countryside of the Yorkshire Dales – but no consolation to Hodge.

For the first time in his life he felt powerless to manipulate his situation. The speed of his transplantation had unsettled him, undermining a lifetime of carefully built self-confidence. His social network was confined to London and Somerville, so now his best choice for company were junior officers in the Pay Corps – *not exactly Oxbridge material,* he groaned to himself daily. A further twist of the knife: he was not even in charge of the payroll office. A position, he found on arrival, reserved for a lieutenant colonel.

But this was not the final twist. To get some perspective on the curious swiftness of his dismissal from MI6, he was desperate to talk to Adrian Russell. Suddenly, Adrian was the hardest man to reach in London. The woman who answered Russell's phone had a mantra, uttered with chilling monotony: Mr Russell was in a meeting. Requests to call back produced no result. After 20 or more attempts, Hodge asked a lieutenant in the office to call on his behalf.

'Does Mr Russell know you?'

'No, but I have information he will value.'

'Let me see if he's available.'

As a suspicious Russell came on the line, Hodge snatched the receiver from the lieutenant.

'Adrian, it's Ken.'

'Oh dear, Ken, most unfortunate. I tried to pull every string at my command. But someone's against you. Best accept it's checkmate.'

'Nothing else?'

'No, Ken. Need to go to a meeting now. Be good to meet you for a drink when you're back in London.' The line went dead.

*

Maxwell now, at last, admitted to himself that withdrawal, viewing the world through the wrong end of the telescope, was a trick he should not trust. Withdrawal had been the key, he now saw, to the failure of his marriage. Audrey was shallow, and selfish, no match for his intellect or intelligence, but that did not mean she felt any less acutely the loneliness of life with Vivian Maxwell. Withdrawal, he now accepted, simply made things too easy – for

Vivian Maxwell.

He resolved to engage more directly with the world, and guessed that staying closer to reality, accepting it unfiltered, might counterbalance the tyranny of the wasps. If it involved discomfort of emotions, then perhaps that would be a price worth paying.

He even pondered the possibility of returning to Somerville. Portia was telling him, again, that the atmosphere had improved another step since lunch at The Connaught. Perhaps he would go back there for a weekend in August, stay unseen in the boathouse, and not visit anyone except perhaps the Selby-Pickforths. Maybe go to the paper shop just once, to gauge his reception. Then, if it felt right, he would return in the late autumn for a week's leave.

*

Leo knew something was wrong the moment she entered the Hatfield crew room, exhausted after delivering a Hudson to Coventry. A strange, taut atmosphere. Instead of chattering, the women were talking in clipped, small voices.

She went up to Chile. 'What's wrong?'

Chile nearly burst into tears, her eyes glistening as she took Leo's hand and held it very hard.

'What *is* going on?'

Chile led Leo into the passage and pointed to the ops blackboard where the day's instructions were written in chalk. There was Chile's name, M. Duhalde, and the time she had landed.

Then there was L. Maxwell and the time she had returned from Coventry. And then there was a smudge, where a name had been rubbed out.

Leo tried to work out whose name. She could just make out a D at the beginning.

'That's what they do if you are killed in a pile-up,' Chile said, then halted, too upset to finish. Then, between sobs, 'Daisy Johnson'.

'Oh Chile, now you'll make cry. We are not meant to. We are meant to behave as if we are proper service personnel, not just amateurs, even if most of us still are.'

Chile said:

'Barrage balloon near Sheerness. Low cloud.'

'Rubbed out', said Leo as she went back into the sitting room for a cup of tea, dazed. 'Just rubbed out. They might have taken the trouble to rub her name out properly.'

Back in the cottage with Diana, Chile and Rosemary, numb banalities were exchanged about what a friend she had been.

'Always doing little things for everyone. Checking the store cupboard for missing things when the rest of us couldn't be bothered. Bringing fresh flowers or lavender bags for our drawers.'

13

August 1941

Dear Brig,

It is another pile-up, I am afraid. Well, not actually a pile-up, but a forced landing in France. Rather a good one in fact, because the Spit is undamaged.

Maxwell's face was morphing from red to white. He wondered if he could carry on holding the letter – though letter was not the right word.

Please get this message to my CO Margot Grey at ATA HQ White Waltham as soon as possible. This is so important. I am extremely worried that this time I really will be sacked from the ATA for losing a plane.

It wasn't a letter, it was a wine list. A long one, 15 pages long in fact, arranged geographically, covering all the great wine areas of France. At any other time, a thing of pleasure. Not now. Nightmare scenarios, besides the obvious intense anxiety for Leo, quicksilvered through Maxwell's brain. *Leo at the St-Cloud?* This thing, this horror, had arrived early that morning via the Caen-St-Cloud courier. Fuller had called to warn him drily – a little too drily – an hour before a messenger delivered it by hand to Maxwell's office. 'A young woman's handwriting, Brigadier. Don't recognize it as any other agent's out there. Perhaps you'll share any intelligence implications.'

In between the printed lines, one for each wine, its year and grower, were lines of neat, livid green handwriting. Leo's handwriting. Green because the invisible ink supplied to Caen-St-Cloud came out the brightest of green when exposed to a chemical vapour whose formula was known only to one technician in the Baker Street laboratory.

Getting it to her is so important. I am extremely worried that this time I really will be sacked from the ATA for losing a plane. The whole thing is so terrible, I don't know how to begin to tell you. Even worse, I have to write this down as fast as I can because the courier is coming in 45 minutes, and he might not take a message again for another week. I am sure I will not be able to write it all down before he comes, it is quite a story, some of which you might not believe. I am going to have to ignore what you always say about telling stories, and instead put some of the last bits first because I must, as you will see.

Maxwell walked up and down his office, the letter still shaking in his hands, pausing to lock the door adjoining his and the outer office. Leo at the St-Cloud? He forced himself to read on:

First of all, the Spit is at grid reference 49 41 13 N 1 16 56 W in a barn in a field near the village of Barfleur. That is the north tip of the Cherbourg peninsula and of course we have sailed past the very spot. The nice French people who helped me hide the Spit and brought me here looked up the grid reference for me on what they call the ee-jay-en, the IGN map, same as our Ordnance Survey.

It is exact. No one will ever find the Spit unless they know the grid reference because it is very cleverly hidden in the barn behind walls made of hay bales. We dragged it there by the tail with a tractor and ropes. I chose to land in a field that had just been harvested – good hard ground. <u>Please tell Margot Grey that the Spit is undamaged</u> and can be flown again. All it needs is some cans of petrol – as you will discover. I think there might be damage to an oil supply line, which I believe can be repaired easily on the spot, because the system is not pressurized. There might also be damage to a fuel line – also not pressurized and easy to mend. I can remember

194

reading about that from swotting up the manual on the way to pick up the plane. Then it will be ready to fly when, as I hope, English soldiers come again to France, to throw out the Germans. One more thing. Anyone can be sure it is my Spit because L.M. is scratched into the paint behind the hood on the starboard side.

Maxwell's mind seethed with calculations. Could he send another Lysander to get Leo out? How soon? At least Labrador and David weren't there – yet. Should he ring Robbo to talk it over? The questions were unanswerable without more information. No choice but to read on.

One thing was clear: the courier route was functioning.

Please also tell Margot Grey that I ran out of fuel over the Channel after being chased by an ME109. There is a lot more to tell about it than that, but for now please just say that. Also, can you please tell her that if I am lucky I will escape from here and get back to England from Tréguier, yes Tréguier of all places, isn't it funny we loved it so much going there on Shearwater, and now it is my escape route to freedom.

Why hadn't she been forbidden to mention Tréguier? Should he think about aborting Zodiac?

In any case, he had better call Margot Grey immediately.
'First Officer Grey?'
'Speaking.'

'It's about my daughter, Leo Maxwell.'

'We're desperately worried about her. She disappeared five days ago on a flight to Hurn. I've rung round every airfield in the country to see if she diverted there. No news. Most unlike her not to report in. We fear the worst.'

'I can tell you what's happened.'

He carried on reading.

Now that I have put down the essential things for you to tell Margot Grey, and that you know I am alive, I will start at the beginning.

Actually, the beginning was four days ago. Something bad happened then that made me and the others at the ferry pool terribly upset and jumpy. A girl called Daisy was killed. She shared our cottage. Perhaps what's happened might not have happened at all if it wasn't for that.

Maxwell noticed that following these words the paper was gently undulated, as if drops had fallen on it. For the first time he could remember, he felt his own eyes pricking. Leo was easily roused, but not a girl to cry easily.

Oh dear, now I have wasted time. I had to stop writing to pull myself together. Can you imagine what it is like to be with someone day after day and then they just disappear? Rubbed out.

196

Anyway I will try to get on with the story now, because there is a great deal to tell about why I am here in Northern France. I think I have 20 more minutes to write, I hope the courier is late.

Next day I drove to Hatfield Airfield as usual with the others and reported to the ops board. My name was down to fly a Spitfire from Tangmere to Hurn Airport, near Bournemouth for a replacement part. Air taxi to Tangmere, fly the Spit to Hurn, overnight at Hurn and then back to Hatfield by train next day.

This would have been terribly exciting if I had not felt so upset. My first Spit. Perhaps I had better explain that it was only a month ago that the first of us women were cleared to fly Spitfires and Hurricanes. Now it was my turn. But the thrill was not as it would have been if Daisy were still alive.

The ATA gives us the sweetest, tiny canvas holdall for overnight deliveries. Just big enough for pyjamas, toothbrush and toothpaste, and small enough to fit into the very cramped space on a fighter.

I had mine with me, ready packed, which as it turned out was a very lucky thing. I said goodbye to Chile and the others and went straight out on to the grass where the Anson was being filled with petrol. The duty ground officer handed me the latest Met. It said that the first half of the morning was clear except for some isolated clouds with showers, so we could leave straight away. But the weather for late morning was a front coming in from the west. Clouds at 3-4,000 feet and heavier showers. Not ideal because from Tangmere in Sussex I would be flying west towards the front. I probably never told you that our regular flying height is only 2,500 feet. So with cloud forecast as low as 3,000 feet that is worrying, because the clouds do not behave as you want. They change all the time, getting thicker and thinner. So that weather could be a problem for me and my Spit later on.

We had a good flight to Tangmere, me in the trainee-pilot seat beside the taxi pilot, doing last-minute swotting up on the Spitfire manual. At Tangmere I was hoping to have a cup of tea in the mess and meet some of the RAF pilots there. Smokey told me about them, one of them is Max Aitken, the son of Lord Beaverbrook, the Minister of Aircraft Production, who helped Pops d'Erlanger expand the ATA after d'Erlanger set it up. Diana told me Max is a very tough fighter and good looking! Anyway, there was no chance to pause because when I checked the Met again the front was moving in faster than expected. I could not get going soon enough so I went straight to where the Spit was standing.

You may be wondering why I am going into all the details, but they are important. They help explain why what happened later actually did.

The Spit was being got ready by a terribly nice man called Roy Bowden. He is the one of the ground crew at Tangmere who works often under terrible pressure to get the fighters ready for the next sortie. Even if there is no sortie again that day, after flying it must be got ready in only a few minutes in case there is another scramble.

He looked worried as I walked up.

'Can you keep a secret miss?' he said.

'I can, yes of course,' I told him.

He took me to the front edges of the wings and pointed at some broken flaps of fabric in several places. 'Do you know what they mean?' he asked. I said I didn't really, this was my first Spit.

'They mean the guns were not reloaded as they should have been after being fired yesterday. After reloading we always glue new patches of fabric over the gun ports.' He explained that he had forgotten to do this job because they were short of people yesterday and that he had been called away to help with another fighter that was needed more urgently.

'It's bad,' he said, 'I should have remembered to come back to finish the guns. Even if the ammunition belts are half used, you have to replace them with full ones. But it was late, we'd been working since 6.30 in the morning, and we'd all had enough.'

I said 'we are not allowed to fly with loaded guns' and he said 'I know'.

'How long will it take to empty the guns?'

'Oh, 15 minutes' he said.

That is when I made my first boob. I could not wait to climb into the Spit, and I was worried about the weather, so I just said to him, 'If you trust me to say nothing about the guns, I would prefer to go now.'

'Are you sure?' he said, opening the gun inspection hatches in the wings. 'There are about eight seconds of ammunition left in each gun on each side. That means you will be flying an armed plane. You can shoot down another plane with just a four-second burst.'

I told him that I thought taking off soon in order to avoid the worrying weather was more important than the rules and could we please go now. Roy was a nice chap, as I said, and so he agreed as long as I promised again to pretend I knew nothing about the guns. He stowed my little bag in the tiny space behind the pilot's seat and then he helped me into the cockpit. Before getting in I stopped to scratch my initials in the paint just behind the hood, which made him laugh. 'I always do that,' I told him, 'it is a sort of agreement between me and the plane, it makes us a pair, which I consider important for flying it well.'

He then did his pre-take off routine, including a shot of something special into the fuel to help fire the engine. He and another ground crew stood at each wing tip steadying the plane as I started the engine and did my own checks. There are 13 of them. I could not possibly remember them all, instead I read them from a little loose leaf book that is strapped to my thigh. Very thoughtful of the ATA to give us this, in fact, completely necessary.

Then it got so exciting that I forgot all about the guns, and if I am truthful, about Daisy too. The TERRIFYING NOISE of the engine. It is SO furious, an angry growl, just absolutely right for fighting Germans. If they could hear them starting up on the ground they would think more carefully about coming over our country.

Oh dear, Cecile, that is Monsieur Lambert's daughter, (he is the owner of St-Cloud) has just come in to tell me I have an extra half hour, but then that really will be all the time I can have. I have a feeling that it is her husband, or maybe her brother who is the courier, but when I ask she won't say.

Maxwell groaned out loud, and had to remind himself yet again that because the letter was in his hands, it hadn't been intercepted, and that therefore St-Cloud was safe. The Lamberts and Cecile had been forbidden again and again to identify themselves or the St-Cloud in courier messages. Perhaps they hadn't checked the letter properly – perhaps their poor English had put them off the task? He read on, half enthralled to have entered so completely into his daughter's world, half appalled.

So I taxied away from the Spit's special sandbagged bay, weaving from side to side as you must with this plane at least when you are new in it, because when it is on the ground the nose is angled so steeply upwards that you cannot see ahead. I was so completely thrilled to be in this beautiful machine as we gathered speed, you cannot imagine. It glues you back in your seat like a sports car, its acceleration is so fierce compared with other planes we fly. In fact it feels as if a powerful person is in charge of you. Very soon, at about 40 mph, I could raise the tail to lower the nose and get a clear view ahead. I increased the boost power exactly as told by the manual for a Mark 11 Spitfire, to +12 and off we went in one marvellous surge, the engine effortlessly growling, it lifted off by itself at 80 mph. Soon after we were off the ground I pushed the throttle forward to increase the speed to 180 mph, perfect for climbing, pulled back gently on the stick, and it tore upwards. It was as if it wanted to be in the sky, my heart was in my mouth and I thought then that even if I did not live another day, that would be enough for me.

If anything, it got better. As we climbed I played with the controls and found that what the other girls say is really true. It is a woman's plane. Though terribly powerful, it is also so delicate and responsive. Soon I was flying along the edge of some of the scattered clouds mentioned in the forecast, with the patchwork of Sussex spread below me in beautiful morning light, peaceful, everything just perfect as if there was no war, just as it ought to be.

I went in close to a small cloud and found the plane answered so neatly to the controls that I could weave along the cloud's edge, one wing misted, the other in the clear. Then I passed a patch where the cloud was thicker, with a little bit of rain inside, and I could see I was going along with one wing wet and the other dry.

Again and again I felt so happy that I could burst. You probably think I am awful, forgetting Daisy and the loaded guns (which actually I did not want to think about) but when you hear the rest I think that you will agree I deserved my few minutes of happiness.

I suppose I flew on another 15 minutes. I could see the east end of the Isle of Wight coming up down to the left. Portsmouth was down on the right and Southampton beyond it. You see, I had a plan for the flight that I thought would get me out of the worst weather. The cloud was building up to the right, over the land, but to the left, over the sea, it was clearer. Up ahead over the Solent, it was really quite clear – it often is over the Solent, the Isle of Wight is known for splitting weather coming in, sending some south over the Channel and the rest north over the mainland.

I suppose you could say that I should have stayed inland, away from Portsmouth and Southampton, because those places are where enemy planes often are because of the Spitfire factory in Southampton and the aircraft repair depot at Cowes on the island. Anyway, I went that way because it seemed best at the time, but of course now I wish I hadn't.

First, it was a speck in my mirror and I did not think anything of it. It was a bit above me. Then it got bigger and I supposed it was another British plane following me, like me, keeping away from the bank of cloud building up over the mainland. Then, such a shock. It SCREAMED past me, above and to the right. I could see the black crosses on its wings and its body. I cannot tell you how angry they made me. A German plane, with black and evil markings over our country. I could see the pilot's nasty little black leather-clad head, turning to look at me. That made me even crosser, and then I was back to feeling as I did before taking off – miserable and nervous.

I thought that is a good thing, he does not know I am a girl because my head is hidden like his inside a flying helmet and goggles, and then my mood changed again to HORROR because he threw his plane, it was an ME109, the German's best fighter, into a climb and a turn to the right, which took him up and then behind me. In other words, getting into position on my tail. This was just as Smokey had described to me that day in hospital. You know what that means, don't you?

Oh no. Now the courier is here and I have got to stop writing. Cecile is standing with her hands on her hips, she is smiling, but I can see she means business. So now there is only time to say that I honestly don't know what is going to happen to me here. I don't know, if I am truthful, rather than just hopeful about escaping, whether I will get home or how long it will take. I have found out that there is something going on here that is going to cause a lot of trouble. I have overheard people talking. I am trying to be hopeful, but have to admit to you now that it all seems very uncertain. Funnily enough, I don't feel terribly lonely and I have made up my mind not to be anxious any more – it does not help. I live from moment to moment. Cecile says she cannot promise I can send a second letter, anyway it will not be for a while. I have plenty of time to write the rest of what happened. That will make the boredom easier. I do nothing except sit in my attic room all day, except for when they allow me out for a short walk in the woods, or sometimes down into the dining room to eat.

Love to everyone from
Leo

*

Two days before Leo had taken off from Tangmere, Labrador and David were called to Woodland House. As for Operation Henrietta, they were handed packed overnight bags and told to climb into the back of the Woodland House car. MacDonald saw them off:

'At last, this is Zodiac. You're being driven to the station. Catch the 10.20 to Waterloo. Then get a cab to Orchard Court, off Bryanston Street, near Marble Arch. Go to Flat 158. Ring the doorbell.'

'Is this where we say goodbye, sir?'

'No, I'll see you at the airfield just before take-off. In about a week.'

The doorbell at No. 158 Orchard Court was answered by Park, the butler, who before the war was a messenger in the Paris branch of the Westminster Bank. He spoke good enough French to greet the Free French agents in their own language, and he had an excellent memory for names.

'Good afternoon, David. Good afternoon, Labrador.' Taking their bags, he asked in silken tones if they would like him to unpack for them. Showing them around the flat, he chattered cheerfully, the smile never leaving his face.

'Here is the bathroom, gentlemen. Black onyx. Rather unusual, don't you think, sir?'

'Never seen anything like it', said Labrador. 'Probably never will again.'

'And that object, sir, is much appreciated by our French colleagues.' He pointed to the black onyx bidet.

'I am fortunate', he went on, 'that I don't have to keep you apart, gentlemen.'

Labrador and David understood. SOE went to enormous lengths to prevent agents on individual missions from meeting each other.

'Your case is, as I understand, rather unusual in that you will be travelling and working together. I shall be spared the effort of serving you tea in separate rooms. Tea, incidentally, will be at 4.45 p.m. in the large sitting room. Major Fuller will be coming to meet you then. It is important to be punctual for him.'

Major Maurice Fuller, a former regular army officer was, by August 1941, the rising star of SOE's HQ in Baker Street. He'd started a few months back with a bare office and no defined duties. Since then he had created an unassailable role for himself as head of SOE's French section, managing operations in occupied France.

Fuller began by sketching out the general conditions in and around Caen. 'Conrad Liedermann. Memorize the name. He's the officer of the local branch of the German security service, the *Sicherheitsdienst*. They have greater powers than the local *gendarmerie*, but not nearly so much as the Gestapo – the SS. His much more sinister Gestapo boss, based in the Avenue Foch in Paris, is Obergruppenführer Conrad Bieler. Remember that one, too.' Then he flattened his voice.

'Your targets are eight Luftwaffe pilots. You'll intercept them as they drive from their lodgings in Caen to Carpiquet Airfield, outside Caen, near the city's western edge. Early morning.' After a pause:

'There are only eight fighter pilots based at Carpiquet. Eliminate them, and the fighter base is useless.'

Again, he paused.

'There is another aspect of your operation which I am deliberately not going to tell you about now. I will simply refer to it as Fireworks – you will use this same code word to your French Resistance collaborators. They will organize and light the fireworks. I can tell you, however, that your part in the fireworks will be simple: as soon as you have dealt with the pilots, you will instruct the French to go ahead with the fireworks.'

Labrador and David stayed silent. Labrador was grimly delighted. Henry tried to keep his mind off what he was being asked to do, trying not to answer the question buzzing in his head. If I had known it would be like this, would I have been so determined to transfer to SOE?

'That's enough for today. Tomorrow and the next day I will flesh out your new identities – at Somerville you were told only the essentials. The next day my colleague Dora Adcock will take you through your documents. You will be surprised at the lengths she has gone for you. The day after I will tell you a little about the safe house where you will live while on Zodiac. It is a remarkable safe house, we are more than proud of it and you will be most comfortable there, eating, drinking and sleeping well, for the maximum of six nights that it may take to achieve your objective. Why it will take a maximum of six nights will also be revealed.'

'Is there an escape route?' David asked.

'I won't tell you, for obvious security reasons, how you will escape after intercepting the bus, and triggering the fireworks, but please be assured, an escape route exists, directly from the safe house back to England. Your local collaborators will only reveal the route at the last moment. I can say, though, that you could be back in London in as few as 72 hours.'

Labrador's identity, Fuller told them, was deliberately to remain close to what it had always been.

'The ideal counterfeit. Your papers will describe you as Jerzy Adamski. Giving your name will be second nature. Your home city is Lodz in Poland, but you were raised on a farm some 30 km outside the city, just as you actually were. To a persistent hostile questioner, you will be able to describe every detail of your village, and your family.

'Your French is appalling, and that is only to be expected. Unlike David, who has had to memorize hundreds of French idioms, you need command only a few basic conversational sentences – if that. This is because you have never learned the language properly. As you know, you're a civil engineer, specializing in bridges. It will be perfectly plausible that you can only speak a few words and phrases of French in a thick Polish accent. But you will need to know the French for certain engineering terms and a handful of other technical words to do with your trade – which I believe you have already mastered at SOE Somerville.

'Your last day will be spent revising with our French teachers here in London. Back to school, I'm afraid. They will go back over the French you learned at Somerville, and test the specialized vocabulary.

'The rest of your story? You have been commissioned, at your request, to travel to Normandy to undertake an inspection of the load-bearing capabilities of the local bridges. Your engineering degree is from the University of Gdansk. You applied to the local *Wehrmacht* to be sent to Normandy to get away from the unhappy memories of the German occupation of your village. And because the modest extra cash for work far from home will help you save for your wedding. Here, Labrador, is the part of your story that you must memorize, and repeat, and repeat, and repeat to yourself. You're engaged. To a pretty girl called Ania Kowalski.'

'Why send a Polish engineer to Normandy, sir?'

'People with your specialized knowledge of small bridges are rare. Experts on big bridges are two a penny. Anyhow, you made it your special subject in your degree dissertation. Chose it because there was so little data on the subject. Thought it might get you higher marks. And, remember, you volunteered. Less trouble for someone.

'Moving heavy equipment – tanks, lorries and big guns – is a constant worry for the Germans in France. The rivers, especially the Seine in Normandy, are crossed by many old bridges. The German logistics people need to know which of the smaller bridges could withstand heavy transport. He turned to David.

'Your cover is much more difficult to maintain under pressure.

Your accent and your story will only stand up to superficial probing. You have to pose as a Frenchman, though not an educated one. Your work is lonely and repetitive. It would not surprise your captors if you were a man of few words. The instructors at Somerville have told me that your French accent is passable as long as you talk briefly.

'You are a water mains inspector employed by the water board in Amiens. You are in the Caen area checking that water supplies are not contaminated. You are staying in the same place as Labrador – the safe house. Only you never speak to each other, it is as if you are strangers. You have a bicycle for making short local journeys, just as Labrador does. If in the unlikely event that you are questioned, your story will be: when finished in the Caen area, you will move to a new *auberge* at Thury-Harcourt, to continue the work there.'

'But I don't know the French for 'reservoir'.'

'Over the next two days we will teach you a list of 50 specialized water supply terms.'

Then, addressing them both: 'There is a one per cent chance – less – that either of you will be questioned, even as a matter of routine, closely enough to test even the outer shell of your false identities. Yet we must allow for the remote possibility. The work, the time, the money that has gone into creating the identities most certainly is not justified by the small risk that you will ever need to fall back on them.'

'So how do you justify it, sir?'

'Good faith. We ask much of you. We in return must go the extra mile.'

Dora Adock's smile was benign but distant as she addressed Labrador.

'I am particularly proud of this.' She handed him a letter in large feminine handwriting. Labrador read, half amused, half embarrassed. It was from Ania Kowalski, describing her delight in their last night together before he left for France – *the gentleness of your caresses, your patient staying power, your instinct to put my pleasure first...*

Dora was one of SOE's most intriguing assets. Some of her colleagues already saw her as the real brains behind the French section. At the outbreak of war, aged 25, her PhD a ground-breaking new appraisal of Middle English verse romances, she had been appointed a university lecturer at Cambridge. Within days she had put her academic career on hold, joined the first service that would have her – the women's section of the RAF – and then transferred to SOE as fast as she could.

The ultimate plausibility of every agent depended on her extraordinary thoroughness and ingenuity. Her Texas-sized memory stored untold information affecting the life of a secret agent in occupied France: on work, travel, food rationing, on police registration procedures and the rest. To the regular documents supplied by SOE's laboratories she added the icing on the cake:

authentic details that clinched a fake identity. Family photographs, old visiting cards, suitably scuffed and dirty, a letter from an old friend or flame, anything which a man or a woman might carry in their pockets and which would lend credibility to his or her identity if searched, including French tailors' tabs, Metro tickets, French matches, even shreds of tobacco from Gauloises cigarettes.

She produced these items from her own private and mysterious sources and tolerated no questions about their origins.

'That's hard to live up to', was all Labrador could think of saying – avoiding eye contact.

'A goal worth your while, Labrador. Make it your priority, after the war.

'David, for you I have something more pedestrian. It is a letter of advice from your father. He is a cautious man of carefully balanced advice, like Polonius in *Hamlet*. He urges you, among other things, to spend money on only one tailored suit, to be worn not in the office but on social occasions only.'

After she had taken them through each piece of their clothing and accompanying theatrical business, she proposed that they went in a taxi to La Coquille, a Soho restaurant.

'When was the last time you were at the same table as a Frenchman?'

'I suppose in June, before we left on Operation Henrietta.'

'Do you remember how the French leave their knives and forks when they have finished?'

Neither could.

'I shall refresh your memory.'

At the Coquille, they were joined by another SOE French Section officer, Jacques de Guyelis. By the end of the evening, surrounded by French people, eating French food and speaking French as well as they could, they began to feel and behave as Frenchmen. They wiped the leftover sauce – 'sauce, remember, not gravy' – from their plates, as demonstrated by Jacques, enthusiastically with a piece of baguette.

They finished their main course, with clean plates, and not one *petit pois* left behind, as an Englishman might have done. Knives and forks were placed not together at half past six, but put, dirty, on the side plate ready for the cheese.

*

Leo turned round in her seat, irritated because the safety straps restrained her, and scanned the sky behind and above for the ME109. By now it would have lined up for the kill. The chance of seeing a speck in such a vast expanse of sky was tiny... especially with the clouds *and* the sun to hide him. Knowing he was somewhere up there, but invisible, deepened her fear to the edge of panic; and she felt her fury start to boil.

She remembered what she'd learned from Smokey in hospital. His plane was faster than hers, and unlike hers it fired exploding shells.

ATA standing orders, drummed into her daily during her first weeks, required ferry pilots to run away if they encountered an enemy, however hostile, and for fuel economy she must keep to the regulation speed – for the Spitfire, 195 mph. Leo pushed the throttle forward and watched the airspeed needle rotate to 290 mph. That would be a start.

Next she turned sharply right, just past Southampton Water, following the next big landmark, the Beaulieu River, as it snaked inland for three miles. Up ahead she saw broken cloud. She wished she could count on him not to notice her turn. She tried to calm her jitters by looking down on the flat New Forest heath and woodland… at least there were no barrage balloons here, or high ground. She passed through a thin bank of cloud, still with no sign of the German in her mirror, and for two wonderful minutes, still angry but feeling a little less tense, allowed herself to think she might now lose him.

In seconds, though, she was out of the cloud, entering a large, clear zone where once more she would be easy to spot.

Above her was a layer of cloud, perhaps at 7,000 feet. Could she climb there quickly enough? She would set the boost to + 8, two higher than normal, and tear upwards towards those clouds at more than 300 mph.

As she reached for the boost control, there was an appalling bang, and a sickening jolt.

Leo stopped being Leo as she experienced her body, already running on adrenalin, sledgehammered by a new and massive injection of the fight-or-flight hormone: a physical hit to her chest, head, even to her fingertips.

The usual Leo was no more. She was now her eyes, her hands and her feet... she was also the Spitfire itself and the air that flowed past... she was a flying machine as much as the aircraft: its essence was her essence as she tested the controls – climb, bank left, bank right, descend. Everything was working normally. How could that be? Maybe it was just a graze? In the new Leo-machine, fear existed, but it didn't dominate, it co-operated with the highly tuned, coldly efficient pilot-plane. The ready-to-flare-up Leo had gone, anger sublimated into icy, deadly, determined calm.

She glanced back. Could she see him now? There he was.

Seconds later, she looked again. He was gaining.

Smokey was speaking again. 'With Bosch right on your tail, you have one more chance. Just one. A Spit turns tighter than an ME109.'

So instead of climbing she threw the Spitfire into a turn tighter than she thought she or the plane could withstand.

The ME109 followed, but from the start, her turning circle was tighter than his. The Spitfire's rudder pedal extensions, designed to raise the pilot's thighs and legs about a foot, now did their work. As the blood drained from her head and chest towards her legs, her raised thighs and knees were a barrier against blood flow to her lower legs.

The Spitfire was a conker on a string, whirling horizontally. It banked steeply, starboard wing pointing almost at the ground, as did Leo's right shoulder. The G force clawed at her: her face felt drawn and heavy, moving her hands was a terrible effort. Then her vision started to go grey at the edges. If this was the end, it was easy. But she didn't black out completely because she felt the Spitfire give a little shiver. A warning sign, a sign that the plane was about to stall, to fall out of the sky because it was turning too tightly. Reflexively, she eased the turn. The plane instantly settled down, and on she went screaming around her turn, holding the Spit, with ultimate precision, just inside its limit, just short of the shiver.

Still deadly calm, she looked around again for the ME109. She couldn't see it behind, but spotting it was hard because they were dipping in and out of small clouds.

Then she saw him, not behind but roughly opposite, the other side of her turning circle: hard to believe because in the air she felt slower than the German, but over the ground, she realised, she was quicker, and gaining. She could see now that it would be seconds before she would be behind him – a racing car lapping the competition, the hunted turned hunter.

Feeling less hunted renewed her aggression, but it was still calmly blue, not red. She caught a clear glimpse of the German in a cloud-free patch, banked on his side like her. The black crosses on the tops of the wings glared at her. Instead of raising her blood pressure, they made her notice what a useful target he was, his whole aircraft laid out in plan view.

In another second he was in her sights. When she pressed the firing button it was not in panic or anger, it was cold and deliberate. She pressed the red button until the chattering guns went silent.

Simple. She had no feelings for the German except the need to get him, and when she saw him wobble and break out of his turn she smiled, as if it was a job well done. He shot upwards, climbing towards the thickest cloud, perhaps at 20,000 feet.

She believed her fire had scared him, maybe chipped him, but not fatally wounded him because she'd shot from at least 400 yards. The best chance of a kill, Smokey had said, was from a hundred yards or closer. Spitfire guns were set up to deliver a blunderbussing shower of metal, spread out in a large pattern. A beginner could kill an ME109, but you needed to be close.

Now perhaps he would think more carefully about chasing her. She eased back the boost and thought about how to get away from the German for good.

Smokey was talking to her once more. 'When being chased, fly low if you can, just 30 feet above the sea. It makes a difference because while you just have to concentrate on one job, flying level, the enemy has two jobs, flying level and keeping you in his sights.'

She turned south, back towards the Solent, followed the Lymington River to its mouth and swooped low over the sea. The crew of two naval patrol boats stared as she screamed past, feet from the surface, towards the Needles, the chain of chalk rocks at the island's west tip. She pressed the Spitfire around them in a tight left turn and carried on south at sea level, thinking only of putting the miles between her and the German, hoping he'd not noticed her duck out of sight on the island's south side.

After perhaps ten minutes she felt less pressured. Time to check the instruments. All were OK but one, the oil pressure gauge, which was just below normal. Oil line damage?

To minimize the engine overheating, she slowed from 250 to 125 mph. The grey-green carpet below slid by half as fast. Still no German in her mirror.

After another five minutes she checked her instruments again. Very low on petrol. Checking the manual strapped to her knee, she worked out that there was enough for ten to 15 minutes flying.

She looked in her mirror again. This time he was there, too far away to fire, but gaining. The last of her energy dribbled away.

She could do another turn, but he would quickly learn that she had no more ammunition, and then she would be cornered. Her heart thudded, she couldn't think. In desperation, rather than calculation, she went automatically into another tight turn, never expecting to see it through – she was fightless, a falling leaf, too feeble to cope with the G.

She saw the grey creep in again at the corners, and possibly blacked out completely, then regained consciousness. She saw her wing pointing at the waves. If a big one came along, she thought fatalistically, perhaps her wing would touch it and the Spit would cartwheel into the sea.

On she clung through the turn until she could no longer take the G force. She straightened out, reconciling herself to seeing him again on her tail.

But no sign.

She dared not think she'd shaken him off, so climbed to 250 feet for a better view. He really did seem to have gone. Perhaps that made sense: he'd gone because he knew she could keep turning tightly, and because he still thought she was armed?

She said a prayer of thanks while checking the instruments again. Oil pressure down, but still steady. Fuel now dangerously low. She guessed that with luck she could fly another 25 miles. By her reckoning, the Isle of Wight must be more than 40 miles behind her. The total distance between the Isle of Wight and the north tip of the Cherbourg peninsula was 65 miles – a figure she knew by heart from Channel crossings on *Shearwater.*

Landing in France was her only choice – and much more attractive than a forced landing on the sea, even if close to home.

On she flew. The cliffs of the French coast grew larger. Not enough fuel to circle for the best landing spot – just put the Spit down quickly. The engine coughed and cut out as she crossed the beach. Her glide path took her six feet above a fence and into a newly harvested corn field. She eased back on the stick for landing, praying that the ground was hard. It was. She rolled easily to a halt.

*

Labrador and David took the train to Newmarket, and were driven to the airfield. MacDonald, and each of their main instructors at

Somerville, went there by car to see them off. An SOE ritual. It was natural for the midwives to be present as their charges finally departed the shelter of the training schools.

As they walked across the tarmac to where the Lysander was being prepared for the flight, they heard another car pull up some yards away, beside a nearby hangar. MacDonald recognized the car. The pennant of the 14th-18th Lancers was on the front right wing, and behind the wheel was Cobb. In shadow, on the back seat, was Maxwell. MacDonald walked over.

'Viv, this is good of you, but possibly a little excessive.'

'I've known David for a long time. The gesture is empty unless – unless – it costs… Something.'

MacDonald understood. This was Maxwell, needing to express himself – as well as he could.

'As you've come so far, why not come out to the aircraft yourself? Say goodbye personally? I could pretend you were in the neighbourhood by chance, and that I had mentioned that David was leaving on a mission.'

'No, Robbo. David has no suspicion of my connection with SOE Somerville, and never should. I shall make do with passing these farewell tokens to you, and watching from the shadows as you pass them on to the young men. The best I can hope for.'

Maxwell handed MacDonald two small boxes with the words 'Collingwood, Bond Street' embossed.

'One pair each.' MacDonald opened one of the boxes.

'Gold cuff links. Usually it's silver. You must have had them made yourself.'

'Give them the L pills first, then the cuff links.'

MacDonald walked back to the plane where the instructors, David and Labrador, were shaking hands in turn, silently, the newly fledged agents too overcome to speak, the Lysander's propellers starting to turn.

Handing each the tiny grey pills, in as casual a voice as MacDonald could command:

'By the way, we always give you one of these just before leaving. Sure you won't need them. Just an SOE tradition.'

Labrador and David stared at the pills.

'The coating's insoluble, so you can hold it in your mouth harmlessly for hours if need be. Crunch it between your teeth, and the effect is immediate.'

Next, he handed them the two Collingwood boxes and strode away quickly.

*

Three times Cecile had turned down Leo's demands to send the first letter back to England. Three times the English girl had radiated such a storm of misery and fury that Cecile went back to Alain asking him to change his mind. Eventually, he had come up with the wine list, pulled from a bottom drawer where he and Cecile kept memorable menus and wine lists from all over Northern France. It could never be traced to the St-Cloud since it was ten years old, picked up on a pre-war trip to Le Touquet from a restaurant long since closed, the owners dead.

The Bissets knew Leo would want to write home again. Cecile discouraged her for as long as she could hold out, then gave in, this time presenting her with a menu from a charming little place near Boulogne, the Auberge d'Inxent. The five different *prix-fixe* menus allowed space for a much shorter letter than the first.

Dear Brig,

I have been told to say nothing that could possibly reveal where and what this place is. I feel ashamed I did that in my first letter – it was bad of me to give them no time to check it through.

This place is very important in the local struggle against the Nazis. I do not understand why, but I do know that whoever thought out this place has got a very ingenious and thorough mind. I am hidden here <u>completely.</u> No one could find me. Every trace of me and how I got to this attic has vanished. If the whole place was searched by 20 German soldiers, they would never find me. And you may be pleased to hear that when the time comes I can escape unseen. The courier's van will be waiting for me, some distance away, the other side of the woods. This is how I am hoping to escape back to England.

My first letter ended where the ME109 turned away from me in order to line up behind me, then to shoot me down. I had some trouble with him, but I escaped in the end by flying low over the sea, south over the Channel. Half way across I discovered I was so short of petrol that my only choice was to fly on and land in France – turning back would have meant a forced landing in the water and losing the Spit.

The Brig paused. Something wasn't right. Leo usually loaded her letters with detail. Why this précis? Why had she gone into such detail in her first letter about the guns being left loaded, yet not mentioned it again? And what about the damaged oil and fuel lines? And feeling so worked up about Daisy Johnson? He read on, suspiciously.

The landing went fine, but as we came to rest I just sat, feeling hopeless. No Spit to fly any more, I had nothing to do. It was most unpleasant, I just had to let events take over.

There was a lane nearby. I remember two people running over from a car that had stopped. 'I am not hurt' I said. 'Par blessay' they said. They also said 'Miraculo'. Then 'Sortay, sortay.' And I knew they were right, there was one thing I could do for myself. Climb out quickly in case it caught fire, like the Walrus, so I did, especially because there was probably a fuel leak somewhere.

I am near the end now.

Maxwell stopped once more to ponder his daughter's delight in droll phonetic renderings of French, in a thick Anglo-Saxon accent. It could be amusing. *But perhaps not now.*

The letter then explained how she had eventually found herself in the St-Cloud, this time without, thank God, mentioning it by name. She'd spent the night in a nearby farmhouse, then was taken blindfolded to a house in a town some way away, presumably the Bisset's house in Caen. From there Bisset's people had smuggled her to the St-Cloud in the furniture van. Cecile had finally concealed her in the attic hideaway.

> *And that is where I have to stop because I have been forbidden to describe exactly how I was then hidden.*

The tone of the last two paragraphs was downbeat, if not gloomy.

> *So that is all. The people here have told me again and again not to worry, that there is a way to get me back to England but that she cannot tell me when. Every time it is the same thing, the less you know the better. I do not like to think too much about why this should be, but I have some ideas and they are not pleasant.*
>
> *So goodbye, Brig. Please pass on all my best thoughts to everyone and hope that I really can escape back to England.*

> *Lots of love from*
> *Leo*

Cecile Bisset took the letter from Leo, went back downstairs, and detoured via the dining room to wave goodbye to her father in his kitchen, surrounded by harassed underlings.

She left the *auberge* to walk ten minutes to the village mechanic's yard, as usual a mess of tractors and cars in different stages of dismemberment, and checked before going in that no one was watching. The mechanic could fix motorbikes too – *useful*. At the back of the workshop she lifted the lid off a water butt. It fitted tightly, and was lined with oiled canvas for waterproofing. In the bottom of the bin was an old sack. She placed the letter inside the sack and replaced the lid. Checking once more that she was unseen, she left the yard and walked briskly to the bus stop. Half an hour later, her brother André would pick up the letter and drive it on his motorbike to Tréguier. There it would be handed over to the Captain of a trawler named *Alouette*. The trawler would chug out to sea for its rendezvous with a British MTB, patrolling ten miles off the coast. The letter would be in Portsmouth the next morning, and in London on the first train.

If she could catch the next bus, she would be back home with Alain in Caen for the six o'clock news. Her husband was a changed man, she reflected. A man with a purpose, at ease with himself. More than just a draper – though why he should need extra status was a mystery to her.

His family, the Bissets, had been Caen's foremost tradesmen for a hundred and fifty years, modestly prosperous, the owners of a four-storey house in one of the best streets of the city's central district, close to the abbey. But yes, more than just a draper these days. His new grey Citroën van proudly announced that it was the property of Bisset et Cie, fine linen, house clearances and removals.

Alain was tuning the radio as she walked into the parlour. A deadpan English voice could be heard intoning the day's *messages personnels* for resistance workers inside France.

'Albert sends his love to his mother.'

'George and Louise have had a healthy baby.'

'Edouard sends greetings to Jean.'

Alain switched off the radio and smiled at Cecile. '*Cherie*, let me say once again that I can only tell you the minimum. It is for everyone's good.'

'Very well, but reassure me that the number of people in our circuit is still only six, including me. The arrival of the English girl is worrying. She is just 23 – extraordinary to be flying a war machine, *n'est pas?* But if she falls into the hands of the Bosch she will quickly tell them everything she knows to avoid torture. We can keep her in the dark as much as we can, but she still knows the existence of the *auberge*. When they get the name from her, they will arrive and – *phut.*'

'It's true about the size of our cell: your father, your mother, yourself, myself, André and the Captain of the trawler. No one outside the family, except the fisherman, and he is far away in Brittany. And the radio operator, who does not know who or where we are. We do not make the same mistakes as others did in

226

the past. Our cell is virtually invisible and we use the radio only exceptionally. I may not tell you where the radio operator is, but he is not in Caen.'

'So how did the farmers know to bring the pilot girl here?'

'It took them a whole evening, trawling the bars, asking if anyone knew if there was a local resistance organizer. When I questioned them about how they eventually found us, they said that someone had told them they suspected our house was associated with the resistance because they lived in the same street. They saw the comings and goings in January and February. A hunch, no more.'

'What is the meaning of 'Edouard sends greetings to Jean'?'

'You know about the escape route, that should be enough. But if you insist: the message means something exciting will happen in the coming days. Afterwards we can use the escape route for the girl – and anyone else who needs it. Now, that's all.'

14

A mile from the French coast, the Lysander reduced height to 2,000 feet and slowed to 80 mph. David and Labrador had had a much shorter and smoother flight than last time, and although most SOE agents preferred to parachute into France, they were pleased not to repeat their experience on Henrietta. The pilot had told them they would touch down in a remote, grassy field on the Cherbourg Peninsula, surrounded by woods.

He beckoned them forwards. Ahead, in the blackness, two powerful torches were flashing in tandem. 'All clear to land. The field is a little bumpy, so fasten your seat belts tightly. I'll open the door. You'll climb out quickly. I'll hand you your bags and the canisters. Give the bags and the canisters to the French, go to the wing tips and help turn the plane to face the way we came in. Then disappear into the woods. Don't watch me go. Anyway, I'll be off the ground again before you can spit.'

Alain Bisset and his brother-in-law André, Cecile's 25-year-old brother, bundled David, Labrador and their canisters into the Bisset & Cie van, setting off for Caen, using the smallest country roads. In the first light of dawn, the van dropped Labrador and David outside Caen station, keeping the canisters for storage in the Bisset townhouse. Labrador and David hailed separate taxis, asking to be taken to the Auberge St-Cloud at Verson, ten kilometres west of Caen. They arrived at the *auberge* a few minutes apart. Already, labourers were slouching into the public bar, a very different environment to the residents' sitting room, for breakfast: a Gauloise, a cup of very strong black coffee and a glass of white wine.

Labrador and David took in the rest of the premises, making their tours independently, as if strangers. A large, lived-in sitting room with brown leather armchairs. A dining room with a window into the kitchen, at this time of day manned by two juniors. These days, the great chef, in his late 60s, allowed himself the luxury of being served breakfast in his own dining room by Mme Lambert.

Up the stairs. Along the corridor. At the far end, on the right, room numbers 11 and 12. Mme Lambert took Labrador into 11. Without speaking, she beckoned him out of the room as soon as he had dropped his bag. Still without speaking, she knocked on the next door, number 12. David, installed a few minutes before, opened it.

She led them, still silent, to a huge painted cupboard against the far wall. She opened the doors, pulled aside some coats and pointed at the pine panels forming the back of the cupboard. She pulled one of them forward with her fingertips, gaining purchase on a gap each side, and lifted it out of the recess holding it at the base. Behind was the outside wall of the house, into which was cut a metal door.

'*Ouvrez*. Open.'

Labrador stepped into the cupboard and turned the metal door handle. Light flooded into the cupboard. The opening, just large enough to step through, led out into daylight on to a metal fire escape platform mounted on the side of the building. Metal steps led from the platform down to the ground.

Labrador and David climbed out on to the platform, followed by Mme Lambert. They watched her lean back through the metal door frame into the cupboard, close the cupboard's front doors, put the coats back in place and then restore the wooden panel.

'Practise many times. I can do it in 40 seconds. With luck, a searcher would not even find his way on to the platform.'

Next she pointed to the steps leading to the ground. 'Do not use them. *Regardez-moi.*'

She climbed on to the hip-high railing surrounding the platform, reached to the left and pulled a loose brick forwards from the wall. She pulled out another brick, higher and to the right, to make a second foothold. With a foot on the first brick she reached above her head into the valley of the roof above, pulling down a length of rope. Using the footholds, and keeping herself steady with the rope, she disappeared out of sight on to the roof.

'*Suivez*. Follow.'

David went first. She told Labrador, last into the roof valley, to reach down and push the bricks back flush with the face of the wall, then pull the rope up out of sight and coil it.

Then, led by Mme Lambert, they walked along the roof to its midpoint, where she paused by a dormer window on the left. She opened it and climbed in.

'*Mademoiselle*, you 'ave *visiteurs*.' Standing by the window, brushing her hair, was Leo, dressed in ill-fitting French clothes. She turned.

'*Qu'es-ce-qui passe, mes amis?* Are you not pleased to have the company of this bold and charming young woman? She can help you climb on to the roof if you need to escape.'

All three stood wordless.

'What is the matter with you English men? Do you not like the company of young women? I can assure you she is *bien amiable. Et courageux*. She has had an *expérience extraordinaire*. She is the equal of any man.'

'Henry…'

'Leo…'

'Labrador…'

Labrador looked at the ground.

'How on earth do you know his code name?' asked David.

'*Vous Anglais. Incroyable*. You seem to know each other. So why not *embrasser sur les deux joues* – how do say? Kiss on each cheek?'

The silence that followed was so uncomfortable that Mme Lambert shrugged and left the attic, saying only that breakfast was still being served.

*

A terse, coded radio message arrived at Baker Street a few hours after Labrador's and David's arrival at the St-Cloud.

Drop successful. L and D installed at St-Cloud. But complication. S-C also sheltering ATA pilot, 23, in attic, after unplanned landing locally. Advice please.

Maxwell had anticipated that this message would be on Fuller's desk at any time. He was prepared.

'Fuller, I need to see you.'

'Urgently?'

'Yes.'

Maxwell hurried round to Baker Street. He had spent months conceiving and planning Zodiac, but accepted that day-to-day handling of the operation must now be Fuller's, except under the most abnormal conditions. Always hard not to interfere, but now impossible.

Fuller placed the radio message transcript in front of Maxwell.

'A confession, Fuller. I've known about the ATA pilot for at least a week. She's my daughter Leonora.'

'Astonishing coincidence.'

'Yes, but a fact. Main thing, her Spitfire is hidden, miles from the St-Cloud. So there's no link to Zodiac if it's found – which is unlikely.'

'How do you know?'

'Those letters you forwarded to me at the Cavalry Club with female handwriting – they were from Leonora. She talked the Lamberts into sending them via Tréguier. She can be... persuasive.'

'What next, Maxwell?'

'They sent it with André on the motorbike. Not the van.'

'That's something, I suppose. The fewer trips that van does, the better.'

'There's one more thing. Leo is a... well, a friend of David's. Grew up with him at Somerville... you know, I have a house there.'

'What sort of friends?'

'Henry has a soft spot... A very soft spot... For Leo. Longstanding. Think he'd like to marry her.'

Fuller's eyes bulged. 'Forgive me for asking, Brigadier, but is your daughter cool headed?'

'She can be cool. And she can be hot headed.'

Fuller took his head in his hands and tried to absorb the reality. 'How did she get to Northern France?'

'Long story. Needs time to tell. Lost her way, one might say. Meanwhile we have a calculation to make about whether David's involvement with my daughter could jeopardise Zodiac.'

Fuller sighed, long and low.

'I can help with a few facts. One, Leo has not made up her mind about David, she has him dangling. It is not an intimate relationship. She has other admirers, and enjoys their attention. Two, Henry is very steady – a little unimaginative. But in this situation, that is a bonus. He is very correct, a strict prioritiser. For now, his number one priority will be Zodiac.'

'Still, if they get into trouble, he will be in conflict with his instinct to protect her. That's if he really does love her.'

'He does.'

'Which means in a tight spot he may debate a decision – internally. He may not make decisions as fast as he should.'

'That's the rub.'

They slid into silence. Fuller was irritated by Maxwell's delay in telling him about Leo. How could he manage Zodiac if facts were withheld? Maybe he should pretend that he needs reminding about Maxwell's briefing? If there are inconsistencies, bits left out or new bits put in, then he could challenge Maxwell for an unedited version.

Maxwell broke the silence. 'I suppose that everything we have done to set up Zodiac in an unusual way works for us now. The St-Cloud attic was never essential – it was a back up. Labrador and David are best in rooms 11 and 12. As long as Leo's in the attic, it's as if she doesn't exist. The escape along the valley and the second fire escape can still be used.' Maxwell let this sink in, then went on:

'And then there's the tiny size of the cell, and the fact that not one person, including Labrador and David, know the full scope of Zodiac and Fireworks.'

'True,' agreed Fuller, 'even Monsieur Lambert has only the most partial knowledge. He doesn't even know about the escape route, does he? Sorry, Maxwell, I'm so troubled by your revelation about Leo that some of the details are escaping me – temporarily, I hope. May we go through them again? Remind me how much Cecile knows, for example.'

'Only about the work her brother André does on his motorbike and about the escape route – starting at the bedroom cupboard and ending in Tréguier. As for her husband, she knows he is involved in resistance work, but nothing of the operation itself. She thinks the removal van, and the expansion of the drapery business into house clearances and moves were done with his savings.'

'And Mme Lambert?'

'Only from the bedroom cupboard to the foot of the fire escape that leads to the woods. Nothing about Tréguier.'

'So to uncover the whole set-up, the SS would have to capture and torture six people?'

'Seven if you add in Leo.'

'And Bisset himself?'

'He has no idea about the pilots. Only that he must light the fireworks when Labrador or David say so. He thinks they are there in a supporting role only – to supply the explosives – so that the French can have all the glory.'

'And André?'

'He's a shilling short of a pound – a bit simple. Incredibly brave, but unreliable – can't think a step ahead of himself. Cecile and Mme Lambert were candid about him when they came to London in February. Said he was a risk, but it would be impossible to keep him in ignorance. So he knows only where the dead letter box is, the name of the trawler at Tréguier, and that from time to time he must give people lifts on the back of the motor bike, all the way to Tréguier. Oh yes. He also drives the removals van – for real house clearances as well as for resistance work.'

'Still, he's the weakest member.'

Fuller asked himself again: Is this the full story? How much more has he witheld? Everything seemed consistent with his first briefing, but with Maxwell, you could never be sure. Silence again, as they both pondered the remaining problem: radio messages. Zodiac's radio operator, the 'pianist' – the final member of the cell, if you could call him that – operated entirely in isolation, from a village outside Rouen, 80 km east of Caen.

Fuller shared Maxwell's intense anxiety over radio messages. Admitting André to the cell and buying the removals van had been done to minimize them. Just one person, André, knew the radio operator's whereabouts. The dead letter box in the mechanic's yard was for radio messages as well as messages for London via Tréguier. It guaranteed that the operator knew nothing of the cell at Caen or of the Auberge St-Cloud.

Both sides in the war were using mobile detection vans,

combined with isolating the local electricity supply, to pinpoint radio operators. Captured radio operators were offered two options: torture followed by execution or to carry on transmitting as if everything was normal. The messages sent from then on were, of course, dictated by the captors.

'How long will your daughter put up with the attic?'

'As long as she can't find an alternative escape route – and that will be hard from up in the roof of the St-Cloud.'

'Will she lose patience and try to escape?'

'Patience is not her strong suit, but her sense of self-preservation is as good as anyone's. If you do decide to go ahead, I suggest you're more cautious than ever about radio broadcasts. Try to rely entirely on the courier route and the *messages personnels*.'

Fuller picked up a sheet of paper from his desk, scanning it.

'Here's just what we need. *Martine is coming to tea*. Meaning, carry on, despite unforeseen problems. Do you mind, Brigadier, if I think about this over the weekend?'

'Personally, I think we should risk carrying on, but I'll accept a decision to abort if you're not on board.'

'I'll telephone you on Monday.'

*

Leo broke the silence. The two men still could find no words. She found it hard enough, and tried to mask her nervousness with speed-talk.

'Don't you think this is the cleverest hiding place? There's more to it than just the bricks and rope to get you into the roof. By the way, I hope you pushed the bricks back flush with the wall. Anyway, it's not just the fire escape that end', she pointed to where they had climbed up. 'It's the fire escape at the *other* end.'

Labrador and David looked nonplussed. Leo continued to gabble.

'Follow me.' She slipped out through the dormer window into the valley and made for its far end.

'If the Bosch was after you, and found his way on to that fire escape,' she pointed to where they had climbed up, 'then he would think you had run down *those* steps, wouldn't he? When in fact you would have escaped down *these* steps.' She showed them a second metal fire escape staircase, leading down from the opposite end of the valley. 'Out of sight. You can jump down on to it in the same way. There's no rope, though.' The foot of the second fire escape staircase was close to woods at the back of the building. 'Three strides and you are hidden. There's a path in the woods that leads to a field beyond. Bicycles are hidden in a shelter in the field. Jump on a bike and follow an obvious track to a lane where the motorbike or the van is waiting. Cecile told me.'

Labrador spoke ahead of David. 'I agree, Leo, it's very clever. Not just thorough, but thought out by someone with a sense of humour. Someone who might enjoy laughing at the Germans.'

'That's right, George, or shall I call you Labrador? One minute you are being chased. The next you have vanished, and there are hidden bells that ring in rooms 11 and 12 if searchers are on their way upstairs. They're operated from the kitchen. That's another thing. Monsieur Lambert, he's the *patron*, and the chef. From his kitchen, through that window into the dining room, he has a view across the dining room, right into the sitting room and bar area, and beyond that into the reception hall. Anyone dangerous coming through the front door, he or Madame Lambert just presses the button in the kitchen. By the way, Cecile told me he has a window because he considers himself an artist – he wants to be seen at work.'

'Well, that's something explained.' David managed a smile. 'Thank you for telling us in detail about the escape arrangements, but I wonder if it might be just as important to tell us how you got here?'

Henry is so... So indirect. Like my father. I know I went on too long, but couldn't he see I was nervous?

She was ready with the censored version of her journey to France.

'I ran into a stray ME109 over Portsmouth. It chased me. I got a bullet in my wing, which caused a fuel leak. The best way to escape was low, over the sea. I was silly, headed due south over the Channel – thought the Isle of Wight would block his view of me. Half way across, I saw I was low on petrol. Not enough to get back to England, so I did a forced landing in France.'

'And the plane? A crashed Spitfire will cause a search for the pilot. I'm amazed you aren't on your way to POW camp already.'

Leo was upset that Henry showed no concern for the danger she had been in. *He is meant to care about me. Why doesn't he say it must have been terrifying? Why does he always have to ask the sensible questions first?*

'We hid it in a barn after dark.'

'Go on.'

'No, I've said enough. Your turn.'

Labrador and David turned to each other. They did not feel like looking at each other. David led, reluctantly.

'In that case, before anything is said about what we are doing here, I have to ask you something.' He turned to Labrador. 'How does she know you? How does she know your code name? And for that matter, what is the nature of your friendship – you do seem to be friends.'

Leo wanted to speak, but she saw Henry's face.

'I met her by the Somer River. Before you arrived at SOE Somerville. Her dog was stuck in the mud and I rescued it. I was fascinated by her, so I asked her to meet for a drink the next weekend. Leo made it clear we were no more than friends. Funny thing – her father – Brigadier Maxwell, has something to do with SOE Somerville. He was often there. I met him once.'

David and Leo spoke together. 'You're mistaken. He's a regular army officer.'

'I had a long meeting with Colonel MacDonald and Brigadier Maxwell in Woodland House. They're old friends. I heard them calling each other Viv and Robbo. They sent me outside their room when they needed to talk privately, but I had my ear to the door.'

'Viv and Robbo?' Leo repeated the nicknames half a dozen times, striding up and down, rocking with laughter. David spoke.

'Your father always struck me as mysterious. Whatever his regular army work might have been it was useful to have a Somerville resident on the spot while SOE Somerville was being established.'

Leo thought back. Now that the idea had been floated, it was not hard to imagine her father having a double life. Much of his time was unaccounted. Again, she felt she should try to lighten the atmosphere, and again the words tumbled out.

'Anyway, the food in the dining room is delicious. I am hoping that on quiet nights when it's mostly French people in the dining room – not those horrible Germans from the airfield – we can all have supper together. Cecile has allowed me to eat with her downstairs once or twice. Behind his window Monsieur Lambert makes the most wonderful things, especially chicken in red wine sauce. The sauce has to be reduced by the chef's underlings for 48 hours. Cecile told me that the boredom reduces them to tears. Imagine, Henry, eating the essence of boredom – only it is not boring. It has *intensité exceptionnel*.'

He was dazzled by Leo's torrent of effervescence. It was one of the things that made him love her. On she went:

'My French is improving, thanks to Cecile. She is becoming a friend, but she finds Leo too hard to pronounce, instead I am *la pee-lot onglay*, or just *peelot*. 'You are the only person around here', she told me, 'who is exactly what you seem to be. So I call you exactly what you are."

David and Labrador were rapt. Leo rattled on.

'Then there is Cecile's younger brother, André. He is the dispatch rider. Nice, but a bit simple. And Monsieur Lambert's wife, Denise. She welcomes everyone to the *auberge* and makes up for Monsieur Lambert's rudeness. Sometimes he comes out of the kitchen to tell the waitresses off, sometimes even some of the guests if they have ordered the wrong wine for the dish they chose.'

'Who else have you... Observed?'

'Cecile's husband Alain. He and Cecile have a house in Caen. Alain runs a drapery, which is also a removals business... I watch them when I am allowed down into the *auberge*, and they all have an understanding. Not to do with what they say, but with how they stand together, how they look at each other. I believe that Alain is the *grand fromage*.'

'*Grand fromage?*' Labrador didn't understand.

'It means the boss. Something Cecile said. Nothing obvious. To do with fighting the Germans underground. She told me her husband had become a different man. '*Merveilleux dans la chambre*' she said. She talks about what happens in her bedroom whenever she can. 'Completely different since he was approached by some important people from Paris."

'She told you *all* that?' Then, turning to Labrador:

'Leo has just told us everything about the local resistance they would not tell us in Somerville or London, probably for the best of reasons. What shall we do?'

In the many weeks that Labrador had now spent alone with David, David hadn't once been edgy or moody. Serious, perhaps, but Labrador had found him essentially a man without temperament. Now David fell into a grave, even forbidding silence that required – and got – the hardened Pole's respect. Leo's too. Labrador felt himself impelled to speak, and to speak constructively.

'It's a security breach, but only from the inside. As for Leo, up in this attic, it's true she's vanished – except on the rare occasions she's allowed out. I suppose they don't matter as long as they are rare enough for the clientele in the dining room to take no notice. I guess Cecile told her those things because she needed to talk, and because she believed Leo would be gone before long.' Leo nodded.

'Yes, they told me they didn't want to take me to Tréguier in the furniture van. They said it was for three or four agents escaping to England together. Possibly they want to take us all together. When the excitement is over.'

Labrador and David opened their mouths together, but Labrador let David speak. He said, very quietly indeed:

'Leo, that's enough. Whatever you have learned, get it out of your head. You don't know anything.'

David had never spoken to Leo so firmly. She didn't find it entirely unpleasant.

'Of course. I'm not that silly.'

Leo almost never spoke to herself: what she was, what she did, what she said were usually one, but this situation made her feel she might break into several parts unless she could reconcile the confusion of her feelings. As she paced her attic prison in the St-Cloud, she said, almost audibly:

'Be honest, Leo. If having them both together in the same room made you feel so agitated, then you can't have forgotten about Henry.'

And it was true. She hadn't, she had put him in a separate drawer and now it was clearly ready to be reopened.

If she went on being honest, she had to admit feeling a little envious of his and Labrador's relationship. They seemed to enjoy a special kind of harmony... as if they were twin brothers. Perhaps it was a fraternity of war, arising from complete trust in each other's courage and competence. She'd sensed, too, an absence of envy or competition between them – and this despite the fact that Henry, alongside Labrador, was immeasurably better educated; despite the chasm of social difference that separated them. She also sensed that Henry had risen above the shock of discovering that she'd met Labrador several times at Somerville. It didn't appear to enter into things, and that made him grow in her eyes.

'Perhaps I'd better think again about Henry being moulded by privilege. His ease with Labrador wouldn't be possible if he had a sense of entitlement.' Perhaps his attitude to class and money chimed with hers.

If she now showed, for one moment, more interest in Labrador than Henry, or the reverse, she could upset their relationship – undermine that special trust, hinder the work they were here to do, which was probably very dangerous. Her reluctance to decide between three admirers looked shabbier than ever. She must remain neutral and make herself as scarce as possible. Anything else would be a very poor show indeed, as the Brig would have said, but not in those words – he would never have used RAF slang.

Two days later, David and his bike went missing. Cecile was agitated. He'd been gone since yesterday at noon.

'He told me he needed a break from the St-Cloud. I said '*Mais oui*, but come back tonight."

Labrador considered the news phlegmatically.

'David knows how to shelter unseen in outbuildings. Don't worry. If he went into Caen, he would have left before the curfew. He probably needs more than just a short break. He'll be back this evening.'

Leo had noticed the missing bike too, yesterday afternoon while she walked in the woods, passing the bike shelter, and again today.

Now it was 6 p.m. Still no David. She was pacing her room, feeling as jittery as when the ME109 had reappeared over the Channel, too agitated to cross examine her feelings.

Then at nine, just before complete dark, she heard steps outside on the roof valley floor. Someone was walking from the far end, the one which led down into the woods. She opened her window, sprang out into the valley, saw David and without stopping to think whether Labrador could be there to see them or not, threw herself at him, whispering into his ear 'You upset us all. Please don't do that again.'

David gently eased her away, holding her briefly six inches from his chest and looking into her eyes, not daring to read what might be there.

'Of course. I'm sorry. Got claustrophobic. Needed 24 hours to myself. No danger.'

15

'Portia? I'm thinking of coming down to Somerville for the weekend. Not to the house, of course. I'll keep my head down – in the boathouse. I won't see anyone except you.'

'Nothing's going on here. I agree – best meet in the boathouse for privacy.'

'Shall I ask Mrs Renyard to make supper for us? Won't be much good, but there's still wine in the cellar.'

'I'll walk over.'

'Try not to be seen.'

Maxwell spent much of Saturday morning working out how much he could tell Portia. He had no doubt that she could keep a secret. In theory, he could tell her everything. He knew that she suspected, in any case, that he had a secret life. But how much would be a burden to her? How many of ones fears could be shared with another? He'd had no practice.

In the boathouse that evening, Portia sensed something different in Maxwell. His movements were quicker, more fluid than last time they met. More natural. He was hardly drawling at all.

'I think you need to talk, Vivian.'

'What's that psalm, Portia? You probably know its number. 'For there is not a word in my tongue, but lo though knowest it altogether.''

'Number 139. It's very moving. All about God's universality. 'Whither shall I go from thy spirit?''

'You are right. I need to talk. Or rather, to try to break the habit of a lifetime.'

'I'm flattered.'

'You know there's no one else I would ask.'

'I hope so.'

'Let me say first that I really do just need to *air* these problems. I don't ask you to solve them. They're mine, and I think I know how to deal with them. But simply seeing your reaction will be helpful.'

Maxwell didn't tell her the full extent of his involvement with SIS and SOE, but enough to explain what followed. As expected, she showed little surprise at his secret life. He told her how Leo and Henry came to be in France, and the dangers they and Operation Zodiac, now faced.

'When Henry applied to SOE, could you have intervened?'

'In theory. But it would have been... unprincipled. Henry had an overriding right to shape his own career. That he chose a way that did not suit me was – unfortunate, but that gave me no right to intervene.'

'I agree. The first step was his choice. But what about the second? Selecting him for Zodiac?'

'Strictly speaking, not my decision. MacDonald, Fuller and the others had the final say. I could have counselled against it. Trouble was, we had no one else of his quality as a marksman. Using someone else would have jeopardized the operation, endangering yet more lives.'

'Fair enough. And Leo? Could you have changed anything there?'

'I tried to stop her joining the ATA. Spelt out the dangers. Again, the final decision could only be hers.'

'If I were your priest, I would tell you that your moral position is not perfect, but about as good as it can be in this world.'

'But how good is it if I want Zodiac to continue? I must admit that part of me is *determined* it should carry on, despite the extra danger to Leo and Henry – in fact, to everyone.'

'I think that's what the Almighty is for, Vivian. Humans have mixed motives, never pure. If you accept that you are unable to judge them for yourself with complete sincerity, then it's more... honest to trust the values of an intelligence higher than yours. Even if you're not sure it exists, the act of trusting still has an integrity, a selflessness – a moral force.'

She let him brood, then said:

'The secrets are a burden. A terrible burden, which you carry for others.'

'You're being too kind. Joining the Service wasn't noble self sacrifice. It was calculated. It suits people like me only too well. I relish the intrigue, the plots... the intricate planning. But the Hodge business was a nightmare, coming on top of the divorce and a testing time at work.'

'Pointless, vicious mischief.'

'Pointless on the face of it, but I'm beginning to see it differently. Whoever was behind Hodge – we never found him, you know – might be surprised to learn that his scheming has had a purpose.'

'What could that be?'

'Nothing like misery for bringing one face to face with reality. I mean properly face to face with reality as it is – not one's own version. It's changed me. I try to deal more directly with the world now. I no longer keep it so much at arm's length.'

'I agree, you've changed.' She sensed that even the new Maxwell found it hard to talk too long about himself, so changed tack. 'On an altogether more worldly topic...'

She waited for his attention.

'There's something *I* need to say to *you*.'

Maxwell's calm gaze, integrity itself, impressed her yet again.

'There is *nothing* – truly nothing – I want more than this evening to be the first night we spend together. Possibly that's why you asked me here. It's a perfect opportunity.'

Maxwell smiled directly.

'Everything seems right. After what you've told me, I now know better than ever what you are, who you are. As well as admiring you, I admire your work.'

Maxwell said:

'It would make me more than happy.'

'As I said, me too. But I believe we must wait a little longer. Your marriage still exists – until the decree absolute – though not morally. But that doesn't matter to me.'

'What does?'

'First, when it comes to you and me, only the best will do. I want to feel that every piece of it shines. Nothing by the back door. No corners cut.'

'And the second?'

'Somerville. If a child came about, and believe me, I want one before I'm too old, it would be illegitimate. Think of the trouble stored up for everyone.'

Maxwell only needed to nod. Later, Portia slipped back to her house, after they had kissed briefly, for the first time.

*

Fuller had instructed Labrador and David that once at the St-Cloud, they were not to be seen in each other's company. Not even a chance meeting in the bar or a drink at the same table before dinner. David needed to cycle over to the farmhouse in order to check that everything was in order, especially the hiding place for the gun, so Labrador stayed in his room. But not for long. Using a spare key to room 12, hidden in room 11, he let himself in, locked the door behind him and climbed through the cupboard to the fire escape platform. He diligently put everything back in place – doors, panels, bricks and re-coiled the rope. Then he walked along the roof valley and knocked on the dormer window that led into Leo's room.

'That's bold of you, Labrador. Visiting a single girl's bedroom.' In his nervousness he lapsed back into his thickest Polish accent. He had a hunch, in any case, that Leo liked it.

'It's your living room as well as your bedroom. And our situation is exceptional. I have come to ask if you are OK. If there's anything I can do.'

'I'd be happier if the two people who've ended up with me in the Sankloo were anyone but you and Henry.'

'I prefer to call him David, please. I only heard him called Henry once before, when I stayed the night at his house in London.'

'So you met his mother, Alice? She's been very kind to me. Since my mother left my father, she's treated me almost as a member of her family. Of course, it's partly to do with Henry liking me. Always has. In fact, he wants to marry me.'

'I didn't realize it was so serious.'

'It isn't, not on my side. I can't make up my mind. Part of me thinks he's not right for me. He's agreed to wait and see. We are not engaged.'

'Have you noticed that although I care for you a great deal, I have always accepted your terms: just friendship.'

'I liked you – like you – for respecting that.'

'But now things are different. We're in danger. We may never see each other again. Not may. It's highly likely we won't.'

'I don't see why that changes anyone's feelings. Does it change yours towards me?'

'Yes. It makes me want to express them even more urgently. Leo, you may be a little innocent, but you must know how men need to express their feelings towards women.'

She reached out for his hand.

'I think you probably guess that I find you physically attractive. Very. It wasn't just about friendship. Inviting you into my bed would be a very pleasant distraction from the loneliness and fear. As you say, we may never meet again.'

'These opportunities are precious, help us live to the full. So yes, I agree, if we had time stretching ahead, we could wait. I would respect your timetable. One must always respect a girl's timetable. But now is different. There is no time left. If such feelings exist, don't throw them away.'

'Yes, in theory I would like to lie on that bed in your arms. Keep that with you always, Labrador, whatever happens. Let it take place in your imagination.' She opened the dormer window and gestured for him to climb out. 'There's one problem. The fear, the strangeness of this all, has made me more tense than I can explain. And tension just makes it impossible to have... those sort of feelings. I hope you understand.'

He climbed slowly out.

The next day, David stayed in room 12 while Labrador cycled to the farmhouse to reconnoitre the scene of the shooting. He rearranged the undergrowth by the road to provide the best possible cover while lying in wait for the bus, and he practised changing, behind the leafy screen, at speed from his civilian clothes into the uniform of a junior officer of the *Sicherheitsdienst*. He had taken with him a trowel, borrowed from the St-Cloud's greenhouse, to dig a hole big enough to bury the German uniform when the work was done.

At the St-Cloud, David climbed out on to the fire escape, up to the roof valley and knocked on Leo's window.

'Do you mind?'

'Come in.'

'I wanted to ask how you're feeling.'

'Trapped. Like a prisoner. Sometimes Cecile lets me go down the fire escape for a walk in the woods. Otherwise I sit here, trying to read.' She gestured to an English translation of *Madame Bovary*. 'Sometimes I pace up and down if I feel especially agitated.'

'We had to read that at school – in French. Are you enjoying it?'

'It makes me very uncomfortable. Emma Bovary pays a terrible price for trying to distract herself from the boredom of marrying the wrong man.'

'Not like you to read a French classic.'

'I know, Henry. I suppose all this – captivity, boredom mixed with danger – has made me think.'

He wondered: perhaps she's changed.

'I understand your boredom. I never dreamt an SOE mission could be boring... I expected tension and excitement. At least regular soldiers have everyday military tasks to keep them busy. I sometimes suspect that the army demands all the kit cleaning and weapon maintenance to distract everyone from boredom. Whereas we wretched SOE agents get non-stop boredom mixed with tension, followed by terror.'

'I shouldn't have complained. You must be under terrible strain – whatever it is that you've been asked to do. I hope you won't have to wait too long.'

'Am I allowed to ask you more about your friendship with Labrador? He did the talking last time. I know he said you were just friends, but is that the full story? He must have been *very* determined to see you. It's difficult getting away from SOE Somerville except on training exercises. If anything happens to me, I'd like to go to my grave knowing whether or not I loved in vain. Just tell me the truth – I won't be awkward.'

Both laughed. He'd said his lines with the lightest, smiling touch.

'Everything he said is true. Besides training, he had an extra job. Keeping Somerville under surveillance. They gave him a timber delivery truck. He stole away in it to meet me for a drink, just four times. We arranged them using a dead letter box in the village shop. I did find him attractive and mysterious, though. He smoulders. But do you understand that a girl can find a man attractive without wanting to *be* with him?'

'I love you more than him.'

'I know, Henry. He's not competition. I spend hours in here worrying that my being here will cause problems between you. I think you have to work closely together – trust each other. I beg you, don't let me change things with Labrador.'

'How do I thank you for making that clear?'

'Don't. I should thank you for being patient with me. By the way, I see you differently since arriving here. I feel that we have more in common. Something about the extra danger we've chosen. I never imagined you would volunteer for SOE. By the way, isn't it funny that the Brig turns out to be involved in SOE?'

'He's a deep one. I wouldn't be surprised if he's behind my entire operation. Much of it feels like him.'

'The way every detail is minutely planned? Like when we go on *Shearwater*. And there's always a plan B and a plan C.'

'And the sense of humour. The idea of searchers breaking into the cupboard, going out through the back, on to the fire escape and then down the wrong end of the building.'

'Cecile told me they were given money by London to put up the second fire escape. Had to scour the countryside for an old and rusty one. A new one wouldn't satisfy London. I suspect London also gave them the money to buy the furniture van.'

'The van – that's one of the few things we were allowed to know about in our London briefing.'

'Can you tell me anything about what you're here for?'

'Nothing, except that it's terrible. Violent. If it succeeds, the Germans will be devastated. Not just physical damage. Mental.'

'The Brig again.'

'Just like him. He'd hate the violence, but he'd order it if he had to.'

'What about the Spitfire? Are you sure you can't say more about that? Running out of petrol half way across the Channel seems unlikely. You must have been out at sea for a reason.'

'Honestly, I want to tell you, but I can't until I have seen my CO.'

'Tell me one day.'

'If I can.'

'Henry, please go now. No. I've changed my mind. Not right now. One more thing.'

For Henry, she found it harder to pick her words. She pointed at the bed.

'There... there is where I would like to spend the night with you. In your arms. It would help with the fear and the boredom. I promise that is what I want, but I can't. The fear, the strangeness of this all, has made me more tense than I can explain. And tension just makes it impossible to have... those sort of feelings... It wouldn't be a pleasure for either of us.'

'Some things are worth waiting for.'

He climbed gracefully out of the dormer window.

Labrador wanted to say something to David face to face, but could not. So he wrote it on a large sheet of lined paper and slid it under the door of David's room.

No need to let Leo affect our friendship. Please don't be angry about me meeting her. I needed to talk to someone. Long way from home. Sometimes only a girl will do when it comes to talking!

A reply came back under his door within five minutes.

Agree. We are both kept dangling, foolish to let it change anything.

Labrador's reply:

Zodiac comes first. Did your work at the farmhouse go well? Everything in place?

Yes, everything just as we were told by Fuller. Do you agree? Same at your visit yesterday?

The same.

Both still felt more comfortable writing their thoughts than talking face to face. Next, David wrote:

I've opened the sealed instructions Fuller gave me as we left – the ones about Fireworks. Alerting Bisset to proceed will be simple, a ten-minute bike ride from the farmhouse. He's chosen me to do it. But it means we must separate when the shooting's over. You come back to the auberge and hide. I join you half an hour later.

Then we escape together, taking Leo?

Yes.

So now all we have to do is wait for the BBC broadcast.

Can you stand any more waiting? I can't. I wonder why they are taking their time? Fuller told us we could expect the go-ahead within a couple of days of arriving. It's already been four.

You forget I am looking forward to the shooting. But I am sorry it's harder for you. Now burn this!

David did.

*

The brigadier returned from Somerville by train on Monday morning, after stopping at Woodland House for an hour. MacDonald also noticed a change in him. Maxwell described the situation at the St-Cloud briskly and frankly. MacDonald agreed that David would put Zodiac marginally ahead of Leo, provided all went smoothly, and that Labrador would put the operation well ahead of any other consideration. No need to abort Zodiac. In London, Maxwell went straight from the train to see Major Fuller.

'I'm still in no doubt that we should proceed. I've run through it with MacDonald at SOE Somerville. He's certain that Labrador and David won't let it come between them.'

'I need another 24 hours, Brigadier. This is the biggest decision I've had to make so far at SOE.'

'The longer you postpone, the harder it is for David and Labrador.'

'I promise the BBC broadcast will be latest tomorrow at six – or not at all.'

After Maxwell left, Fuller went to the radio room.

'Message for the Rouen pianist. 'Will Cecile ask the pilot if she considers David in a fit state to proceed? And does Cecile think his friendship with Leo could come between David and his work?"

Cecile knocked on Leo's dormer window.

'Now I understand the *silence* when Labrador and David were introduced to you. You knew David already. A special friendship. But how special? Is he in love with you? Not *impossible?* Why did you not tell me about him? The only man you ever talk about is the RAF pilot with the funny name.'

'Smokey. Yes. We are friends. In fact, he told me about aerial combat – it helped me deal with that ME109.'

'Exciting pillow talk, I am sure, *pilote.*'

'All we did was kiss.' Then, as if pleased to change the subject:

'I've known Henry – I'm sorry, I mean David – since we were children. He wants to marry me. I'm not sure yet.'

'*Tu pauvre.* You poor girl.'

'I feel bad for keeping him waiting. But maybe that's kinder to both of us in the long run.'

'*Très sage. Très mure.*'

'What does that mean?'

'It means you are using your head as well as your heart. You English. So practical. A French girl: she wants to be wanted. Enough. *Marriage. Après,* when the excitement wears off, a lover perhaps – for him and for her. Not perhaps. *Probablement.* Anyway, thank you. You have just told me the reply I must send back to London.'

The German detection car, on a random patrol in the eastern suburbs of Rouen, picked up Cecile's return message. It was too short to pinpoint the sender's location, but it was the first coded radio message intercepted in the area for many months. It set alarm bells ringing not just at the local *Sicherheitsdienst,* but in Paris. Jakob Liedermann reported the incident directly to Obergruppenführer Bieler.

'One coded radio broadcast is enough to suggest terrorist

activity, Herr Ober.'

Bieler was irritated by Liedermann's habit of making self-evident statements without suggesting the necessary action. He saw his junior, before the war a policeman and part-time choir master in the Bavarian mountain village of Oberammergau, as dreamy and soft.

'*So?* What will you *do?*'

'Do you require me to wait for one more transmission, Herr Ober? Then we have a chance of isolating the operator. Or do you wish me to record several more messages so we can attempt to decode?'

Again, the Prussian SS officer was irritated. As usual, Liedermann was bringing him a problem, not a solution. Why do I have to do his thinking?

'You Bavarians. Dreamers. *Bergfolk*. Mountain people. Isolate him, of course, at the next transmission. Isolate the street he's working in by switching off the power. Then search every house. You'll find the radio if you are thorough. Then bring him in. We can get information out of him far quicker than breaking a code – *of course.*'

'Yes, Herr Ober.'

'Have you enough barriers to block every main road in the area?'

'No.'

'I'm sending you two lorry loads. Make sure they are kept at strategic points for rapid deployment. If there's a terrorist incident, no one must leave the area without being interviewed.'

Wir Preussen. Us Prussians. *Wir sind die Manner der Tat.* We are the men of action.

At seven the next evening, David and Labrador turned on the radios in their rooms, tuning to the BBC. In his office on the rue Foch in Paris, Bieler did the same, as did Liedermann in Rouen. Since the first intercepted message, Liedermann had deployed three extra radio vans to patrol the area east of Rouen where the first message had been detected, around the clock. Nothing more had been picked up. The *messages personnels*, in the perfectly modulated voice of the BBC announcer, were more of a provocation than usual.

'Henry's dog is better today.'

'Eduard's father has had a stroke.'

'Brigitte sends her love to Veronique.'

'Martine is coming to tea.'

David switched off his radio and went downstairs to the kitchen where Cecile was helping her father.

'Time for me to meet Georges. Tell him I'll be in the walled garden.'

Half an hour later, Georges arrived at the *auberge*.

'This should be a celebration, Cecile. The end of many months of waiting. Bring a bottle of champagne to the walled garden. But don't let anyone see you.'

As David made his way past the bar and through the dining

area, it was starting to fill with early diners, some of the Luftwaffe personnel from the Carpiquet Airfield, other army officers from the German military headquarters in Caen. He did not look at them. He found Alain admiring rows of onions. They spoke slowly, in French. David had little difficulty in understanding every word.

'Good evening, David.'

'How do you do, Georges. At last we meet. I've been told as little as possible about you, of course. And, I hope, the reverse.'

'Indeed, *bien sûr.*'

'My instructions are simple, as expected, but one thing has changed.'

Bisset looked at him intently, refilled both their glasses, and led David a little further into the walled garden. Both checked once more that they were not being followed.

'Fireworks remains exactly the same, but London has decided to mount another, less dramatic operation nearby, just before yours. Therefore, you must wait until I authorize you to proceed with Fireworks. The sign to proceed is a box of matches handed over by me personally. A very modest joke, don't you think, but still a joke. In case something happens to me, then this box of matches handed over by a substitute will also be authorization to proceed. The time, 5.30 to 6.30 a.m., and the rendezvous, remain the same.'

'Which day?'

'It could be any morning from tomorrow onwards.'

Bisset looked mystified.

'In fact, not any day. Excuse me. It will be tomorrow, the next day, the day after, or the day after, or the day after that, or possibly the day after that. It could happen, in other words, on any of the coming six days.'

Bisset looked no less troubled.

'I know, it seems odd. No way to run an operation. But I assure you, Georges, that everything has been very precisely planned. There is a reason it could be on any one of the coming six mornings, but I am not permitted to explain why. Trust me.'

David knocked on Labrador's door, and was quickly let in. Labrador:

'So, the time has come.'

'But it hasn't. The torture of waiting only *might* be coming to an end. It might go on for six more days. I can't bear the banality. Eight men to be killed in cold blood, and we are bored. It's shocking.'

'I'm a simple soul compared with you. More like an animal. I sleep. I wake. I eat. I do not think about anything much. You keep using that word, banal. I am afraid it describes me.'

The next day, and the day after, there was no bus.

*

'Fuller.'

'Yes, Brigadier.'

'Two nights since the Martine broadcast. Four more to go. How are you dealing with the tension?'

'It's all I can do not to send a radio message.'

'I know. We must resist the temptation. Our reward will be a proper account when they're back at Portsmouth. Could be only six days from now. You're discovering what it's like running agents on a major mission.'

'Dull torture.'

'Indeed.'

*

The third morning passed with no bus. David and Labrador returned separately, as usual, to the *auberge* and went up to their rooms. They both rested until late morning, had coffee downstairs, again separately, then read in their rooms and exercised in the woods. They did not disturb Leo, having both told her that now it was best for them to stay apart, but that their return to England together was days away.

She drew the obvious conclusion. Her only way to deal with the heightened tension was to pace up and down her room, not just some of the time, but most of the day. She was too agitated to sit, or to finish reading *Madame Bovary*. The fourth day passed, still with no bus. The tedium and tension were paralysing. Even

Labrador, alone in his room, was beginning to feel it. To distract himself, he got out the cuff links. He weighed them in his hand. Small, but heavy. They were simple ovals, linked by a gold chain. Plain on the outside, but inside there were tiny markings. Perhaps David would know their meaning. He knocked at the door of room 12.

'Have you looked at the cuff links MacDonald gave us?'

'Yes. Gold. Pure gold – what we call 24 carat. They're generous. I didn't know SOE ran to that kind of thing.'

'I never owned anything like them. After the war I'll have to buy the right sort of shirts. Have you looked on the inside of the oval part? What do the markings mean?'

'We call them assay marks. They say who made them, where, and the quality of the gold. That's odd... There are some extra markings on mine.'

He strained to see them clearly. 'I can see an H. And a D. And a G... and another D. Heavens. Henry Dunning-Green. David. What can you see on yours?'

They compared them. All the assay marks were identical, but Labrador's had, in addition, a J, an A... and an L. The initials were stamped in random order, among the assay marks, as if to avoid them being noticed. Labrador spoke.

'This is the most special thing I have ever had. Whoever ordered them made must have been thinking just of me – and you.'

'Whoever it was needed to say we mattered.'

'Maybe he also wanted to thank us?'

'Maybe he wanted to distract us while we waited? Give us something pleasant to think about?'

'I don't think MacDonald would have done it.'

'No.'

They sat in silence, turning the cuff links over in their hands, enjoying the feel and the weight of the gold. Then, they swapped them.

David took the rifle from its hiding place under the farmhouse kitchen floorboards as Labrador changed into his SD uniform in a bedroom.

'I wonder what the occupants would feel about us being here?'

'Pleased. By letting us use the house, they are serving their country. Fighting the Bosch.'

'I hope they can return soon.'

Labrador crossed the road and hid himself, for the fifth time, behind the screen of undergrowth. David positioned himself at the open bedroom window, curtains partly drawn, and steadied the rifle on the sill.

Then they heard the engine of an approaching bus. David sweated. Labrador was icy. When the bus was 50 yards off, Labrador stepped into the road and waved it down. David whispered to himself, he looks as if he really means business. Not like me.

The driver, used to random road checks, even on minor roads, pulled into the side and started to assemble the paper work for all eight pilots. The SD liked ID papers and permits in a particular order. Labrador gestured for him to get out.

There was the whine of a bullet, a tinkle of glass, and then three more whines and three more tinkles.

Labrador shot the driver in the head with his pistol while the windows were being broken, pulled him to the verge and heaved him into the ditch. Then he crawled at speed back to the driver's door of the bus, while David's rifle punched four neat holes in the temples of the four pilots sitting on the side of the bus nearest him. They lolled, rag dolls.

The four remaining pilots, breathless with shock – their faces, if David could have seen them, a terrible pallor – ducked to the floor of the bus and were crawling to the exit door behind the driver's seat. As they fell out, Labrador cut each of their throats. One tried to scream, but could only gurgle.

David watched unwillingly as the last pilot tumbled out. Labrador treated him differently. He produced a length of wire with wooden handles at each end. He wound the wire round the man's neck, pulled violently, then dragged the body by the wire to the driver's door, where he secured the wooden handles to the steering wheel. David closed his eyes, hoping not to be sick. The man's body jerked, half in, half out of the bus, trying to gain a foothold that would take the pressure off his neck, but already his strength had gone.

As planned, Labrador stayed behind to change back into his civilian clothes, bury his bloodied uniform and replace David's rifle beneath the floorboards. No one appeared to have heard the shots. David had already left on his bicycle, eager to put the scene behind him, negotiating minor roads and lanes in the direction of Carpiquet Airfield – a route he had memorized again and again. He met André in a lane a kilometre from the airfield, and handed him the box of matches. André headed for the airfield and David rode back to the Auberge St-Cloud.

In the back of the van, Bisset was unpacking the explosives from the canisters parachuted in with David and Labrador. Next, he changed into the uniform of an SD airfield guard, made for him in London by Dora Adcock's department. André drew up on his motorbike and handed him the box of matches.

It was around 6.30 a.m., as anticipated, still quiet on the airfield. The guards didn't expect the pilots to arrive for morning duty until about 6.45. Most of the guards were inside their hut, drinking coffee and smoking. Four were left outside, patrolling the hangars, one patrolling the fuel dump.

Bisset let himself into the airfield at the gate nearest the fuel dump with a key copied from a set carried by one of the guards. Getting the key had been the most worrying part of his work. He had had to bribe a cleaner to remove it from a guard's pocket while off duty, take it to the fence and wait while a locksmith, brought there by Bisset, made a wax impression before then replacing the key. The cleaner had got cash for her work and an explanation:

the duplicate key was needed to steal fuel from the dump, for the use of local tradesmen.

Bisset, acting just as the guards did – he had studied them day after day from his van – ambled in no hurry to the fuel storage tanks. Once among them, he taped a plastic explosives charge to each of the six inlet valves. The fuses were set to detonate in eight minutes time.

He strolled away, nodding a friendly but silent hello to the guard who passed, and let himself out at the gate, locking it behind him. Bisset smiled at André, who was in the van's driving seat watching for him. André got out and drove away on his motorbike. It was noisy, probably a hole in the exhaust. *I must tell him to get it mended.* Alain moved leisurely off in the furniture van. The fuel tanks exploded.

16

David got back to the *auberge* soon after 7 a.m. and climbed the stairs, still in disbelief that it had gone so smoothly. He'd heard the noise of the explosions at Carpiquet, three miles distant, and seen black smoke confirming his guess all along that Fireworks was an attack on the airfield's fuel dumps. The humdrum efficiency of his early morning work sat grotesquely with the violence. Now the sound of sirens added to his disturbed mood.

He knocked on Labrador's door. No reply. He went downstairs to ask Cecile for a spare key, and she looked worried as she handed it over. David opened the door of room 11. Everything seemed to be as Labrador had left it. Either he had not got back to the *auberge*, or he had been in and gone out again. Neither theory was comfortable.

He went back down to Cecile.

'I've got to search the lanes for Labrador.'

'Alain has phoned to say that lorries are arriving in Caen stacked with road block barriers. He thinks they may try to block every road leading out of the area. It's odd that they can concentrate so many barriers, so fast. Not expected.'

'In that case, get *la pilote* out of here now, before they block the road between Caen and Avranches. Say goodbye to her from me.'

'We don't want to use the van except for groups. Too many single journeys risk someone noticing.'

'Cecile, please *do it*. If the *auberge* is searched and by chance Leo is found – I know it's unlikely, but we must allow for the worst – then Leo is the hardest to explain. She has no cover story, no papers. She knows far too much. Get her out fast, right now before the road is blocked. Once the van reaches St-Brieuc, let it pause while Labrador and I try to catch up. If we can't, then we'll go all the way to Tréguier by public transport. We have travel permits. Or maybe André will take us one by one on his motorbike.'

News of the fuel dump attack had reached Liedermann in Rouen as David was arriving back at the *auberge*. Liedermann would not learn about the bus for another two hours. He phoned Bieler, who listened in silence, then asked:

'No radio broadcast picked up, before or after?'

'None.'

'Go ahead with the barriers. Block every main road leading

273

out of Caen, in any direction. Stop and search every car. Arrest anyone where there is the slightest ground for suspicion. Lock them up in your prison in Caen and interview them one by one. Isolate prime suspects and then call me. I will come to help you with the second interviews. Also, interview everyone living within half a kilometre of the fuel dumps. Ask them if they saw or heard anything unusual.'

Cecile had the measure of Leo. She knew *la pilote* would not want to leave for England without Labrador and David, so she had her story ready.

'You must leave quickly. Pack the little bag. I will take you to the transport rendezvous.'

'What about Labrador and David?'

'They are going by a different route, for extra safety. There are more police out there than we expected. You heard the bangs? Three people travelling in a group is very hard to explain, especially in the back of a furniture van, when one has no papers.'

'How soon before I link up with Labrador and Henry again?'

'A matter of hours. The van will stop once it's well outside Normandy, inside Brittany. At St-Brieuc. We have friends there. They will call us and we will tell them how and when Labrador and Henry will join you. When they join you, you will continue to Tréguier together – only another hour's drive.'

Cecile ushered Leo quickly down the back fire escape and into the woods, explaining that the van was not in its usual place, and that it was better not to use the bicycles in case Labrador and David needed them. Twenty minutes of brisk walking took them to the furniture van, parked in a lane south of the main road connecting Caen with Avranches, Alain at the wheel.

'Any more news about the barriers?'

'None. Be cautious, Alain. I think you should stay away from the main road, even if it takes longer. Use the small roads all the way to Vire, then take the secondary road to Villedieu. Only then the main road. You'll be well past any barriers at Villedieu.'

'Au revoir *pilote*.' Cecile suddenly realized how much she would miss Leo. Rather than slow the departure with a tearful farewell, she shut the van's rear doors before Leo could say her own.

17

Bieler spat his words. They bored into Liedermann's head.

'*Nie wieder.* Never again.'

'Certainly, Herr Ober.'

'So how will you make that happen?'

'The airfield bus will carry armed guards. Airfield security will be stepped up. The same recommendation has gone to every Luftwaffe base in occupied France, especially the north.'

'Recommendation? It should have been an order. What came of the road blocks?'

'We stopped 120 vehicles in the days following the incidents. Just five couldn't give an alibi straight away, so we arrested them and put them in cells overnight. Then they were interrogated according to your instructions, Herr Ober, under threat of a beating. One we beat anyway. His cries could be heard by all the others waiting in the cells. I know you like us to demonstrate our determination.'

'The result?'

'All of the five confessed they had been with mistresses.'

'Are your men sworn to keep the shootings secret? On pain of labour camp?'

'They know that, Herr Ober... However...'

'What?'

'Leakage may be inevitable. British intelligence in London will announce the success of their operations to the press — not immediately, but as soon as they have full details. You know how quickly such stories travel back to France. The resistance leaks them to the public. That is the purpose of the shootings, is it not? To spread fear among Luftwaffe personnel, and boost the morale of the French?'

'They are not resistance, they are terrorists. But yes, it will get out. Until then, it didn't happen. We don't want to give the terrorists a day's more satisfaction than necessary.'

'The bodies left for Germany yesterday in complete secrecy. The bus has been hidden. When will the Luftwaffe supply replacement pilots? I need to make sure the extra airfield security is in place.'

'Weeks. No point, in any case, until the fuel tanks have been replaced. What other steps are you taking?'

'We are interviewing every householder within a kilometre of the fuel dump, asking them if they heard or saw anything unusual around the time of the explosions. A long job, but at least we have the reward to offer.'

'Yes. 10,000 francs. Generous. Too generous for a conquered people. But you can do more.'

'Sorry, Herr Ober?'

'Reprisals, of course. Why do I have to spell it out? Hang a couple of men. Anyone. Announce that unless someone comes forward with information leading to the arrest of the terrorists, you'll hang two more next week, and the week after. Actually, I think you should hang eight straight away – one for each pilot.'

Liedermann had to gather all his courage. 'That could make our work more difficult.'

'Why?'

'Elsewhere in France, where reprisals have been made, the local people close ranks and refuse to speak at all – even the greedy ones who might have been tempted by the reward.'

'To me that's the sign of a people who haven't been taught to respect their masters. To me, that means harsher reprisals are required.'

Liedermann hoped silence was his best option. Bieler conceded, grudgingly.

'However, we will do it your way for now. I will settle for just two hangings. But remember, I would prefer eight.'

'Very well.' But Bieler was not finished.

'*Auch…*' he raised his voice, yet again, 'Also… I order you to raise the stakes in your householder interviews. Take in one man immediately. Give him a beating. Then call me and I will personally supervise a second interview. With my pliers. He will be released with bloody bandages on his feet. Toe nails are an insignificant body part, but disproportionately useful for concentrating the mind.'

'That will make people clam up completely.'

'Then we'll do it again. Until we get a result.'

Leo's journey to St-Brieuc, in the back of the furniture van, was mostly uneventful. Bisset successfully skirted the single remaining road block on the Avranches road, 20 km west of Caen, rejoining the main road west to Brittany at Villedieu-les-Poelles. The late August sun beat down on the van. Wedged in behind an upright piano and stacks of chairs covered in sheets, Leo was well hidden. To unpack the van, first several heavy, hideous concrete garden statues would have to be removed from just inside the rear doors. Seated in an armchair, she was comfortable enough, but hot and irritable. At one point, the van pulled in to the side of a road, in a town, Leo guessed, because there was traffic noise all around. Then German voices, speaking in poor French:

'What are you carrying?'

'Household items. I am moving house.'

'Open the rear doors.'

Bisset obliged. 'Do you want me to unpack? I'll need some help.' He gestured at the statues. Laziness got the better of the SD officer and Bisset was allowed to continue. A little further along the road, Bisset stopped and told Leo how close they had both come to arrest.

'You stayed quiet, *pilote* – you did well. Keep it that way.' Before she could reply, he had closed the doors and was on his way. Her irritation mounted.

Reaching St-Brieuc, Bisset parked outside his contact's house and went in, leaving Leo locked in the van. As he reached for the door knocker, he heard her banging on the van wall. He went back to the rear doors, checked there were no onlookers and climbed inside, closing them behind him.

'*Pilote*. Did you listen to me just now? Do you want us to be discovered? If a passer-by happened to be a *gendarme*, or an SD officer, we would be finished.'

'Cecile told me there are far fewer Germans in Brittany. I assume we've got to St-Brieuc, yes?'

'Yes. I have to go into my contact's house to make a phone call. For your sake. To get news of David.'

'Can I come too? I'm roasting in here.'

'Sorry. You must stay here. I'll be ten minutes at the most.' He got out and shut the doors without waiting for her answer. Leo's irritation mounted another notch.

'Cecile?' She answered the phone at the second ring and said without preamble, 'David has found no sign of Labrador – of course. He must have left straight after the explosions, before the Germans could react. Planning it all along, I suspect. I think he went into Caen and caught a train to Paris. Wouldn't surprise me if he's on the way to Poland by now.'

'Probably. Do you agree David mustn't leave until all danger of road blocks has gone?'

'*Absolument*. Bad enough to have taken the *pilote* so soon. David must stay another four days, maybe five.'

'What shall I tell *pilote*? She's expecting him to follow tomorrow.'

'You're not used to dealing with women like her. Take it gently. Tell her he's coming tomorrow. Say that there's a possibility of delay, which is out of your control. Give her hope, but give yourself a let out. Don't tell her the truth until she's actually aboard the *Alouette* – with the engine running.'

'David?' Cecile knocked on the door of room 12. 'Leo is safely at St-Brieuc. Only another hour's drive to Tréguier. She's almost free.'

'When can I join her?'

'There are still random road blocks. Alain avoided one this morning, only by using the utmost prudence. We must wait until the Bosch have given up on the blocks entirely. Another four, maybe five days.'

'That means Leo will leave without me.'

'I'm sorry.'

'She won't like it. You know she never takes no for an answer.'

'We know... But trust us, David, this is the safest way. I'm sorry it means more waiting. You've done enough.'

'In that case, will you send a radio message for me?'

He could see her reluctance. 'It's just 20 seconds.' He wrote it down.

'Did you think of asking at Caen station about Labrador?'

'Yes, but I soon gave up. I was worried my questions would arouse suspicions. The place was riddled with SD.'

'I guess he caught the 8.03 to Paris. At that time everyone was still in shock from the explosions. It took them at least another hour before they started questioning people at the station and putting up road blocks.'

'I've checked his room thoroughly. Not just once. He left behind two changes of clothes and his holdall – as if he wanted us to think he was still around, but his papers were missing. And one other item. Something personal. Something he would want to have on him all the time. So yes, he could well have left by train straight after – '

He checked himself, then said it anyway.

'Zodiac.'

Cecile glanced again at the sheet of paper with the radio message.

'Yes, David. Zodiac. I can see that word written here. 'Zodiac 100 per cent successful. Labrador missing."

'I may as well tell you. It'll be public knowledge in Britain and France 48 hours after you've sent that radio message. Zodiac was the operation Labrador and I were sent here to achieve. Separate from sabotage at the airfield. Of course, our orders were not to tell you about Zodiac.'

Cecile held up her hand. 'Don't talk about the airfield. I have my suspicions, and I don't want to know.'

'Quite right.'

'But Zodiac?'

'Labrador and I killed eight Luftwaffe pilots. The entire squadron.'

'How?'

'In their bus on the way to the airfield.'

'*Magnifique.*'

*

Maxwell, Fuller and Vera Adcock assembled in Fuller's office. First, Fuller produced the full radio message received from Rouen the previous night.

'Zodiac 100 per cent successful. Labrador missing. No evidence arrested. Assume returned to Poland. Leo Maxwell on way to England. My return delayed at least a week. Safer to travel at intervals.'

Next he produced aerial photographs of Carpiquet Airfield. Enlargement had made them hard to decipher. 'The experts say they show all six fuel tanks destroyed.' Then, turning to Maxwell:

'You know Labrador personally, I'm told.'

'Yes. I met him when I was setting up the Somerville training schools.'

'Do you believe he preferred to escape to Poland than come back here? Why return to misery? Could he have joined the other side?'

'I'd stake my entire career on his being loyal. He loathes Germans and Germany. And he could get to Poland easily – he has all the papers. As you know, the identity you cooked up for him made it only too easy to go home. Psychologically? Yes, I think so too. Zodiac was only the beginning, as far as he was concerned.'

Dora Adcock spoke next. 'They must both be short of clean clothes. I only gave them three sets.'

Maxwell replied:

'I saw to it that the St-Cloud did their laundry. Even if Labrador travelled in what he stood in, it was clean and respectable.'

'If all goes well for your daughter, she'll be in Portsmouth any day. What's the weather like in the Channel?'

'I'll check.' Maxwell continued, 'When she arrives, she'll have to go straight to her CO at ATA HQ, White Waltham. She has some explaining to do. We won't be able to talk to her for a day or two.'

'Will you do it?'

'I'm not always the best at getting information out of Leo, but I'll try.'

*

As Bisset drove away from St-Brieuc, he could not avoid comparing *la pilote* with Cecile. The English girl announced with every gesture that she was her own mistress. Cecile's demeanour was always neutral, she was almost always biddable. The English girl spoke directly, Cecile in the conditional. 'What if…' 'Supposing…' He knew that when his wife wanted something badly enough, she would eventually get it – but to be manipulated by her was soothing – a gentle massage. Could the English girl do that? *Non.* After the phone call to Cecile in St-Brieuc, he got back into the driver's compartment to hear tapping, once more, on the dividing partition. Gentle tapping at least, not banging.

This time, the girl was using a very different tone of voice. 'Alain, you must be tired of driving. Would you like me to take a turn?'

'This is a heavy machine. You would not enjoy hauling on the wheel.'

'Don't worry about that. Some of the aeroplanes I fly are like tanks. Really, I love driving.'

'I'm sorry, if we get stopped, you have no papers.'

'Well, if I can't drive, may we go for a walk? I need a change of scene. I've been looking at this furniture for hours.'

He shrugged and gave in. It was getting dark and the side streets were quiet. In any case, the girl was right. Germans were scarce. He helped her out of the van.

'We're a strange pair, don't you think?' She slipped her arm through his. 'You're obviously around 50 and I'm just 23. Perhaps we should pretend I'm your mistress?' Bisset checked his pique. He was just 40.

Next, she started talking in French – more or less grammatical

French, but in her thick, Churchillian accent. 'I'm so worried about David. Can you understand that I don't want to leave him behind?'

'David is trained. He can look after himself, and the Auberge St-Cloud is the safest place for him now. He'll follow soon.'

'When?'

'I hope, tomorrow – just as I've always said.'

'Does that mean I will have to wait in Tréguier?'

'The boat leaves in the evening. And we have somewhere for you to stay. A pleasant *auberge* overlooking the harbour.'

'I don't want to leave David behind.'

'Why is he so important to you, *pilote?*'

'There are things I want to say to him. We became friends at the *auberge*. Thrown together. Surely you understand?'

'I'm sorry, if you are asking me to keep you at Tréguier several more days in case David can't come tomorrow – it's most unlikely. Maybe a day or two – we'll decide tomorrow evening. We're fighting a war. Romance comes second.'

He felt Leo stiffen with anger. She withdrew her arm, increased her pace, and strode ahead.

'I don't like the view of your back. Your profile is better.'

'You will put up with whichever view I present.'

They returned to the van in silence, Bisset furious. No woman had ever spoken to him in such a way. But then, she was not like any other woman. He pitied David. Instead of helping her into the van, he stood by with the doors open, then shut it firmly, though without slamming – better not let her know she'd annoyed him that much. Locking the door with a sharp click was enough. But as he drove the final 80 kilometres to Tréguier, Leo felt his displeasure through every lurch of the van's sloppy suspension. He cornered a touch too fast, and applied the brakes a shade more impatiently than necessary. Leo's anger went on building.

When they reached Tréguier, Bisset felt better, but not Leo. It was 11 at night. He got her out of the van and escorted her into a harbourside *auberge*, standing back aloof as she was checked into her room.

'I'll be back at ten tomorrow. Stay in your room til then.'

Before she could speak, he was gone.

*

Cecile knocked at room 12. 'David, please join me, my father, my mother and André for dinner downstairs. A celebration.'

The table was laid in a corner, with a view of most of the other diners. Among them, there were two groups of German officers from Caen and senior airfield personnel from Carpiquet. The atmosphere at their tables was subdued. At the Lamberts' they were cheerful – but not too cheerful. To the casual onlooker they appeared to be a family party, entertaining an honoured guest. David felt deeply uneasy that he was tempting providence by celebrating behind enemy lines. The others found M. Lambert's best dishes and finest wines vicariously enjoyable. To begin, his rabbit pâté; then the *coq au vin*; then *purée des marrons* with whipped cream and the last, raspberries from the kitchen garden. David behaved like a Frenchman. His hosts respected his respect. At the end there was a silent toast to the Englishman. As Cecile got up, she remembered to remind André that his exhaust needed mending.

*

Leo ignored Bisset's instruction to stay in her room. She was wandering the streets of the riverside town at half past eight next morning, irritation still buzzing in her head. She climbed to the top of the little hill on which the town was built, lingering over the view down to the River Jaudy. It brought vivid memories of visits on *Shearwater*. Tréguier was the Brig's favourite Breton port: peaceful, sheltered from most ways the wind could blow, with simple bars and restaurants lining the town quay, and pretty half-timbered houses. 'Only one thing wrong with it,' the Brig had once said. 'It's the birthplace of St Yves. The patron saint of lawyers.'

Now her feelings about the place were tainted with anxiety about leaving Henry behind and suspicions about Bisset's good faith.

At ten she was waiting for him inside the *auberge*.

'There's no sign of the SD or even *gendarmes* in the town today. So you may wander the streets, admire the view. Please meet me again on the quay at six.' He pointed to where the *Alouette* was tied up. 'Your day here won't be a hardship.'

'I know.'

Leo counted the hours. At six, standing beside the *Alouette*, she noticed the crew preparing for sea. *They obviously mean to leave with or without Henry. What's going on?* Bisset approached.

'I just spoke to Cecile again. I am sorry, but there is still a danger of random road blocks. It's not safe to move David yet.'

'Then I have decided to stay here. David gave me cash. I have enough for a few nights. Why, anyway, is the boat being prepared when you promised me no final decision until tonight?'

'You must leave. Without papers you're a danger to everyone. The Bosch will do terrible things to make you talk. We'll all be sent to labour camps. If we're lucky.'

'I would never reveal information under torture.'

'I agree, the Gestapo would find you... Difficult to interview... But I do not choose to take the risk.'

'Risk!' Leo erupted, an incandescent lighthouse broadcasting fury and disapproval. 'I'm prepared to risk myself. Why not you? I didn't ask to be here, yet I accept the danger. You chose to join the resistance. That was brave. Now where's your backbone?'

Several of the crew left their work to watch the exchange. Bisset had to be restrained from pushing her off the quay. Leo was escorted aboard, clearly amused by Bisset's anger. Bisset hissed:

'They've already hanged two young men in reprisal. They say they'll hang two more next week unless someone comes forward with information. Is that risky enough for you?'

Bisset turned his back on her, unhooked the lines securing the boat, threw them aboard and marched towards his van. Leo made her way to the bow of the *Alouette* and stood defiantly aloof as it chugged away from the quay, heading downriver towards the sea.

*

'The hangings haven't helped, Herr Ober. There is defiance everywhere.'

'What about questioning people near the airfield?'

'One result. A woman told us she'd heard a noisy motorbike soon after the blasts. Heard, but didn't see.'

'Find every local motorbike owner.'

Over the next 48 hours, Liedermann did as he was ordered. One by one, every motorcycle licence holder in the area was traced through the regional licensing office in Rouen. Some were brought to Liedermann's office and pressed for alibis. The rest received a visit at home from the SD, including the Lamberts at the Auberge St-Cloud.

The motorbike André used was licensed in his father's name. Questioned by the SD, Monsieur Lambert could produce four members of his kitchen staff and details of several overnight guests who had seen him at breakfast between seven and eight on the morning of the explosions. The SD officer then asked to hear the bike's engine running. Lambert went outside with the officer to kick-start it.

André had collected it from the mechanic that morning, fitted with a new exhaust.

18

The *Alouette's* passage down the River Jaudy was deceptively peaceful. Lush, gently sloping land rose each side. It was almost as sheltered as the upper reaches of the Somer River. They passed the oyster beds and the Corne lighthouse, where the river widened into its estuary and merged with the sea, and a shingle spit where she saw small white sea birds diving energetically into the water, emerging with small fry in their beaks. She'd noticed the same birds on the Somer River, and they made her feel connected with home. The Brig would know their name, probably their Latin name too. Perhaps they're an omen: *maybe, at last, I really am going home.* The superstition was short lived.

As soon as the fishing boat was over the river bar, she started to buck. A moderate, but steep swell was driving in from the south-west, the hangover of a storm in the Bay of Biscay. Sickly yellow light leaked in at the horizon under an otherwise grey dome of sky. The grey-green sea frowned, turning close to black where fresher and fresher gusts of breeze sent the ruffles racing. Leo stuck to her rollercoaster perch on the prow until long after it was safe, then made her way astern along a leaping, crashing deck, without a stumble, to the relative safety of the central cockpit.

She stood watching the boat's progress, and the Captain and crew's handling of her for 20 minutes. When the mounting blasts of spray had thoroughly soaked her, she went into the wheelhouse. She studied the chart on the table, and checked tide times in the nautical almanac. The skipper was frozen to his wheel, wrestling to hold a straight course, unable to think about anything else, disabled by panicky fear that his engine was too feeble to hold the boat straight, muttering that he never had, never would again, venture out in such conditions. Every sixth or seventh wave crashing into the port side knocked the *Alouette* completely off course. The engine screamed as it fought to push the boat back on course again – when the stern lifted clear of the water, the propeller bit on foam and air, racing hysterically. The crew, one by one went off duty, miserable with sea sickness, taking turns to retch over the guardrail. Leo went to the wheel and spoke quietly to the Captain.

'If we go on making leeway like this we'll hit Les Casquets.'

'Leeway, *Mademoiselle?*'

Leo tried to explain leeway in schoolgirl French, this time with her best accent. 'The effect of wind, waves and tide hitting a boat broadside. We go forwards a little, but also sideways – faster than we go forwards.'

He understood. 'Ah yes, *Mademoiselle*. I fear it too. Once past Guernsey we get Les Casquets. I fear them beyond everything. Not just one rock. A whole village of shallows and rocks. They mince much bigger boats than ours. *Horrifique*. Can you manage the wheel for a few moments? I will calculate.'

While Leo took the wheel he used the chart and tide tables and plotter to project the boat's passage forwards. It showed they would pass well to the west of Jersey, the southernmost Channel Island, then close, but not too close to Guernsey. Corrected for the extra tide – as much as six knots near the Casquets – their line went straight for the Casquets, 13 km west of Alderney.

He took the wheel from Leo and turned the boat south-west, straight into the gale. 'Pray that the engine keeps us stationary.'

'I doubt it, while the tide is against us, but let's try.'

Leo turned to face the land, and located the Corne lighthouse. She lined it up against a church tower, further inland, and watched. Minute by minute, a gap widened between them, proving that over the sea-bed the boat was still travelling north-east, on course for the Casquets.

'Is there a sail?' She pointed at the boat's mast and boom. 'A small one for steadying the boat under power?'

'Yes, but we haven't used it for years. We've never been out in these conditions.'

While Leo took the wheel again he staggered below, returning with a dirty brown folded sheet. Stopping every other minute to regain their balance, or to be sick overboard, the Captain and a couple of crew manhandled the sail into place, threading it into a groove on the gaff and tying it to the boom with reefing lines. Finally, they hoisted the sail by heaving on a halyard that drew the gaff up the mast.

Leo held the boat accurately head to wind while they hoisted. The sail flapped violently, threatening to tear. The moment it was up, she edged the boat gently away from the wind, letting the sail fill until it set, half out. The boat heeled, digging into the water. She sensed the force of the water biting on the rudder transmit to the wheel, held it fast and waited. The boat wallowed less now, and started to drive slowly forwards.

She turned again to the land and searched for the lighthouse and the church tower in the remnants of the light. After another ten minutes of sailing just west of north they were still in line. She glanced at the compass, noted the bearing and said to the Captain, now as sick as any of the crew:

'I think we can clear the Casquets now.'

He looked at her as if he did not care whether they hit the rocks or not, slumping incapable in a corner of the wheelhouse. Leo carried on at the wheel, granite faced. Now, unwillingly, she recognized that she'd behaved badly on the quay. She should not have taunted Alain. Her obsession about going home with Henry had ruled everything. Two innocent men hanged. It looked different now. *If I'd known, I wouldn't have said those things.*

The *Alouette* staggered on. Leo could feel her making headway, but could not tell how much. As darkness closed in she felt escalating fear take hold of her as it had while being chased by the ME109. Her world narrowed to a feeble circle of illumination cast by the masthead light. Inside its 20-yard radius, black water was punctuated by seething white water crashing into the hull. Then there was a twilight zone of grey and dirty white. Beyond that, blackness. The fear of a monster wave, unseen in the blackness, all but crippled her. She clung to the wheel. Obsessions. Traps. Obsessed with flying. With hurting Germans. With my feeling that Henry might not be exactly right. What's so bad about not exactly right? Why not be grateful for more or less right?

Out to starboard, she fancied she could hear increased sea noise. Was it the sigh and roar of swells breaking over the Casquets? Was it her imagination? Had the Captain calculated the bearing with enough allowance for tide? She thought she had counted off the lighthouses on Jersey and Guernsey, and that the light flashing ahead and to her right was the Casquets lighthouse, but now she couldn't trust her memory. In any case, seeing the Casquets lighthouse was not enough. She needed to know how far off it was, and without help from the Captain, there was no way to estimate its range. Not knowing was another order of fear, new to Leo, even after the dogfight: it was terror.

She clung harder to the wheel, trying to believe in the course calculated by the Captain. She was paralysed, waiting second by second for the violence of the bang of the hull on a reef.

At around 5 a.m., the blackness in the east grew less, then paler in maddeningly slow stages. Eventually the sun rose over a depressed and fitful seascape. She looked more or less due east and saw the black hulk of the Cap de la Hague, the north-west cape of the Cherbourg Peninsula, backlit by the rising sun. They had cleared the Casquets.

An hour after dawn, the wind eased a little. In calmer water the boat was almost pleasant to handle.

'*Capitaine*. Please get up, even if you are unwell. How far from Cap de la Hague is the rendezvous?'

'Ten kilometres. Due north.'

An hour and a half later, in moderate wind and watery sunlight, Leo asked the Captain to take down the sail and fire a distress rocket. After a minute, an answering rocket shedded red smoke ahead of them.

In 20 minutes, the *Alouette* was alongside the MTB, and Leo went aboard. The crews of both boats saw a sober young woman clamber up the ladder, resisting offers of help and asking politely if they would understand if she did not talk, but went straight below.

From Portsmouth Leo went to Maidenhead by train via London, pausing in the city to leave a message for her father at The Cavalry Club – he'd never given her his office number – and, from a public phone box, to call Margot Grey's secretary to request an urgent appointment.

'Call again from Maidenhead. We'll send the car.'

White Waltham Airfield, a vast grassy expanse with no runways had been home to a flying club before the war. Leo walked past the bar and sitting room with its wicker chairs to her CO's office and sat outside waiting for the summons.

*

'Liedermann?'

'*Jawohl*, Herr Ober.'

'Take down the barriers. The terrorists must be gone by now.'

'May we also stop calling on householders near Carpiquet?'

'I suppose so. Instead, send out random patrols for anyone on a motorbike. Especially a noisy one. A motorbike with a rider and a passenger.'

*

At the Auberge St-Cloud, the Lamberts, Cecile and André were still shattered by the near catastrophe of the SD's visit.

'David, they're taking the barriers down, I think for good. Tomorrow or the next day André will take you to Tréguier on the motorbike. It's a long way – nearly 200 kilometres – but you can break it at the safe house in St-Brieuc.'

*

Margot Grey was neutral, deadpan, grave. Leo, expected to stand throughout, was too proud to mention that she'd had no sleep.

'You may as well tell me the whole story, Maxwell. I don't believe the version your father gave me. If you were being chased – and I accept that's possible – why not stay circling in cloud? Or above cloud? Or fly off close to the sea, parallel to the land? Even chance a landing at Hurn for that matter. You were very close.'

So Leo told her everything. She didn't feel shame or guilt, so why hide anything? Her account was fluent, accurate, undramatic. She sensed the older woman would only respond to the plain facts.

'Admirably described. But problematic. You should understand that a missing aircraft means a full accident enquiry. Your fate will not just be in my hands. There will be an RAF officer, a civil servant from the Air Ministry and an ATA officer.'

'I understand.'

'As for the dog fight, I don't blame you.' Still the deadpan face. 'Most of us would – I hope most of us would – have been capable of the same. But I have to run an organization. I can't let pilots think that I make exceptions, because that may encourage others to do as you did. Perhaps even to compete. Until we've decided how to handle it, you'll discuss the incident with no one. If you do, I'll dismiss you from the ATA without notice.'

Leo nodded mechanically, suppressing her urge to argue. She minded most that the interview had taken 15 minutes of her CO's time. In the last four weeks she had lived her life three times over.

'Meanwhile, stay in your lodgings until the enquiry is complete. It will take ten days. I've arranged for an air taxi to take you back to Hatfield.'

The cottage was as she had left it. Diana, Chile and a new girl replacing Daisy were out ferrying aircraft. Leo went straight to bed, not bothering to open a letter addressed 'Leo Maxwell' by hand propped on the kitchen sideboard. The handwriting was Smokey's.

*

There were no goodbyes at the Auberge St-Cloud, but instead another compliment for David: breakfast with M. Lambert and his wife, served by Cecile. It was strictly small talk, dominated by the chef's complaints about restricted wartime ingredients, and the cost of black market provisions.

'*Au revoir,*' murmured David. 'Thank you for your hospitality.' Perfect French. Then, in a whisper. 'I'll return after the war.'

Lambert spoke as quietly, close to David's ear. 'We salute your inner strength.' Then strode back into the kitchen.

From the women, a kiss on each cheek, then on to the back of the motorbike, engine running, at the front door. They sped through the lanes south of the main road west to Avranches, joining it east of Vire. As they turned on to the main road, André spotted an SD patrol car, a motorbike and two officers 50 yards ahead. They looked as if they had stopped a motorist for questioning.

Without thinking, and before David could tell him to carry on as if they had no fear of the SD, André turned the bike round and sped back down the approach lane, away from the main road. One of the SD officers noticed. He left a colleague to finish questioning the motorist and motioned another to join him. They mounted his motorbike, and followed.

*

After breakfast the next day, Leo opened Smokey's letter. Chile and the others had been mystified, and a little upset, at Leo's scant account of her adventures in France, and her disinterest in opening the letter. It explained that in her absence he'd been posted to the Far East. That he'd discovered, despite efforts 'at the ATA's highest level,' no information about how she had disappeared. 'All I know is you're missing. Therefore, I refuse to give up hope.' That he'd wished, every living hour, that she'd be home before he had to leave.

However, most of it was about Smokey: his belief that his latest promotion was no less than his due; his impatience to get to grips with the enemy in a new theatre of war; his belief in his leadership qualities. The swagger in his tone sat uneasily with Leo.

*

André accelerated down the lane. David clung tightly to the seat with the fingers of both hands and braced his legs on the foot supports, glancing behind every few seconds. The Germans' bike had just appeared at the far end of the lane – perhaps half a kilometre behind. Ahead were a series of tight bends. André threaded them faster than was safe. The bike heeled crazily. Driver and passenger leant into the turn to compensate. Next, the road was straight, through open fields. Ahead was a patch of woodland.

When David next looked behind he saw that their follower hadn't gained.

'In the woodland, stop the bike and run away. I'll continue on my own. Faster with just one.'

'No, I'll stay.'

'I insist. If you are taken, you'll lead the Germans to the *auberge*. Anyway, it's faster with just one of us on this machine.'

André stopped the bike and evaporated into the woods. David tore away. As he left the woods, he saw in his mirror that the German had closed in on him. In minutes a village came up ahead. David roared through, as fast as he dared. Past it, he twisted the throttle again to its maximum, but the Germans were still behind, and gaining.

In his mirror he saw the German pillion rider raise his right hand to aim his pistol. The noise of the machines muffled its crack. David felt pain in his right thigh, and slowed reflexively. Now the Germans were yards from him, the gunman raising his pistol once more. David stopped his bike and lifted both hands.

'A wise move, my friend.'

The German parked his bike and ordered his passenger to ride it away. He strode over to David, put his pistol to the back of David's head, and mounted David's rear passenger seat, steadying himself with the other hand.

'Go. *Allez*. Follow my instructions and you might survive.'

David rode off slowly, wondering how long he could bear the pain in his thigh. He felt his shoe fill with sticky wetness and his trouser leg clammily warm with blood.

'Continue to Vire. We will arrest you formally at the *gendarmerie*. You have questions to answer.'

On the outskirts of Vire, without warning, David accelerated violently and swerved the bike wildly across the road. The German's pistol hand moved automatically down to the seat to give himself extra support against the sudden G force threatening to tear him off his perch. Henry elbowed backwards with all his strength into the German's other arm and kicked with his good leg at the German's shin. His synchronised blows dislodged the passenger, who flew through the air, landing yards from the bike. Winded, he was moaning, unable to move.

David's swerve had been too sharp. Rider and bike crashed to the road, David rolling clear, standing up and, to his surprise, able to limp. Another shot rang out. David felt a sledgehammer blow to his back, but was astonished to find he could still walk. He turned. The German had managed to stand. Now he was advancing. David took his pistol from his pocket and aimed with both hands at the German's right leg. The German screamed, fell, and rolled from side to side clutching his leg.

David dragged himself off as fast as he was able, turning down a side street, and then another and then another, then banging on a door when he could bear no more pain. Eventually, it was opened by an elderly woman. She took in the young man and the pool of blood gathering at his feet and motioned him inside.

'Can you find a doctor?'

'There's one five doors along.'

In another half hour, David was installed in the doctor's top-floor bedroom, all traces of blood removed from doorsteps and road by the elderly woman and the doctor's wife. There was no sign of anyone following – yet.

The doctor laboured over David, hands shaking, more disturbed by the minute because the moaning, shaking young man was too overcome with pain to provide information about his followers or the likelihood of being traced. There was a neat entry wound in the left of his back. No evidence of smashed ribcage bones. And a neat exit wound in the chest, implying the bullet had passed above the left lung, missing the heart and major blood vessels. Lucky. No need to extract a bullet, but there must be damage and risk of infection. The leg was simpler: a deep score of a wound in the muscle, but near the surface. It was bleeding less now and after 15 minutes of gentle pressure the bleeding stopped. With his wife's help, the doctor bandaged the wound very tightly, then returned to the back and chest.

Disinfectant, a pad of gauze and plaster was all he could do. David heard the doctor tut-tutting, then moving away. He returned with a syringe. The morphine took less than five minutes to work. With the pain in his leg and chest easing magically, David surveyed the doctor and his wife's anxious faces.

'This is hard for you.'

'Yes. We have no idea who you are. We don't want to know. But we fear that before long the SD will knock on the door of every house in the street. They will search our house, and when they find you, all of us – me, my wife, my children – will be taken for questioning. Beatings. Torture. Labour camp. Execution. They happen here every week. We're sorry for you, but you're not welcome.'

'I understand. But please do one thing. Search the streets for drops of my blood. Clean it up completely. Then go to the motorbike. Have someone take it away and hide it.'

David explained its location, then they left, locking the door behind them. Downstairs, they conferred in whispers, as if the police might be listening at the door.

'The bullet in his back went close to a lung. Unless he gets hospital treatment, chances are he'll die slowly from internal bleeding.'

'And we'll be left with the body.'

'All deaths have to be registered before burial. There'll be an investigation.'

They ate supper in silence and later climbed back up to David's room. He was moaning and muttering again.

'As I thought. The morphine relieved the pain for an hour or two. No longer.'

At two in the morning, after lying awake beside his wife, the doctor went back to check David's condition.

'He's much worse. His breathing's very shallow. I think he will die in the night.'

But he didn't. He floated through the hours on a raft of pain and confusion, thinking in turn of Leo and an imaginary sailing race on the Somer River – Leo and he in the same boat, swapping between helm and jib. It helped to take his mind off the feeling that suffocation lurked with every breath, that it would overtake him if he stopped even for a second trying to beat it.

He survived that night, but the next day grew worse. In the evening, the doctor told his wife that he had no chance of surviving another night. 'Swelling, bleeding, fluid, damage to the heart and lungs by protracted shallow breathing – they will kill him soon.'

'Then let him die here. We can get rid of the body. No need to report it.'

'How?'

'Sacks. We have them in the garden shed. Fetch three. I will cut the ends and sew them together to make a tube. Those old bricks in the garden – they will go inside. Enough to sink the body bag in the river.'

The next morning, the doctor entered Henry's room. Henry was half lying, half sitting. 'Give me water. Please.'

'Extraordinary. We thought you would die in the night. Someone is smiling down on you.'

'My breathing is easier.'

'You are a lucky man. So are my wife and I. If you had died in the house we'd have been arrested. We were making plans to sink your body in the river. Look.'

He showed David the body bag.

'Could you make a call for me?'

'Where to?'

'The Auberge St-Cloud at Verson. Ask for Cecile.'

'What do I say?'

'That David is alive and free. Tell her to pass it on to Baker Street.'

'So you're a spy? Your code name is David?'

'I can admit that much.'

'Is that all I tell this woman, Cecile?'

'Yes. Radio messages have to be short.'

*

Leo was back in her CO's office. She read conflicting messages in Margot Grey's face.

'First, Maxwell, bad news. But perhaps not that bad. You were found responsible for putting a Spitfire temporarily out of service but not for the loss of an aircraft.'

Leo stayed silent.

'You won't be dismissed, or even grounded. But because of a previous incident – the Walrus – you must do some retraining. Until complete, you're only cleared to fly groups three and two – not group one. No Spitfires. I know it makes no sense – you know as much about flying a Spitfire as any of us. But be thankful. We can have you back flying all groups in three weeks.'

'Thank you. I suppose I'm lucky.'

'You are. But there's a condition. You continue *never* to speak of the dogfight. If it gets out, for whatever reason, even if by an innocent slip of the tongue, you'll leave the ATA for good.'

'Very well.'

'And now for something less gloomy. If I understand correctly, it may take a weight off your mind. A radio message – sent to London from France. Are you with me? Your father rang me. He asked me to pass on the message to you – on the condition you tell no one.'

'Please tell me quickly, I can't wait.'

'It's very short, but even so I'm going to write it down for you. Your father told me you might prefer it that way. That you might want to absorb the information in your own time.'

She handed over a slip of paper. *David is alive and free.*

Back in the cottage, Leo let herself be overwhelmed with relief that Henry was still alive, then felt tensely impatient for more news. At last she admitted to herself that since she'd left the St-Cloud, he had occupied more of her thoughts than Smokey. Flying, Smokey, Labrador: all three, things of the moment, taking more than their fair share. Crowding out Henry. Doesn't mean he's any less of a man. Still in France, alive and free. That means he's had an ordeal...

*

Maxwell and Fuller were in Baker Street, trying to complete the picture.

'Labrador vanished and assumed back in Poland. The killings at the farmhouse just the start of his crusade of vengeance. It's not surprising: we kept him too long at Somerville. He must feel a need to catch up on lost time.'

'Zodiac 100 per cent successful. That must mean all eight pilots executed.'

'And that David was probably safe when that message was sent.'

'And that Fireworks went up according to plan.'

'Then we have Leo coming home first, without David. What do you make of that?'

'She was the wild card. No papers. They were desperate to get her out – even if it was risky just after the operations.'

'Safest to keep David behind until SD activity died down.'

'Next we have Leo back in England, telling us she heard from Bisset that there were two reprisals and the threat of more.'

'Did she give you any idea of Bisset's morale? Is he fired up by his success? Keen to do more?'

'She was evasive. I think she might have had an argument with him.'

An awkward silence. Fuller sometimes felt Maxwell's presence as a mild irritation, despite his ideas being so good, his work so thorough. But to have things complicated by his bloody-minded daughter...

'And now there's the latest radio message. David alive and free. Implies he was caught, then escaped. Perhaps that he was injured, but recovered. Which means the SD or the Gestapo were on to him. Injured, but not tortured. Hard to escape if you've been tortured. My guess is that he was in a chase. Got shot at, was injured, then recovered. He's probably being sheltered somewhere. Let's hope that the Auberge St-Cloud isn't compromised.'

'Your daughter has to sit here and wait for him to turn up – assuming she cares. And he's a marked man.'

'She's been through worse.' Fuller caught in Maxwell's tone, drier than dry, a distinct injunction on going any further.

'Any hint that Leo learned about Zodiac?'

'No.'

'So if we release the story now, we can reckon on complete surprise.'

'Let's do it. Might make the Germans think everyone is away safely – and stop the search for David.'

'Or the reverse. But yes, the propaganda comes first. If we delay any longer, Downing Street will start telling us our job.'

*

'So your men lost the motorcyclists? Even when one of them was wounded? *Cretins.*'

'It is perhaps difficult for you to understand, in Paris, the hatred in Normandy for the German security services. No one in the neighbourhood of the motorcycle crash would say anything about it. We do not have the men to search all 50 houses in the neighbouring streets.'

'At least you must have the motorbike's registration number?'

'The officer who was thrown off the back was too stunned to think of such a thing. Of course, some of the witnesses might have noticed it. But would they remember it when asked?'

'What's become of the motorbike?'

'By the time our officer had been removed, and a truck sent to recover it, it was gone. At the bottom of the nearest river, I suppose.'

'And now we are taunted daily in Caen?'

'Yes. Cars drive around hooting eight times. Eight crosses on dirty windscreens. Eight crosses on any German language poster or official notice.'

'Senior Luftwaffe officers call me daily from every airfield between here and Calais. They tell me the pilots are living on their nerves. They have to cope, not just with waiting for combat but fear of being murdered in cold blood. On or off duty.'

'Devastating, Herr Ober. But the damage has been done. I hope you decide that further reprisals are pointless. It will make my work here easier. By the way, there's been one more radio message.

So short it could hardly be detected.'

19

David took three weeks to regain enough strength to travel. The doctor and his wife shared the danger of his presence with their neighbours, moving him from house to house at night. The doctor looked very happy indeed when David finally asked if he could use the phone.

'Cecile. It's David.'

David... Merveilleux. You sound strong again. The doctor told us he thought you would die.'

'How soon can you send the van? I'm sorry that it has to be the van – I'm sure you don't want it to go to Tréguier yet again, but the motorbike can't be used any more.'

'Of course we will use the van. You saved André, and you saved St-Cloud. How could we not send the van?'

'Come by daylight. As if it's a normal removals job. I've asked the doctor to let Alain take furniture from his house to make it look authentic. He will deliver it back later.'

As David stepped into the van, the doctor and his wife presented him with the sacking body bag, rolled up, tied with string.

The morning after the next, David was stepping ashore at Portsmouth. The sea had been calm, the MTB crew jovial and welcoming. He caught a train to Victoria and a taxi to Orchard Court. Park answered the door as if he had been away for a couple of hours.

'David, sir. A pleasure to see you again.'

'I need a few hours sleep. Please tell Fuller I'll be ready to talk this evening.'

As soon as Maxwell heard that Henry was back, he planned a welcome party at The Rectory for the following Saturday. His first call was to Margot Grey.

'Could you allow Leo special leave? Her old friend – the one I mentioned – has got back from France. He's had a remarkable escape. I know she'll want to welcome him home. Could you spare her Friday, Saturday and Sunday?'

That afternoon, after a gruelling day delivering a Hudson bomber to RAF Holbeach in Lincolnshire, Leo was back in the crew room at Hatfield Ferry Pool. Slumped in an armchair, she picked up a newspaper. It was three days old, but she scanned the front page all the same.

Success of daring SOE operation in Normandy

Details are emerging of a remarkable operation in occupied France. Codenamed Zodiac, it took place at Carpiquet Airfield on the outskirts of Caen.

A small team of SOE agents flagged down a bus taking eight Luftwaffe pilots to work in the early morning at Carpiquet Airfield, where a squadron of ME109s is stationed.

All eight were executed. Soon after, local French resistance agents blew up the fuel tanks at the airfield.

The ME109 squadron at Carpiquet is no longer operational and the airfield will be unusable for many months.

Two British agents are still in Normandy, but understood to be safe.

Heads turned as she exclaimed: '*Henry*. It was *you*. And Labrador.'

At home in the cottage there was a message to ring her father at The Cavalry Club.

'Brig. I've just read the paper – three days old. Carpiquet. It must have been Henry and Labrador. Please don't tell me you can't comment.'

'It was. I can. And now, are you sitting down? David has returned.'

She was silent. He thought he could sense her struggling with her feelings. In a few seconds a shaky voice asked:

'He's in one piece?'

'Very much so.'

'What about Labrador?'

'Vanished. We think he's gone back to Poland.'

'I could have told you that.'

'Henry's been debriefed, so I can tell you as much as you like.'

'Go *on* Brig. Spill it out… None of your dreadful pauses.'

Maxwell, as careful as ever to give Leo no clue that he worked for the Service, told her that he'd learnt Henry's story from his old friend Jeremy Gunn, head of SOE, after running into him at The Cavalry Club. Now that the operation was complete, successful and public, Gunn had been happy to give his fellow officer the inside story.

The Brig's account was as lucid and economical as Leo could have wished. Understated, of course, but for once her father's dryness did not irritate her. The facts were enough. 'He saved André and the Auberge St-Cloud by insisting André escaped. Then he endured the ride with a pistol at the back of his head, blood pouring from his leg. Then he had the presence of mind to gamble everything on throwing his passenger off the bike. Next, he didn't murder the SD officer in cold blood when he could have, so easily. Instead he immobilized him, despite the shot in his own back.'

Maxwell finished with Henry's near-death experience, lying unwelcome in the doctor's house. Finally, the body bag, which

Henry had handed over to Maxwell and Fuller as a souvenir.

'He didn't want it – said it held bad memories. We spent hours getting the full story out of him. He was loathe to say anything that made him look like a hero.'

'Which he is.'

'Indeed, Leo. The unassuming hero. Quite a man.'

They were silent.

'Would you like to join a small party at The Rectory to welcome him back? Saturday?'

Many a father would have connived to make it a surprise party, Leo reckoned, but not the Brig. He wanted her to absorb the news in her own time. For her to be in charge of herself when she saw Henry again.

'I'm not sure if I'll get leave.'

'I've already asked Margot Grey. She understands.'

'Brig, you've been scheming again.'

'I'm sorry. But this is special.'

The small party that gathered for dinner at The Rectory that Saturday at the end of September 1941 included Geoffrey and Alice Dunning-Green; Emily and Charles Maxwell; Leo and Henry; the Brig – and Portia. Now that Hodge had gone, Sir Geoffrey was considered the most insensitive man in Somerville, but her presence made even his very short antennae twitch.

Maxwell had debated whether to ask the Selby-Pickforths.

Including them would have been a useful way of thanking Pat for her loyalty during the bad times leading up to the AGM, but in the end he left them out. They got on with Alice Dunning-Green – everyone did – but were no good with Sir Geoffrey. In his company, Pat usually managed to refer obliquely to Sir Geoffrey's lack of a reputable family tree by mentioning someone else's. Sir Reggie, who'd earned his title as a reward for decades of honest service on a modest salary at the Home Office, was not above alluding to the fact that Sir Geoffrey had purchased his.

Maxwell relished briefing his guests in advance about the reason for the gathering. He told them of Henry's experiences even more drily than he had for Leo, which made the story seem all the more remarkable. Alice had been overcome: through sobs she had told the Brig she needed to put the phone down and ring back later. Each was told that a condition of coming to dinner was – strictly – not to mention Normandy. 'As if it had never happened. Henry and Leo would hate any fuss.'

Of Leo's story he told Leo's censored version – that she had been chased by an ME109 across the Channel and forced to land in Northern France. Exciting enough for Somerville. That she had sheltered in the same safe house as Henry. Again, exciting enough for Somerville. It set not only Alice's mind racing with questions, and hopes. So Leo and Henry were fêted, and warmly – though not physically – embraced, as if for no particular reason.

'Very Maxwellian.' Portia whispered to Alice. 'Charming, though.'

'True. He thrives on people having to read between the lines.'

After dinner, the men went to the drawing room and the ladies upstairs. Henry slipped away, refusing a cigar, saying he wanted to see the river again after so long. 'I'll be back.' When Leo came downstairs, she noticed that Henry had gone. Maxwell watched her closely while keeping up a conversation with Portia.

'I need some air – a stroll down to the river. Haven't seen it for ages.'

Not a glance.

Henry was at the end of the jetty, experiencing something new that he would later describe to Leo as an 'extraordinary nowness.'

A sense crept over him as he pondered the river of being profoundly, deeply in the moment. He was one with the river, as soothing as ever, brimming full with the last minutes of a spring tide. One with the clear sky, vibrating with starlight. One with the hoot of an owl. He felt an unfamiliar sense of lightness. That he was not only at one with all these things, but that he actually was them, and that it was always meant to be so.

Better still, his life's obsession was as strong as ever, but mercifully no longer in absolute command. *Leo matters, but then so does everything else. If we can be together, then so be it. If not, awful, but so be it too.*

Leo had tiptoed up behind him. It was only as she came within three feet that he sensed her – he didn't have to turn – he knew who it was. But he did turn.

'Yes.'

20

1945 – Epilogue

Alain Bisset and Cecile stopped resistance activities for good after Zodiac and Fireworks. Cecile had had twins: the danger wouldn't be fair to them. However, days after the Normandy landings in 1944, the Auberge St-Cloud was a hub of warfare once again as a temporary command post for Henry's regiment, The Rifle Brigade.

After Zodiac, Henry was posted back to his regiment and served in North Africa and at the Normandy landings. He never again had to cope with such danger, tension and boredom as he had at the St-Cloud, but Labrador left an aching gap, softened only by his cautious longing for the day when Leo and he would be together for good. He ended the war a very young Lt Colonel.

Leo carried on flying until the day the ATA was disbanded in 1945, vowing like her friends to be back in the air as soon as they could find civilian flying work.

M. and Mme Lambert retired from running the *auberge* in 1945, leaving it to Cecile and André. André met a simple local girl, married her and lived happily with her in the St-Cloud under the eye of Cecile.

Adrian Russell's career as a traitor blossomed. He passed countless British and US secrets to Moscow, and indirectly sent dozens, if not hundreds, of British and American agents to their deaths. By the end of his career, he had everyone fooled – MI6, the CIA, even his handlers in Moscow – one of whom would describe him as an aristocrat among spies. He was eventually exposed in 1962, when he defected to Moscow.

Kenneth Hodge was never seen in Somerville again, and never seriously mentioned. Word was that he'd been reduced, after his divorce from Phyllida and a downturn in his legal work (competition from the post-war crop of hungry, younger lawyers), to looking for a wealthy elder woman.

The effects of Russell's mischief, realized by Hodge, his greedy puppet, survived them in ways they hadn't intended.

The Brig really had changed – had been changed – by the wounds of autumn and winter of 1940-41. The crippling anxiety of the undetectable fifth columnist; being a victim, then an exile; the humiliation as everyone stared at their plates during his toast – all of these, combined with the divorce, had made a new Brig.

His drawl rarely surfaced now, and his manner was almost always engaging and direct. Before the war, Somerville had respected him but found him hard to know. Now he was respected and liked by most. Those who enjoyed his ultra-dry humour even thought he could be good company.

Exactly how much this enhanced his relationship with Portia was hard to gauge, as both were still the most private of people. But together they radiated harmony out into their community. Patricia Selby-Pickforth fancied that Somerville might become a unique survival in the post-war world of gentlemanly values and manners – perhaps even chivalry. Adrian Russell and his Moscow handlers, had they been interested, had they known, would have been confused and irritated at how happy Somerville was to change slowly, a little behind the times.

Maxwell and Portia married soon after D-Day, in July 1944. It was the quietest wedding anyone could remember. The local Roman Catholic church was little more than a tin hut, so the guests were family only. A reception was postponed until after the war. They didn't have a honeymoon. The Brig moved into Portia's house and gave The Rectory to Charles, also just married, as was his sister Emily. The Brig and Portia never moved into the Castle.

In 1945, Maxwell retired from MI6 and devoted himself to helping Portia run the Somerville Estate, offering her his investment portfolio as a partial guarantee for the estate's bank borrowing. Portia was astonished at his wealth. Maxwell made the arrangement conditional on her never telling anyone about the guarantee, or how much money he had inherited from his father and elder brother, Edward, who had died childless. Portia paid off the estate's debts over the next 15 years by expanding the river's appeal to visiting yachtsmen – without spoiling it – and by charging higher prices for moorings. No one in the community except Portia, Leo and Henry ever suspected Maxwell's involvement with SOE Somerville or wartime intelligence.

Late in 1945, Leo and Henry got married after a long engagement. It was one of many post-war weddings, but for Somerville it was *the* wedding. Everyone went to London for the service in Chelsea Old Church and the reception in Claridges. Leo seemed happy to the Brig, but he still worried that her addiction to excitement would one day make her restless.

Henry discovered, to his unimagined delight, that Leo was not much interested in his money. She was as frugal as her father, and almost always turned away Henry's offers of new clothes, foreign travel and domestic help.

'Spending makes me nervous.'

'You've made me happier than I could believe. It means you've married me for myself.'

'True, Henry. I hope it makes up for keeping you waiting so long.'

To remind herself that what she now possessed might so nearly not have been hers, she badgered her father to give her the sacking body bag. Henry never knew that she kept it hidden in a bottom drawer. She did, however, tell Henry (only him) about the dogfight with the ME109 but, obedient to her CO's order, not until after the ATA had been disbanded in 1945. She described it in the driest of deadpan terms, avoiding triumphalism just like the Brig when with Portia and Flavia he had toasted the exit of Hodge.

Labrador's fate remained a nagging mystery to Leo and Henry. Henry, at least, had come to terms with Labrador parting without a farewell. At first it had troubled him, but soon he could understand that Labrador had probably stayed silent for security: if David had been picked up and tortured after Fireworks – entirely possible – then the SS could have caught up with Labrador before he reached Switzerland. Perhaps swapping the cufflinks, in which Labrador had taken the initiative, was Labrador's way of saying goodbye. But his eventual fate?

The Sunday after Christmas 1945, the Brig, Leo and Henry were walking the riverside path.

'This is where Labrador first plucked up courage to talk to me. He rescued Brownie from the mud.'

'What's your guess, Brig? Is he still alive?'

'Jeremy Gunn told me that SOE put out feelers, but found no trace. Poland was a cauldron in the war. I think he perished in it.'

As the Brig was now his father-in-law, Henry put the question he'd never dared ask. 'Did you have anything to do with Operation Zodiac?'

No reply. But the Brig did look at him, fleetingly, and smile, before going on:

'Labrador was at the mercy of his obsessions, more than any of us. They were all he had: no chance to connect with any other reality. The training school was partly to blame, of course, cooping him up in a bubble world – not to mention Somerville – another bubble world – for so long.'

As the Brig spoke, Henry removed one of his cuff links and held it out to the Brig on the palm of his hand, assay marks to view.

'This is all we have of him.' The Brig peered briefly at the tiny markings, but it was clear to Henry that he knew what to expect. He looked at Henry again directly, smiled, and nodded. Leo was too busy with her dog to see what had passed between them.

In fact, the Brig thought he knew what had happened to Labrador, but would never tell Henry or Leo.

Keeping an agent so long at SOE Somerville, partly for selfish reasons, continued to haunt the Brig as one of the most regrettable decisions of his life. To leave a man with a revenge obsession isolated for so long had ensured that he became less than human.

Through Jeremy Gunn, Maxwell had pieced together Labrador's movements, and formed a theory about his eventual fate between August 1941 and late 1944. The account, he knew, was part fact, part reasonable conjecture – but the Brig was disturbed by the ease with which reasonable conjecture, once expressed in words, took upon itself the status of fact. It was the same process, he saw, as that which had made him believe Hodge was a

German sleeper, even though the evidence was inconclusive. He'd told himself he wouldn't make the same mistake again, but here it was happening once more, as if out of his control. That part of his mind where hunches and ideas gained the dignity of theories, helped by the reasoning process, and above all expression in words, appeared to have a will of its own, a need to rule.

He'd contacted the Free French leader in Paris who had harboured Labrador and the other Henrietta saboteurs. The Frenchman had confirmed that in the late afternoon of the same August day as Operation Zodiac, Labrador had turned up in Paris, sought him out in his usual bar, asked for shelter, and for help in escaping to Poland.

Maxwell didn't discover the exact route he'd taken, nor had the Frenchman, but he assumed it was long winded: probably from France through Switzerland, across North-east Italy, the Northern Balkans and finally via Hungary into Poland. It was probably early winter 1941 before he arrived home.

More certain was the trail of blood Labrador had left behind him once back in Poland. The Polish resistance – the Polish Home Army – would have welcomed him. A successful operation reported by them to Polish contacts in London mentioned a new recruit from England, and the affair bore Labrador's signature. Not far from Labrador's village in Lodz province was Belsyce Castle, taken over by the German army as officer's quarters in 1939. It had a magnificent medieval hall with a long dining table at ground level overlooked by an all-round gallery at first floor level, with a thick oak balustrade. While 16 German officers were enjoying a St Nicholas Day dinner on 6th December, resistance fighters entered the castle and crouched out of sight in the shadows of the gallery. When the Germans were too drunk to respond, the firing had started. In seconds, all 16 had been executed.

A second operation also had Labrador's mark. Blowing up troop trains was run-of-the-mill SOE work, for which agents were trained to lay explosives along many yards of track in order to maximize damage. In mid-1942, a train carrying German troops to the Eastern Front, on the main line between Warsaw and Minsk, was lifted from rails near the Polish border with Belorussia by a sequence of explosions along 50 yards of track.

Then? Maxwell could not be sure, but he suspected Labrador to have been involved in a sequence of reckless sabotages and assassinations in 1943 and 1944. Finally, reports from the Polish resistance placed Labrador at the heart of the 63-day Warsaw uprising in the closing months of the war. Sixteen thousand Polish fighters had been killed as the Germans cleared the capital of opposition – helped to do so in their own time by Stalin, who had halted the Russian advance outside the city.

Towards the end, isolated pockets of resistance held out, typically in ruined buildings and basements, the last favoured by resistance fighters for picking off Germans passing at road level. Maxwell assumed Labrador to have been one of these basement snipers: he couldn't prove it but now, unless he took a hold on himself, he believed this was the truth, as if carved on Labrador's headstone. When the Germans identified subterranean snipers, they dealt with them by entering the building from the rear with a flame thrower, battering their way into the basement and incinerating the contents.

The Brig revived the S.R.S.C. in 1947, and was voted Captain once more as if the events leading up to his resignation in January 1941 had never happened.

Six months later, Portia's father died. Everyone had to move up a rank. Portia, as the new Countess of Taunton, automatically rose from Vice Commodore to Commodore. The Brig stepped up to Vice Commodore, a role ideal for keeping fingers in pies. Henry became Captain. Leo took over his job as Sailing Secretary.

No one ever talked about how badly Somerville had wronged Maxwell in 1940-41, or ever alluded to his shaming and exile.

Portia and the Brig relaxed the membership rules of the S.R.S.C. step by step, over several years, just as they had planned, without the need to be prompted by the likes of Hodge. No one minded: in fact, members had no choice when they saw how warmly Portia and he welcomed newcomers – people who would never have been admitted before the war.

There would be many more almost perfect days by the water.

Postscript

Adrian Russell is almost entirely based on Harold Adrian Russell Philby, better known as 'Kim' Philby, who betrayed his country to the Soviet Union. He spent about 12 months at SOE Beaulieu as an instructor teaching propaganda and subversion in 1941-2.

Brigadier Maxwell is the fictional counterpart of Brigadier Buckland, who was a Beaulieu resident and who helped set up SOE Beaulieu by using his connection with the Beaulieu Estate to get the houses. His real-life character was nothing like Maxwell's.

The Head of SOE, Colonel Colin Gubbins, later General Sir Colin Gubbins, has his fictional counterpart in Colonel Jeremy Gunn.

Colonel Robert MacDonald had a real life counterpart in Lt. Colonel J.W. Munn, who was the first commandandant of SOE Beaulieu, but his character as described in this book bears no relationship to what it was in life.

The character of Lord Taunton is largely based on that of the present Earl of Harrowby. Lady Taunton is invented, but has one feature – the glass eyes – in common with 'Win' (Winifred), Lady Dent, married to Sir Frederick Dent, a Beaulieu resident in the 1930s. Lord Harrowby's wife Caroline, unlike Lady Taunton, doesn't drink.

Neither the Earl of Taunton nor his family have any resemblance to the Montagus of Beaulieu. John, 2nd Lord Montagu of Beaulieu, was roughly the same generation as Lord Taunton, but died long before the outbreak of the war. His heir was 13 in 1940.

Dora Adcock is the fictional counterpart of Vera Atkins. Park, the butler at Orchard Court, has not been renamed. Major Fuller is the fictional counterpart of Major Buckmaster, head of the French section of SOE.

David's (ie Henry Dunning-Green's) experiences on the way back to England from Normandy are closely based on those of Robert Mortier ('Maloubier'). He joined the Rouen Circuit in 1943 and is thought to have been the youngest SOE officer sent into the field in 1939-45.

Operation Zodiac is based partly on the SOE operation, which never materialised, to execute the German pilots based at Meucon Airfield in Brittany.

Operation Henrietta is almost entirely based on Operation Josephine, the successful SOE operation that destroyed the power station at Pessac near Bordeaux.

The O'Grady case, which heightened Maxwell and MacDonald's worries about a fifth columnist in Somerville, was a real event: Dorothy O'Grady, an Isle of Wight landlady, was condemned to death for spying in 1940, but reprieved.

SOE Somerville is real-life SOE Beaulieu, moved to an imaginary location on the South Coast of England. In fact SOE Beaulieu began work in 1941, after a setting-up period starting 1940. In this story, it's been moved forward a year to be already in operation by the summer of 1940.

Milton is Lymington, Beaulieu's neigbouring small town; Stretford is Milford on Sea, next stop along the coast from Lymington; Hampton is Winchester.

The names of the SOE Beaulieu houses have been changed. For example, The House in the Wood and The Rings, the officers' mess and the administrative HQ, have been combined in a single building, Woodland House.

The S.R.S.C.'s real life counterpart is the Beaulieu River Sailing Club. In 1939-40, the B.R.S.C. did not sail at the mouth of the river, but instead further up the river, and in those days there was no Up River or Down River race.

Acknowledgements

One important book especially influenced the writing of this tale: *The Master and his Emissary*, by Iain McGilchrist. I am much in his debt for his comprehensive elucidation of the tendency of the left brain to connive and to dominate: how it is a virtual world, masterminding language, reasoning and theorising, but poorly connected with the real world, and consequently makes us prey to obsessions.

Two people pointed me towards writing this tale, one deliberately, one accidentally. The first, Clive Lester, a Beaulieu resident, suggested to me (while running sailing races on the river) that there was an original story to be written bringing together SOE Beaulieu and the ATA.

The second, Anne, Lady Chichester, set me thinking by a chance remark about the fictional potential of SOE Beaulieu. As Anne Douglas-Scott-Montagu, eldest daughter of the 2nd Lord

Montagu of Beaulieu (see above), she had grown up at Beaulieu in the 1930s and had known Brigadier Buckland (see the Postscript, page 329). None of her family, she told me, had any idea that he was leading a double life during the war years, setting up the spy training schools, but superbly acting the part of being a regular army officer and just another Beaulieu resident. Both Clive and Anne died while I was writing the book.

I am also more than grateful to Richard Poad, Chairman of the ATA Museum at Maidenhead, and to Squadron Leader Mark Ponting, for their expert advice on Leo's dog fight, worked out with the help of the superb Spitfire simulator at the ATA Museum. Richard has done a supreme job keeping alive the memory of the men and women of the ATA and raising awareness of their contribution to the Second World War.

I must also thank Maxwell Beaverbrook, grandson of the 1st Lord Beaverbrook, for introducing me to the late Roy Bowditch, an armourer at Tangmere – he is the basis for the character of Roy Bowden and he explained to me in detail before his death how easily a Spitfire could accidentally be left armed – a pivotal moment.

Thanks also to Sam Jodison, who reviewed the original synopsis and the first 50 pages – and his colleagues at Cornerstones for invaluable advice.

Next, to Cindy Bodycombe, who reviewed the story stage by stage – acutely but tactfully critical; likewise Katy Gordon, Araminta Whitley and Eleanor Pyne for their professional editorial input.

A few friends and relations read the story before it was published and made valuable suggestions, almost all of which have been incorporated. They were Sara Steele, Paula Norris, Charles Nettlefold, Alastair Seaton, Robert Sutton, Mark Fox-Andrews, Roger Bevan, Fergus and Felicity Duncan and Alastair Colgrain.